OUT OF THE ROONS

ISOBEL RAVEN

Out of the Roons
Copyright © 2019 by Isobel Raven

All rights reserved. No part of this publication may be reproduced, distributed, or transmitted in any form or by any means, including photocopying, recording, or other electronic or mechanical methods, without the prior written permission of the author, except in the case of brief quotations embodied in critical reviews and certain other non-commercial uses permitted by copyright law.

Tellwell Talent
www.tellwell.ca

ISBN
978-0-2288-1744-4 (Paperback)
978-0-2288-1745-1 (eBook)

In memory of Elizabeth and Claire,
who read the chapters in their earliest drafts
and encouraged me to keep on telling the story.

Table of Contents

Introduction vii

Book I   Elve 1
Book II   Hom 117
Book III   Elve 179
Book IV   Hom 243
Book V   Elve 297

Acknowledgements 329
Thanks 331

Introduction

Rather foolishly, I have set this novel in the fourth millennium. That's a thousand years from now. I've invented no amazing new hardware: nothing that does anything more than the stuff we already have. But I have pictured possible cultural change, especially language change.

What will happen to English in a thousand years? Will people still speak and write English as we know it? Would the English of 3015 be as unintelligible to us as is the Middle English of Geoffrey Chaucer (1340-1440)?

In the Roons presents a familiar language with spelling that has been jerked around by the interference of governments and global business. It has become Inglish. You, the reader, will have to put up with reading a little Inglish in this book, and you will hate it. But persevere. You'll get onto it rather quickly.

Don't recoil from "sposta", "hafta" and "gonna" in the mouths of almost all the characters. These universals in our present spoken language can very well become Standard English, and very soon, too. Especially "gonna".

You will not be pleased to read "taked" and "goed" in the mouths of children. This is a result of government-decreed regularization of verbs. The kids take to it right away.

The Glorius Noo Wrld Reepublik uv Azhu and de Amerikas (the RAA) not only legislates the exclusive use of Inglish, it tries to legislate nearly everything else too. You will see how well that all turns out.

BOOK I
Elve

1

The brownish-grey envelope came by courier two days before Elve's seventy-fifth birthday. It was not a surprise. The Glorious New World Republic of Asia and the Americas (GNWRAA) had been very efficient in implementing their plan to prevent massive overpopulation of the habitable world.

Elve took the grey paper out to her balcony where the light was good. The message was written in Uniscrip, a simplified version of traditional English spelling adopted several decades ago. Elve, educated in Traditional Orthography (Trad), read the message while mentally transliterating to Trad. She reminded herself that "th" was now represented by "d" and waded in.

27.07.40 MNA
Elve 29.07.-40.43.79
Congratulashuns on reeching ur seventy-fifd brdday! U ar entering de glorius goelden faze uv ur lief. GNWRAA welcums u to taek part in de Nue Wurld Populaeshun Redecshun Plan. Dis represents ur oppurtunitee too bee a nobel wrld sitizen, wrdy uv all gloree, onr, and reespect.

Elve understood the letter to be dated in the fortieth year of the MNAGNWRAA, that is, the Magnificent New Age of the

Glorious New World Republic of Asia and the Americas. Approved abbreviation: MNA.

The Common Era in which Elve had been born and educated had been officially ended at 2975 years. So this was really July, 3015 in Elve's reckoning.

The letter went on:

> **Widin de next five yeers, ue ar rekwested too maek de foloeing araenjments for ur glorius ded.**

There followed a list of requirements for planning her own death on or before her eightieth birthday. The plan was to be submitted to the Death Officer at the local Hospice for the Glorious Departure of Loyel Sitizenz.

Elve laboured through the document. She hated Uniscrip.

Ue hav de foloeing opshuns for ur maner of ded.

1. **Ded bie leedal injekshun**
2. **Ded bie leedal gas**
3. **Natchral ded, bie widdroel uv food, wotr, and medicaeshun**

Sweat trickled down Elve's temples. It wasn't just the tropical heat that was typical summer weather in Urb 43.79. Contemplating these ways of dying inspired dread.

Elve was far from feeling that her time had come. Her health was robust. She walked to accomplish all her errands and worked in her garden every day. Her little patch of earth was doing well. From her third-floor balcony she could see her row of spinach in her allotment below.

She was fortunate in living in a structure that had withstood disaster remarkably well. Only the north end had been nicked by a missile. It was just twenty storeys built of steel and brick.

It was said that there had once been immensely tall glass-clad towers in old Tranna. They had succumbed to wild temperature variations and the onslaught of vicious hailstorms that arose some centuries ago in the Age of Natural Disasters.

Elve's condo looked out on Miller's Lane, a street of low brick and cement buildings. Her road, once a broad paved thoroughfare, was little more than a track, with a few heaving bits of asphalt as a reminder of its former integrity. Directly across from her balcony rose the ruin of a luxury condo, ravaged by both weather and war. It was called Statesfield.

The morning traffic was beginning to gather— children on their way to school, men and women with gardening tools, mothers with babies tied to their backs, also carrying tools, bags, and baskets. Some women carried their burdens balanced on their heads. The schoolchildren wore pyjama-like garments of greyish blue, the others similar clothes of a dark grey. As the road filled with pedestrians, it seemed to crawl with large ants.

The drabness was punctuated, however, by bits of colour provided by the ubiquitous polybags. Polybags were made of polyester fabric dug up from garbage dumps of previous centuries. The GNWRAAA guarded all these dumps, especially those found with troves of discarded garments and bales of fabric, the offloading of surplus goods by manufacturers and retailers during the Centuries of Growth.

Most of the people, like Elve and her family, were of a mild brown colour with dark hair. Here and there Elve saw people of various darker shades. Much rarer were fair-skinned blondes. The hair of everyone, male or female, was cut short at earlobe level. Government policy.

As Elve watched, a donkey ambled down the track pulling a cart built on a velo chassis. It was said that cars operated within the government compound, electric velosines owned by the Glorius Noo Reepublic Comishuners and Onerd Marshals. But in Elve's neighbourhood, people made clever use of the chassis and bodies of salvaged velos to make carts of many kinds.

Something moved high in the clear, blue sky. A silent white shape with needle nose and swept wings. Elve watched, puzzled, as it hovered and then disappeared into the heights.

She went inside. She consulted her calendar, trying to get used to the ten-day schedule of the GNWRAA. Elve was used to the seven days named in honour of historical international corporations from which the world economy had developed: Kochday, Buffday, Amday, Donsday, Walday, Yuday, and Baysantoday. The three new days of the week were named Maoday, Kimday and Washingtonday in honour of historical figures of the founding nations.

If this is Kimday, Elve thought, Jema might be coming for dinner. Jema was Elve's middle-aged daughter.

Elve yearned for her ComD (communication device), a digital booklet confiscated by the government a few years ago. Its utility was much diminished at that time, since the net was all but useless, but she could have still called Jema on it. Maybe even called her sons, cut off from her ken for thirty years.

Jema did indeed arrive late in the afternoon. She brought Elve eggs and soya bean cake in yellow Porgel packs. These would round out their dinner of stir-fried tofu and vegetables.

As the women prepared their meal, they talked of their routine activities and those of Jema's three adult children: Reba, gone to the Northern Tundra; Odro and his partner, Doro with their twin baby boys; Nura, eighteen and daily expecting induction into the military.

As well, Reba's five-year-old boy, Hom, who had been left in Jema's care.

Elve and Jema faced each other over Elve's antique table, a survivor, along with four chairs, of a long-ago era of chrome and arborite. At first they ate in silence, pausing occasionally to dry sweaty fingers on their garments.

"My 'glorious death' letter came today," said Elve.

Jema didn't bat an eye. "The RAA is on the ball, aren't they." There wasn't a hint of sarcasm in her voice. She clasped her hands over her heart. "Oh Mom, we'll have such a glorious death ceremony. The best. I can just see you now, in red for good luck, sweeping down the aisle on my arm. You'll be such a gorgeous corpse!"

Elve had less enthusiasm for the project. They finished their meal and cleaned the dishes with the two cups of water that could be spared for the work.

They sat down again with the official document. Jema read it to her mother.

Opshuns for the Glorius Ded Seremoenie uv Loyel GNWRAA Sitizenz

Jema was clearly unimpressed with the Baesik and Grand options. She moved quickly to the third: the "Glorius, Grand Seremoenee" which included unlimited numbers of attendants, flowers, music, and a great procession to the place of burial (the nearest desert). Price: 1000 New Yuan.

"It doesn't hafta be like this," said Elve. "Funerals haven't always been by governmental decree."

"What do you mean?"

"People once died whenever death came from natural causes. I can even remember my great-grandmother's death. I was very young. There was a funeral in a beautiful church."

"A church?"

"They're mostly museums now, the few that survived the Centuries of Wars. But this was a church, I think, a temple of some kind. I wish I'd asked my grandmothers more about it. Now I don't know."

Elve had several sources of ancient knowledge: a few threads gleaned from her great-grandmother, Jamila, who died when Elve was seven. Bereft of her parents at the age of three, she had been raised by her two grandmothers, Atlanta and Kumi. Her formal education was complete before the Great Cleansing, when sources in Trad and all other languages were purged from the internet.

She had, as well, a little collection of books hidden in a metal box in the back of her storage closet. The origin of this collection was long forgotten, and only by some miracle had the books escaped destruction in the Age of Natural Disasters and the Centuries of the Wars.

Elve had hoped Jema would become interested in the books. She felt that they held something important that should be preserved and passed on. Although the GNWRAA hadn't explicitly forbidden the possession of paper books, she sensed that if the authorities found her little library, they would quickly destroy it.

Before Jema could read at all, Elve read to her *Rhymes of Mother Goose* and *Anne of Green Gables*. Jema asked her mother to reread these so many times that she could recite many passages by heart. But she could not be persuaded to learn Trad. Her rejection was vehement. Trad spelling was wrong, even evil. It belonged to the Old Time before the GNWRAA, a time, she learned at school, of darkness and ignorance.

At the table, Jema continued to concoct grand plans for Elve's "glorius ded".

"Who do you want for attendants? As many as you like. Your friends here in the building? We can find a magnificent gown at the RAA Emporium."

The government-operated store was indeed the only place where they were might find a magnificent red dress. The government controlled commerce vigilantly, and persons openly setting up a shop of any kind were likely to disappear.

"We'll invite everybody we know," said Jema. "All our friends and neighbours."

Elve couldn't enter into Jema's enthusiastic planning. A sumptuous death ceremony held no attraction for her.

"The only guests I would want besides you and the kids are Max and Mungo," she said. She longed for her twin sons, whom she hadn't seen since their eighteenth birthday. On that day they'd been collected by a brigade of soldiers and marched away to begin the obligatory years of military service.

"Where do you suppose they are now?" said Jema. She had loved her older brothers, and their being ripped out of her life was the one thing she held against the GNWRAA.

"They should have been discharged by now. They should have come home. But there has been no word."

Elve had a source of information, a connection she didn't divulge to Jema. She often walked the half-hour journey to visit an elderly woman in a cleverly camouflaged shack in the Humber ravine. She had met the woman while both were picking wild apples there.

Her friend, known only as "O", had a contraband radio. With it she communicated with other ham operators dotted about the continent. Her east coast contact picked up messages from London; her west coast contact could pick up Hong Cong. She managed to piece together a fragmented picture of world events—the wars, for there were always wars, a bit of insider GNWRAA news, disasters natural and man-made.

Elve still hoped at every visit for some news of Mungo and Max. But there was none.

Max, she thought, was probably loyal as Jema to the GNWRAA, and might have risen in the ranks to become a permanent officer. He was both enterprising and skilful. A tinkerer who could fix things—anything. As such, he would have been invaluable in the field. He attracted firm friends, was a natural leader. Max would be OK.

But she greatly feared for Mungo, her quiet, thoughtful son. He had read all her ancient books, poring in puzzlement over the pages of a tome entitled Holy Bible. Its leather binding and gilt-edged leaves marked it as an unusual volume.

Putting together what he gleaned from Holy Bible, *Alice in Wonderland* and *Anne of Green Gables*, Mungo had formed a haphazard picture of times radically different from the one he knew. A blue schoolbook called *Life and Literature* only compounded his puzzlement.

Mungo and Elve tried to picture these foreign worlds. "Do you think those times really existed?" the boy asked.

"I think they did, or maybe some aspects of them did," said Elve. "But I can't get it sorted out—the real and the fiction."

Mungo turned again to his sources. Then the military came for him.

Elve feared for Mungo. He knew too much. He knew the wrong things. He longed for something that the GNWRAA hoped to wipe out. He might question orders, might be too creative and most certainly would not "fit in".

"Max is still alive somewhere," Elve said to Jema. "He would be a good soldier. If he died honorably in battle, the government would have let us know." Her face creased in a worried frown. "But Mungo. Mungo isn't safe."

"He didn't have a pure love for the RAA," said Jema. "He got crazy ideas from those old books of yours."

"Ideas are very dangerous." And Elve realized as she said this how true it had become over the course of her life.

Some ideas were necessary, of course. Ideas on how to make old things last, how to scrape by when the cupboard was bare, how to grow food and preserve it with minimal electricity

Abstractions like love and liberty and compassion had passed out of the language. But not hope and misery.

Jema grinned. "Mungo is very smart, though. He knows when to keep his mouth shut. I bet he's still alive somewhere. He'll turn up when you least expect it."

Elve brightened. "I hope you're right. Sometime before I hafta do this death thing."

"It's your sacred duty to the RAA, Mom. The honourable and glorious thing to do. We all hafta do our part to keep the population within the viably sustainable limit."

Elve cringed to hear her daughter spout the fixed phrases of the RAA.

Jema stood, wiping her temple with her sleeve. "This hellish weather has to stop soon." She collected her Porgels from the kitchen and bundled the vegetables that Elve had set aside for her into a polybag.

"Think about what you want. You should have a really beautiful ceremony. It's your day. Bye, Mom." She saluted and let herself out.

Elve didn't move to embrace or kiss her daughter. A team of government psychologists had determined that such expressions were deleterious to the development of "Loyel Sitizenz." The Good of the State being the highest priority in ensuring the Good of all the People, parents were most urgently enjoined to abandon all overt expressions of affection, an urgency backed with police action in flagrant cases.

From her balcony, with the sun setting in a hot, red ball, Elve watched Jema set out down Miller's Lane. She returned to her dreary room and sat down. Overcome with despair and loss, Elve laid her head on the ancient, bruised table and wept.

Elve was a morning person. She liked to rise at dawn to enjoy the coolest part of the day.

"Weeping may endure for a night, but joy cometh in the morning," she quoted from the gilt-edged tome. A light breeze came in at her balcony door, so she went out. Her years sat lightly on her still erect shoulders as she stood, resting her arms on the rail.

Her heart lifted, and resolve informed her, body and mind.

"I will not do it." She said it aloud. Then she said it again. What could they do to her that they didn't already hope she would do to herself? Prison or death, the GNWRAA's usual criminal punishments, didn't look any worse than "Ded bie leedal injecshun," following a ridiculous ceremony.

No. She wouldn't spend one iota of her remaining strength in executing the government-dictated death procedure. What she would do, she decided, was begin to transliterate her precious books. She would rewrite them in Inglish/Uniscrip so that Jema and others of her generation could read them.

Paper and ink and binding materials would be a problem. The government controlled the production of paper very strictly. Elve had resources. Friends who would help, some nearing their own death sentence. Some who could read the old script. O, who could make all sorts of things, probably paper and ink as well. Pens too. Already, plans for a writing group formed in Elve's mind.

She knew who she could trust. While eating her porridge, Elve constructed her mental list. The next morning at dawn she set off for O's home in the ravine. Together, they would mobilize a corps of the condemned. And they would write. Write for dear life.

2

At dawn on Maoday, Elve put on her conical straw hat and set out to visit O's hidden lair. She plotted her path as the crow flies, sometimes using the remains of the streets of the old city, at other times following the paths beside the sullen creeks. At this time of year, they were mostly mud-bottomed ditches, but here and there a spring-fed stream flowed under trees that had achieved a reasonable size. Elve drew in the odour of fern and wild rose, grateful for these oases of revitalization.

As she drew near O's hut, which crouched under a cover of wild grape vine, she paused to check in every direction to be sure no one lurked in her vicinity. She listened for the snapping twig, the swishing branch that might necessitate the abortion of her mission.

Elve bent low under the shrubbery and descended the three wooden steps to the door. She scratched it softly. When it opened, there were two more steps into O's sunken shelter. Here dim greenish light filtered through leaves partially obscuring a skylight window. A pungent mix of odours filled the room, scents from bunches of herbs hung from the ceiling to dry.

"So you've come," the old woman said. "There has been some unrest in the north. Have you heard of it?"

"Not a word. Not a cloud in the sky," said Elve, handing to O the polybag of foods that she always brought. "But then, we are always last to know. Nothing comes through to Miller's Lane."

"The word is faint and intermittent. It may mean nothing."

Elve sat on a stool by the wooden block which served as a table. In spite of her great age, O moved to the cupboard with a firm step. She scooped water from a bucket, preparing to make tea. O was fortunate in owning a functional solar panel of Pre-RAA manufacture. She always had electricity.

"Peppermint, this morning," said O, bringing the tea to the table. For a time they sipped the hot brew in silence.

O said, "Of Max and Mungo there is no word."

O always used this wording to maintain the hope that one of these days there would be word. Elve replied, according to the ritual, "Not today, but someday soon."

There had once been a wisp of information. A year ago now.

An unidentified source said that a traitor named Max was to be executed for the assassination of the Honoured Prime Minister of the Administrative Echelon of the RAA.

It was RAA policy that only single names, chosen from the official list of names, should be used for the naming of children. A person was designated by that name, plus six digits indicating birth date, and four digits indicating the GPS location of their birth.

So this news of Max could have been news of any number of Maxes. Elve swung helplessly between hope and despair.

Elve picked up the cups and took them to the dry sink. "My death letter has come," she said. "I have five years to plan my funeral."

"How good of them to give you five years. They will not come for me. I was never registered. I am a non-person, and I like it that way."

"Don't you ever wish you could at least go to the Emp?"

"What do I want with the Emporium? This ravine and the generosity of my friends provide all I need."

"But aren't you tired of hiding?"

"I'm used to that. I'm getting along very well without ID. But I do mourn one of my losses. More than makes any real sense. When I was very young, I had three paper books written in the Dutch before we all had to learn English. My grandmother taught me to read them. They were lost when my family fled Europe during the last uprising."

O's eyes seemed locked on that distant time. "I find that I long for my books. They were story-books about flight to outer galaxies and other possible worlds."

"How fantastic! Do you think the stories were true?"

"No, they were called science fiction. But I think some elements were factual. Which ones, though." O smiled and shrugged.

Elve used the water remaining in the boiler to wash the cups in the basin. "It's time I told you about my books. I have five of them. They belong to the era before the Time of Natural Disasters and the Centuries of the Wars. Mix of history and fiction. Fantasy too. They're written in traditional spelling, of course."

O's face shone. "I know Trad. I went to school well before the legislated adoption of Uniscrip."

"I was counting on that. I need your help. I want to copy the books into Uniscrip. I want everyone to be able to read them. They are about people like us, but living in a different way. A way without IDs and checkpoints and government-approved names."

"Can this be done openly? Are there regulations?"

"There are no laws that I know of. The RAA knows nothing about books. It's unlikely that the police have ever seen one. But the officials will look suspiciously on anything they don't understand, and I've no doubt that the project would get us into trouble." Elve resumed her seat. "The materials will be hard to come by, as well. Paper is very scarce. I wonder about handwriting. Are you adept?"

O grinned, pleased with Elve's subversive idea. "I was very good at one time. I think I could resurrect my old skill."

"We would need ink. It's years since I've seen the kind of stick pens we used. I don't think they're made any more."

"Oh? What do they use at school?"

"It seems that at the schools they don't teach any kind of writing. They rely entirely on memorizing from the screen—unison recital, singing, that sort of thing. The kids are required to sit on their hands. I taught mine at home. They all liked to write when they could get their hands on something to write with. I had to stop the boys from scraping messages on the walls with my best knife."

"I think I could manufacture ink," said O. "There are chokecherries in the ravine—terrible flavour, but very dark juice. I'll experiment with that. The season is right and they are plentiful. For pens of some sort, we can ask Lem at the east bridge on old Bloor. He comes to me for news and I know we can trust him. He whittles intricate little things from wood. He made this tiny spoon for me."

O stood up and went to her cupboard drawer. She brought out a wooden spoon no longer than her forefinger, its bowl perfect in form, and the handle worked with a simple design. "I use it to mix the more poisonous powders."

"How lovely!" Elve fingered the smooth bowl and pretty decoration. "Do you know Boatman? Boat? He lives in his fishing boat moored at the old Credit docks and brings fish to me at our agreed place. I pick up the fish and leave the money in the niche. His catch is sposta go exclusively to Camp 46 for the army. He is old like us, and I think he can be trusted, but I don't know what he could contribute to the project."

"Boatman isn't one of my people. But there are one or two others. People of the time before. Probably they can write. And I trust them."

"It wouldn't be wise for us to meet. Ask them discreetly if they're willing to risk joining the team."

"I'll think about paper too," said O. "It seems to me that it could be made of any fibrous stuff and some sort of glue."

It was time for Elve to leave. She wanted to get home before the sun delivered the worst of its noonday heat. She picked up her polybag and sun hat. The women touched hands, and Elve left the house, looking sharply in all directions before venturing into the ravine

3

Boatman fished all night. He had a decent catch, enough to spare a couple for each of his secret customers. In the early light, he distributed the fish to agreed hiding places. In the rocky cavity lined with fresh leaves which was Elve's spot, he found, along with two yuan, a small flat, black rock. Elve's code stone. It indicated that she needed to talk with him. It could mean a number of things, including info re threatening police activity. Or it could be a harmless invitation to share a meal. He hoped it was the latter. He would go up immediately after his delivery to Camp 46.

Trundling his small cart, he walked from the camp towards Elve's building, using a dry creek bed as his main route. The noon sun beat on his frayed straw hat, and sweat dripped from his grey-stubbled chin. A dark triangle seeped from his shoulders down the back of his grey tunic.

At midafternoon, he found Elve at work in her garden, pulling weeds. Tomato vines ran rampant, rich with plump, satiny fruit. Small beets were just ready for harvest. The young carrots as well. Elve straightened as Boatman approached, wiping her hands on her loose, grey pants.

"Yo, Boat," she said, unsmiling. He returned the greeting, stone-faced.

Elve dumped her pile of weeds onto her compost heap and added a few spades of soil. She picked four tomatoes and pulled small bunches of the vegetables, laying them in Boatman's cart. A jerk of her head sent him on up the road with the cart.

Elve picked some vegetables for herself and went around to the back door of her building. The ornate front entrance had long been closed up with a bank of gravelly dirt. She went inside and climbed the three flights to her rooms. She had three: two bedrooms (one the size of a broom-closet) and a kitchen/living room. Rooms that had once been part of her suite were now blocked off and occupied by Sor, a young mother, and her son.

Shortly after Elve entered, there was a soft knock on her door. She opened to Boatman, who had circled back to the building with his cart. He now carried the vegetables along with two fish in a basket.

"Ovid has your cart?"

Boatman nodded. Ovid was a sort of building superintendent who presided in the garbage room/workshop off the back entrance. He did his best to keep the ancient heating system working in the winter months. He did repairs as materials were available and sometimes replaced burnt-out bulbs. It seemed that he could be trusted, but it was important to stay on his good side. He knew everything about everyone, and there was hardly a resident who was "clean", that is, engaged in absolutely no unlawful activity. So for a rael (one-tenth of a yuan), Boatman was able to leave his cart hidden from curious eyes in Ovid's workshop.

While Elve trimmed the vegetables, Boatman cleaned the fish. He cooked them out on the balcony on an improvised solar grill, one of Max's creations, amazingly still functional. Elve provided a sort of dark bread procured at the Emporium.

They drew the bamboo shade against the western sun and sat down to eat.

"What's up?" said Boatman.

"Can you write?"

"I could, years ago. I had a job that called for writing. Before the RAA, that is."

"By hand?"

"Yep."

"In Trad? Before the Great Spelling Reform?"

"Part of the GSR. I had a job changing signs from Trad to Uniscrip. Painted thousands of road signs. Peeterboroe, Kingsten, Winepeg. You name it, I wrote it. That was before they changed all the names to numbers, like Tranna to Urb 43.79."

"Before the size and shape of the world became a mystery. My kids never saw a map or a globe when they were in school. The boys got me to show them the world I remembered from my school days. Jema wouldn't even look at my attempts at map-drawing. She sensed that there was something disloyal to the RAA in them."

"So the kids nowadays think the world is flat?'

"Uh-huh. With a magic mountain in the middle where the RAA resides. Over there where the sun rises," Elve said, gesturing to the east.

"And how does the sun get back to the east every morning?"

"The magnetism of the RAA pulls it across under the earth, up through the magic mountain to rise again each day." Elve demonstrated the sun's magic ascent.

"Surely they can't make the kids believe that!"

"It gets easier with every generation. Jema swallowed it, hook, line, and sinker. Her children believe it, too. Now my great-grandchild sits on his hands in school, watching the Youth Training TV. Teachers merely turn on the TV and patrol the classroom making sure everyone is sitting on their hands. Then they go out to march around the parade square."

"Yeah. I've seed them out there. Rain or shine. Anyway, come to the point. What's on your mind?"

In answer, Elve went to her storage closet and moved the bundles that concealed the tin box. She brought it out to the table, opened it, and laid out the books, tattered and scorched, their bindings loosened and pages askew.

"Gawdamity, what are those?"

"Books. Have you ever seen one?"

"Looks like these were snatched from the fire."

"Must've been. My last English teacher, a very old man, gave them to me, all that he had. I've kept them hidden all these years except when I gave them to Mungo and Max to read. Jema hardly touched them."

Gingerly, Boatman picked up *Anne of Green Gables*. On its blackened cover he could make out the illustration: a young girl, seated, red hair in long braids, wearing a straw hat and clutching the handles of a large, cloth bag.

Boatman opened it and his eye fell on the line "Mrs. Lynde says Canada is going to the dogs the way things are being run at Ottawa . . ."

"Hey, I painted signs for Ottawa. They changed it to O-T-E-W-A-W. And Canada got changed to K-A-N-E-DE. Some linguist geezer said the ' a's were schwas and had to be represented by the letter 'e' in the new system. Made no sense to me."

"Doesn't matter now. Canada is a thing of the past and Ottawa too. But I remember the day when we watched on TV. I was four years old. It was supposed to be a super, great, wonderful day. They took down the maple leaf flag at the government building in Ottawa and ran up a flag representing the Greater United States of the Americas. That's gone now too. All swallowed up in the RAA. We've seen a lot of changes in our lives, haven't we?"

"Too many. I wasn't born then, but I've seen enough. So what's the deal? What're we gonna do with these books?"

"We're gonna rewrite them. In Uniscrip. So people can read them. So they'll know that it doesn't hafta be this way. With police breathing down our necks all the time. With IDs and heaven help you if you're caught without one. Even if the stories are all made up, they demonstrate that the world could be different. That the RAA hasn't existed from time immemorial."

"The kids believe that?"

"Oh, yes. That's what they're learning."

"Hm. Well we better get on with it. What're you gonna use for materials? Paper is as scarce as crude."

"I know. We'll hafta make it. And the ink too. And the pens. I have a couple of contacts. People with know-how and imagination."

Boatman scratched his chin thoughtfully. "It'll take forever."

"I have five years before the RAA does me in. I can make a start, along with my friend, O. Others will hafta carry on the work."

"There's a woman lives by the river," said Boatman. "About my age, I guess. Has ten years to go, or so. She harvests reeds in the shallows and makes stuff out of them. Hats and baskets, mostly, and they hafta go to the Emporium. But she showed me some good stuff—cloth that she made out of reeds. Like you say, know-how and imagination."

"Reeds. Papyrus. Like ancient Egyptians. D'ye think?"

"Don't know anything about Egyptians, but I could sound her out. Tomorrow, maybe."

"Leave me two white stones if she says she'll try it."

"Two whites for yes. Two black for no go." Boatman stood up. He opened the bamboo shades revealing the western sky decorated with little clouds edged in peach and gold. "Should get home before dark. Wanna quickie?"

Boatman and Elve enjoyed a relationship of mutual comfort entirely devoid of passion. They found the occasional fuck a pleasant exercise. Elve nodded and they moved off to her bedroom, his hand careless upon her still nicely rounded rump.

Elve checked her fish niche every day for a week before there was word from Boatman. Two white stones. Reedwoman was in!

At her next meeting with O, Elve took *Anne of Green Gables* with her. It was small and easily concealed in a polybag. She hadn't yet met the police on her journey to O's hideout, but there's always a first time, she thought.

O's eyes filled with tears when she saw the book. She held it with a certain reverence, as an artifact from a lost civilization. "Imagine," she said, "at one time everyone had books and could read what they liked."

"Now we have TV. No entertainment. Just the RAA's ads for themselves. They call it "Nue Wrld Gloree", but I call it the "Hour of Power". H of P. It drives me crazy."

"Thank goodness I don't have TV."

"Out where I live, the police do random checks when the show is on to make sure residents are watching. Our duty as 'Loyel Sitizenz' of the RAA. Everybody scrambles to sit in front of it if we hear them at the door. Otherwise, we ignore it as much as possible."

The women sighed and sat silent, pondering the new reality.

Elve straightened her spine. "Have you made any progress with the ink?"

O stood up, excitement clearing her brow. "Look, Lem has made me pens already. One from a twig and another from a gull feather. I've been using them to test my ink.

"Chokecherry juice is working not too badly. I have added vinegar to keep it from going mouldy, and a tiny bit of starch as a thickener. You have to shake it to distribute the starch, which collects in the bottom of the bottle. But the starch dries and makes dust all over the writing. I need to find something else." She showed Elve the scrap of paper on which she had tried out her experimental inks.

"Excellent! We might just blow the dust off. Boat is on board with this too. He knows Trad and Uniscrip and has writing experience. He knows a woman, another from the years before the RAA. She is skilled in making things from reeds. She might be able to help us with the paper. I guess we should get together at my place."

Fear shadowed O's aged face.

Elve understood. O dared not move beyond her hideout and the shelter of the ravine.

"Can we meet here then?"

O considered. To reveal her location to strangers and have more than one person visit her at a time involved a great deal of risk.

"Send the others to me separately. I will collect all our information and communicate it to each. When we get the materials, I'll work here. That's the best I can do."

Elve nodded. The work would have to proceed very cautiously. It would take a long time. She didn't have a long time, but more writers might be discovered along the way. She had to begin.

Elve clasped the old woman's hands and took her leave. She kept to the shelter of the ravine for at least a kilometre before climbing up towards an old road. She paused before joining the pedestrians loaded with bags and baskets and babies going about their errands of the day.

Many of the women wore bright headdresses. They had repurposed their prettiest polybags, winding them artfully in a style Elve had only seen long ago in pictures of Nigerian women. A wonderful way, Elve thought, to cover the ugly haircuts required by the RAA.

A rare gust of sweet air bathed her cheek. Strengthened, she turned for home.

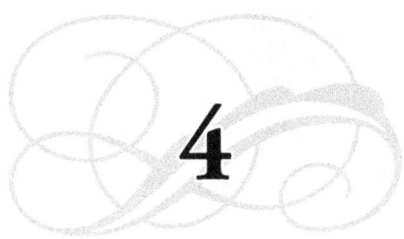

4

Elve had become accustomed to the sounds and appearance of the ruin across the road. In the untold years since its destruction, the east façade remained relatively unscathed. She would contemplate it from her balcony in the early mornings. Her spirit responded to its architectural beauty, to the many colours of its unusual facets shading from black to sun-warmed gold.

The building had suffered a direct hit from a rocket in the last days of the Statist movement. At least, people guessed that Statists were the source of the attack, since they were the only group that threatened Canada in the past. By and large, Canada had few enemies, and the protective wing of American military power deterred attacks from groups that coveted her large expanses of habitable land.

The old façade rose in gritty strength, a two-metre thick wall of grey concrete with ranks of empty windows framing bits of sky. East winds whistled through them creating a spine-freezing eeriness, and it would seem that the façade was in imminent danger of collapsing. Many swore that they'd seen it sway.

Such ruins were usually picked clean of anything useful, with scavengers scrambling among the rubble before the dust had cleared. But not this one. The danger of being crushed in the fall of the façade, and the ghostliness of the keening wind discouraged all but the most doughty. After three pickers met their deaths there, the place acquired a reputation as a site of supernatural malevolence.

The ruin became the home of a colony of ferocious feral cats. Their nightly yowling enhanced the menacing ambience of the place.

Elve wasn't afraid of Statesfield or its cats. Taming the barn kittens had been one of the joys of her childhood summers at Grandma Kumi's farm. Grandma Atlanta, too, had kept an orange tom, regal of mien, but more than amenable to preferred strokes.

She thought she might find something in the ruin that would be useful for the writing project. Plastic pens, perhaps, since when all else degraded, plastic endured. Paper might still be found, paper that could be mashed up and bleached and become new paper. Metal that could be fashioned into useful tools. What tools they would need she didn't know.

She saved the offal from two lots of Boat's fish, hoping it would be enough to keep the cats occupied for a decent interval. Precious time that would allow her to explore. Slinging a large polybag over her shoulder, and carrying the stinking offal in an old pot, Elve set off as soon as it was light. The cool of the September morning would soon dissipate in the relentless sun.

She skirted the hulking façade, intending to enter the ruin at the tumbled-down north end. The explosion had left the south tower still standing, the stacked rooms of the upper floors exposed by the shearing off of an interior wall. Elve stood, daunted by the mass of charred concrete, twisted metal, and shards of glass that lay between her and the tower. Chunks of drywall lay about as well, the white plaster backed with paper: pink, yellow, and blue.

There among the ruins, between slabs rough with lichen, nature's implacable urge to growth was asserting itself. Grass and low shrubs flourished in soil that had formed in the crevices. Virginia creeper covered significant areas. Tiny maples and a young birch tree had found sustenance for their roots. Atop the highest pile, a twisted pine challenged its unforgiving environment.

These witnesses to life's resurgence restored Elve's courage. She began to pick her way through the rubble. Three brindled cats watched from their perches, but made no move to attack. She spread her potful of offal on a slab, and leaving it for the cats' delectation, moved as nimbly as she could toward the promising rooms. There had been a time in her youth when she leapt from rock to rock on the lakeshore like a young goat, but those days were gone.

Once Elve was out of the way, the largest tom moved in on the food. He was soon joined by several others. The toms shoved the females and kittens aside and there was considerable clawing and yowling. There was just enough food to keep them all interested for the time being.

Elve discovered that the south stairwell still led upwards, only partially blocked by debris. She climbed the crumbling flights dimly lit at intervals by slits in the concrete wall. She thought that she would begin her exploration at the top and work her way down. A draft chilled her neck, and the wind, singing its constant obligato through the empty windows, rose in an unearthly whistle. The shaft must be open to the sky.

She stopped, sensing danger. She would go no higher.

A thin edge of light outlined the door in front of her. She grasped the knob and pulled. The door opened. There was sudden brightness and clamour.

She threw up her arms to protect her head from a flapping, screaming bird. The peregrine. She had seen a pair often, circling above the ruin. Now she had disturbed one of them from its roost on the doorsill. Joined by its mate, the falcon continued to swoop and scream.

Elve saw that she had nearly stepped into empty space. This is where they fell, she thought. The other three.

She waited for her terror to subside.

Her plan needed a rethink. The higher floors were the most exposed. Anything in them would be in a state of disintegration from dust, wind, snow, rain, mice, mould. The basement with its windowless rooms was much more likely to yield something useful.

Still breathing heavily and clinging to the handrail, Elve made her way down the stairs to the basement. With no source of light, she felt her way into darkness so thick you could slice it. Spiders had been industrious. Their webs stuck to Elve's face and hands. She brushed at them in futile gestures.

In the darkness, she splashed unawares into a layer of fetid water.

There were doors. Feeling her way, she tried several, turning the knob and putting her shoulder to the task. They were solidly locked.

Of course, she thought. These would be doors to locker rooms. Locked doors to locked lockers. She leaned on the wall, considering her situation. Light. Tools and light. Her mission couldn't get anywhere without tools and light.

Coming back through the cobwebs, Elve tried to talk herself out of her discouragement. Boat would have tools. She had a solar lantern. But the difficulties surrounding her project laid a burden that she couldn't shake.

She now had no protection from the cats. But as she scrambled across the rubble, she spotted several curled or stretched on sunny blocks, looking like very ordinary pussycats. But their ears were pricked, and one sprawling belly-up opened a lazy eye. Elve knew that the animals were aware of her presence. Pretending to ignore them, she continued steadily on her way, retrieved her pot at the feeding slab, and came out of the ruin without incident.

She was met with peculiar looks from passersby as she crossed the road to her building. Looking down, she realized that she was covered head to foot in cobwebs. I must look like a ghost, she thought wryly. And shivered, thinking how close she'd come to unpremeditated suicide.

5

Elve left the small, black stone in the fish niche. Boat came the next day after his delivery to Camp 46. He brought two fine trout and they made a meal as usual.

As they ate, Elve recounted her adventure in Statesfield. Boat was horrified.

"You went in there?" Those cats might've torn you limb from limb."

"The cats were easy to manage. The door out to thin air was something else. That and the darkness in the basement. I nearly suffocated. Have you any tools to jimmy open locked doors?"

"Hmph. Maybe. Or something to pick a lock. I've picked a lock or two in my day."

Elve suspected some shady doings in Boat's past. She didn't ask. It was better that she didn't know, in case of interrogation by police. There were so many laws (and new regulations all the time) that only newborn babes were innocent of transgression. Simply by sharing a meal of Boat's fish she was culpable in the eyes of some policeman, though another would turn a blind eye, even without a bribe.

They settled on a time two days later for their exploration. Boat would bring whatever tools he had to gain entry into the lockers. Elve would provide more food for the cats and her precious broom to knock down cobwebs. (Brooms were among the many products seldom available at the Emporium.) The solar lantern too.

The power came on and with it the H of P. Obligatory for all citizens of the RAA to watch. It was the usual talking head, a long-faced "white" man with large teeth and sanctimonious air. Behind him, the puce and gold flag of the GNWRAA and the motto, "In de Glorius Reepublik, Wee Ar Ol Wun." He introduced himself as de Sekretery for de Reespekted Ministree uv Fuking and Famly.

"Some irregularities have been noted in the observance of the Orders of Fucking in the GNWRAA," he intoned. "Citizens are hereby reminded that the following rules apply to all citizens not affiliated with the armed forces or the government. The Fucking Rules are simple and easily followed. There will henceforth be no more such irregularities on pain of fine or imprisonment."

At this point, a poster entitled "Fuking Rools uv de GNWRAA" appeared onscreen. A stocky woman in the puce army uniform stood beside it with a pointer. She pointed to each word as she read with strident voice:

- **Ol adult Sitizenz hav de inaeleeenabl rite too fuk, exsept does hoo ar inkarseraeted.**
- **Notwidstanding dis inaeleeenabl rite, strict rools aplie in ol caeses.**
- **Maels shal not fuk der muders, der muders' sisters, or der foders' sisters.**
- **Feemaels shal not fuk der foders, der foders' bruders, or der muders' bruders.**
- **Maelz shal not fuk maelz.**
- **Feemaelz shal not fuk feemaelz**
- **Der is to bee NOE FUKING by peepl under de aej of aeteen.**

Elve and Boat grinned at each other. "I guess we're old enough to escape the wrath of the Fuking Polees," Elve said.

"Fat chance any woman has of knowing who her father's brothers are," said Boat. "She likely doesn't even know her own father."

"My kids were lucky that way. They had their dad quite a few years. Jema was ten when my partner fell afoul of the police."

"Executed?"

"Yes. For illegal trade." Her voice was calm, resigned.

There were more rules.

- Joogs (oefishely conjoogated cuplz) mae hav too and oenlee too children uv eeder sex. Unconjoogated peepl wil uez guverment-suplied condums at ol tiems too preevent pregnansee.

"Oops! We're not conjoogated. What if you knock me up?"

"If you get knocked up it'll be an act of the gods, and you'll be set up on a pedestal by the holy RAA."

"A chosen vessel. I can see it now."

With unspoken agreement they were moving towards the bedroom. In its gloom, for it had no window, they shucked their grey pyjamas and lay down together, face to face.

Boatman caressed her hip and thigh where the flesh was firm and velvety under his touch. She took his penis in her hand. It lay inert, a soft, warm worm.

"Damn the RAA and their fuckin' fuking rules. Takes the rod right out of a man," said Boat.

"Never mind, he's very cute this way." Elve patted the useless organ affectionately.

So they had a nap instead of sex.

As planned, Boat turned up two days later. In his cart he had a maul and a crowbar; in his pocket an assortment of small sharp items suitable for probing a lock. Elve was armed with a pot of scraps for the cats, though nothing as delectable as the fish guts she'd brought the first day. The lantern she tucked into her polybag. Broom in hand she was ready to sally forth.

Boat blanched at the incessant soughing of the wind but followed Elve's lead into the forsaken ruin. The broom and the crowbar served as walking sticks, aiding their progress across the rubble. As before, cats watched from a little distance and didn't approach Elve's food offering until she and Boat had taken themselves off by five metres or so.

Elve found herself balking at the entrance to the south stairwell. She didn't want to go in there. But Boat, having safely passed the gauntlet of cats, was getting into the game. "Come on, old girl," he shouted over the wind, "Let's get on with it."

They entered the basement corridor. Elve fought the cobwebs with her broom. Boatman followed, holding the lantern high. As they progressed, they found the corridor strewn with more and more debris. They found three doors, two on the right and one on the left. At this point, the pile of rubble left only a crawl space at the top.

"I can get through there, no problem," said Boatman, eager for the challenge.

A small plaster chunk broke off from the ceiling above and fell into the pile, causing a delicate rattling of stones.

"Uh, I guess not."

By the lantern's sickly light, they inspected the ceiling. Another bit detached itself like an autumn leaf, landing on Boat's shoulder. Caution vanquished valour. They retreated to the entrance and considered their options.

"It all looks solid enough for a ways into the corridor," said Boatman. "Let's try the nearest door."

So they tried the first door on the right. Locked, as Elve knew. Boatman applied a powerful shoulder. The door resisted just as strongly. He was about to attack with the maul.

Elve yelled, "Don't do that!"

Boatman leaned on the maul. "So what am I sposta do?"

"I don't know, but don't go at it with the maul. The whole place might fall down."

"I'll have a go at picking it, I guess." Boat reached in his pocket for the subtler tools. "Probly all seized up."

Elve held the lantern close. Boatman thrust a thin wire into the keyhole in the centre of the doorknob. It went in easily. He pulled it out and fashioned a tiny loop at the end of the wire. It was still small enough to enter the hole. With thumb and finger, he rotated the wire. There was a soft click. Boatman turned the knob. With screeching hinges, the door moved inward.

After a few swipes of Elve's broom, they could make out a double row of slatted cages. Lockers. Lockers stuffed with all manner of objects—the flotsam and jetsam of life of another era. A treasure trove, Elve hoped.

The first locker was fastened with three heavy padlocks. They passed it by. Boat went to work on another fastened with a simple combination lock. He solved it by ear and hauled open the door. Two small cages clattered out to the floor.

"It's Fibber Magee's closet," Boat yelled. This reference to a sitcom of the distant past was something he had picked up in random Galaxy explorations.

Under the dust, Elve and Boatman could make out skis, an exercise bike, a miniature tree, golf clubs, a binocular case, a paint box, also a barbecue, a spectacularly ugly lamp, a small metal table, and two folding chairs. On the table, a sturdy zippered sports bag.

Curious, Elve lifted it. Heavy. She brushed it off and tried the zipper. It yielded.

Tools! Heavy shears. A hammer. A rubber mallet. In a velvet-lined box, two thick, straight needles and a curved one. A staple gun. And more.

"Sacably kristus! We gotta take these home."

Good tools were scarcer than diamonds. The Emporium carried tools of all kinds, sleazy items that broke down after one or two uses. Any implement saved from the days before the RAA was indeed a treasure. With an agreeable nod, Elve zipped the bag.

The paint box contained only a bit of dried up pigment. But there were two good brushes, which Elve tucked into the zippered bag.

Boat opened the case to find a perfectly preserved pair of fine binoculars. With a grunt of satisfaction, he closed the case and slung it around his neck.

Elve raised her head. She felt the hairs on the back of her neck rise. Something wasn't right. "Boat, we should get out of here."

Boatman was moving in on the rest of the contents, hoping for more booty. He looked at his companion. "OK. Let's go."

The heavy sports bag was hard to manage along with their tools and the lantern. Elve found that she could balance it on her head. She wasn't skilled in this form of bearing, but the bag settled itself in a stable sort of way. She used a hand to steady it and kept the broom for a walking stick. Boat managed the chairs along with his tools.

They picked their way among the rubble towards the open end of the ruin. Cats with raised hackles and switching tails raised eerie calls from slabs above them. Elve couldn't interpret their unusual cries.

They stashed the bag in Elve's storeroom. Boat went on his way, the binoculars hidden under a rag in his cart.

As Elve went about her evening chores, she thought she felt something move under her feet. Then she thought she was imagining things.

The sun fell into a mass of threatening cloud.

In the night, heavy rain began to fall. Elve woke, aware of a distinct tremor. Dishes rattled in her cupboard, but the tremor was weak and brief.

She got up and went to the glass balcony door. Rain driven by a fierce wind slashed across her view. She couldn't see the familiar façade across the road. A roll of thunder began, low and distant. It continued and rose in intensity in tandem with a powerful tremor.

The roar exploded, mingling with the shrieks of wind in the gaping windows. Lightning snaked and crackled, illuminating the façade with one last incandescent glow. The wall shuddered, wavered, and in the darkness, fell.

The earth stilled. The tumult faded. Only the rain continued to pour.

Elve sat down at her table, trembling, grateful.

6

When Jema visited as usual on Kimday, Elve noticed her daughter's unusual silence and tension. They prepared their meal with the few, necessary words and sat down at Elve's scarred table. Food fell from Jema's trembling fork. She gripped the table's edge.

Elve looked at her questioningly, but said nothing.

Jema cried out, "It's Hom."

Hom was Jema's little grandson, born to her daughter Reba, who was born of Jema's first impetuous partnership when she was just eighteen years old. The relationship didn't last, and neither did Jema's subsequent partnerships.

Reba, as unlucky in love as her mother, also entered on a short-lived partnership when she was eighteen. Hom was the result. Reba moved to the Northern Tundra Region with a subsequent partner, leaving little Hom in Jema's care.

This arrangement wasn't unusual. Many households consisted of grandmothers and aunts caring for children of failed partnerships. There was no legal mechanism for requiring the men to support their offspring, and every reason in the world for them to pursue exciting new sexual partners, sexual satisfaction being their inalienable natural right. It was, under the RAA, a woman's right as well. So the grandmothers were stuck with the babies.

Elve prodded. "Hom?"

"He's just started school. Of course he has to sit on his hands. He's an active kid, and doesn't seem able to do it. He reached up to scratch his nose (not the first time), and the teacher whacked his hands with a ruler until they bled. If he does it again, he may be 'deemed ineducable'."

Both women knew what that meant. "Ineducable" children (ineds) were quietly dispatched by lethal injection at the local hospital. The regime had no room for imperfect specimens.

"Bring him to me," said Elve. "If anyone asks, say he was an ined."

"But what will I tell the Admin? His absence will be noted. RHA Garg knows he lives with me. It's in the records."

"Say that you're sending him to live with his mother in the Northern Tundra."

"I'm not a good liar."

"No, dear Jema, you're not. But you need to get better. It's a survival skill."

At this, Jema shoved her plate aside. Tearing at her grey tunic, she howled with despair.

Elve was at a loss to console her. But instinct prevailed, and she rose to lay a comforting hand on her daughter's shoulder.

When Jema returned the following week, she seemed subdued and uneasy.

At the table, she announced, "I did it. But it's no good."

"How so?"

"When I talked to Garg, she ordered me to turn in Hom's ID. She said that she alone is authorized to send it to the kid's mother. Upon Reba's request."

"That isn't right. That ID should always be on the kid. He can't go anywhere without it."

Jema shrugged. "That's what she said. So I turned it in to her."

It would not have occurred to Jema that she could question the policy of anyone in authority. She was, Elve thought, probably unable to even think of such a thing, given her devotion to the RAA. And since the Respected and Honoured Administrator is appointed directly by the State Secretary for Moral and Practical Training, she has the power of the RAA behind her.

Jema had worked at the school ever since her release from the armed forces after her obligatory years of national service. She was the Honoured Supervisor of Custodial Operations, organizing and supervising platoons of senior students who performed most of the cleaning and maintenance work in the school. The job was an envied appointment, earned by Jema's exemplary diligence in memorizing virtually all the laws and regulations governing the Loyel Sitizenz of the GNWRAA. She aced every test.

Jema had managed to accomplish all this while hiding any sign of her painful knee. At the age of twelve, she had had a fall in the ravine that left her with a need to limp. This she simply would not indulge. Aware that the RAA hated deformity, she endured in order to live.

Elve sat with a resigned air. "You did what you had to, I guess. Will Hom be safe with you? What if you're caught with a kid who's sposta be in school and no ID?"

Jema could only shrug.

"Bring him to me," said Elve. "He can stay with me until we get ID for him."

"You think so?"

Quashing her own doubts, Elve found the strength to be encouraging. "This is a decent neighbourhood. People mind their own business pretty much. I can keep Hom here without anyone questioning or reporting us. When he has settled in, I'll undertake his schooling. He'll be OK."

Jema brought Hom to Elve in the morning before she went to work. She presented him hastily along with a yellow polybag containing his few belongings.

"I told him he could stay with great-granny until his hands got better."

Hom was a small brown boy with downcast eyes. He kept his hands behind his back as if to escape further punishment. Elve's hand on his shoulder was gentle, but he didn't look up. He evaded her attempt to take his injured hands in hers.

"Just call me Granny," she said. "Come and we'll have bread and jam.

An immediate need was to introduce Hom to Ovid, the super and informal guardian of the building. He let legitimate people in and kept others out.

On the first morning of Hom's residence, Elve chose three choice beets from her store, and giving them to Hom to carry, took him down to Ovid's quarters on the ground floor. She didn't find him in the tool shop or the garbage area, so she rapped on the heavily studded metal door of the furnace room. The door rolled back into the wall and Ovid stepped out, shutting the door with a powerful motion.

He was a short, wiry man with a shock of grey hair. He might have been sixty years old. His watchful look relaxed when he saw Elve. She suspected that she was one of his favourites, and he was known to have favourites. She motioned Hom to give Ovid the beets.

The man accepted the beets, laying them beside the tools on his workbench. "What can I do for you?' His voice retained a rolling lilt, a remnant from his origins in the British Isles.

Elve presented the child, her hands on his tense shoulders. "This is Hom, my great- grandson. He is staying with me for the present."

"I guess he'll do, if he's one of yours." Ovid eyed Hom appraisingly. "Take your hands out of your pockets, lad, and stand up like a man."

Hom let his hands fall to his sides, but didn't raise his head.

"What 'appened his hands?"

"Correctional policy at school. Hom failed to sit on his hands, so the teacher beat them with a ruler. Steeledged."

"Ah they would do something like that. Not the first I've heard of."

"So you'll be seeing us around. He can help me with the fall work in the garden."

"Be careful when you're out and about. The police will want to know why he isn't in school."

"I'll say he has a contagious disease. Ringworm. That'll do, at least until his hands heal."

"You do what you gotta do," said Ovid, retreating through the studded door. He disappeared into the murkiness of the furnace room.

Elve treated Hom's hands with aloe and his spirit with a soft voice and tender touch. His hands began to heal, and with that healing he became a lively child with gleeful dark eyes under hair that sprang up, black and straight from his open brow. He was sturdy and erect, though not tall. He wore Elve out with his constant flow of questions and observations. Elve had only five years left. What could she make of him?

Without his ID card, Hom was *persona non grata* to the GNWRAA, subject to immediate dispatch without recourse. The RAA welcomed any opportunity to reduce the population.

7

The care of Hom, undertaken in instinctive sympathy, proved to involve more trouble than Elve could easily manage. She hadn't thought it out. She hadn't anticipated the demands a hungry, active, chattering lad would make on her resources: food, patience, and ingenuity in thinking up ways to keep him busy. If she didn't keep him busy, he was ingenious in devising things to do, like setting the four chrome-and-plastic chairs in a circle to see if he could jump from one to the next like a frog on lily pads.

His hands healed quickly, the right as good as ever. But the left had only thumb and two fingers with normal function; the outer two were curled and stiff, almost useless.

Hom wasn't much handicapped by this deformity. He helped enthusiastically in the garden, pulling up the dead stalks and consigning heaps of fallen leaves to the compost bin, while Elve bent to the tomato vines. Enthusiastically, until his five-year-old's enthusiasm waned, and he looked about for more exciting things to do. He was especially fascinated by the ruin across the road. Nothing had been done to clear it up. It was still the domain of yowling cats and the circling peregrines.

"Can I go over there, Granny? I want to see the cats."

"No—no—don't ask. It's a terrible place. The night the wall fell was a night out of hell."

"What's hell?"

Elve straightened, her hands full of green tomatoes. They would never ripen now, but she would fry them with rice and onions. "Hell?

Well it's the very worst place." Elve searched for a definition of this commonest of words, common, yet empty of its once powerful notion as a place of retribution after death. Belief in any kind of afterlife had disappeared from the common culture long ago. Only a few weirdos professed it in every generation.

"Where is it?"

"It isn't a real place. It isn't any *where*. It's an *idea* of the worst place of all."

"If it isn't real why can't I go there?"

Elve spotted two officers on bicycles approaching from the south. "Shtup! Get behind the bin. Get down! Quiet now."

With her knee, Elve pushed the child into the small space between the bin and a sheltering lilac bush. Fortunately, its leaves had not yet fallen. She dropped the tomatoes into the bin, keeping her back to the road.

The officers dismounted and approached. "Huah," they shouted. Elve turned towards them. They were strangers. Men with small heads and spherical bodies. Tweedledum and Tweedledee.

"We greet you in the name of Hiz Sooperbnes, owr Glorius and Preshus Onerabl Leeder uv de GNWRAA."

"May his Onerabl Preshus name live forever." Elve mouthed the formula obediently.

"Checking IDs. Government policy."

Elve wiped her hands on her tunic. She fished in its vee-neck where she kept her ID on a lanyard.

The officer read off the card. "Elve 29.07.2940.43.79 ," "Check," the second man said making a notation on a digital device called an Apsam.

The officers mounted their bikes. Elve watched them leave with thumping heart, thankful that Hom hadn't betrayed himself. When the officers were out of sight, she pulled him out of his hiding place.

"Why do I hafta hide, Granny?"

"You're sposta be at school, buddy. And you have no ID."

But another reason nearly escaped her lips—because we live in hell, my sweet wee lad.

When Boatman paid a visit bringing three good fish, he was startled to see the youngster seated at Elve's table. Hom had fashioned an animal from odds and ends in Elve's junk drawer: a scrap of tinfoil, rubber bands, and a couple of twist ties. He was pretending that the animal pulled a cart, with an egg slicer standing in for a cart.

"I need string," Hom said, "to make the donkey pull the cart."

Boatman obligingly dug in the pockets of his baggy pants. Among an assortment of small objects, he found a short piece of stout string. "How about this? Will it do the trick?"

Delighted, Hom attached the donkey to the cart and began to trot the beast around the table with appropriate donkey and cart noises. Carefully, because the construction was delicate and likely to founder at any time.

"Seems to be a likely kid," said Boatman, settling in at the counter to fillet the fish. "Where'd you get him?"

"He's my great-grandson," and Elve went on to explain Hom's family tree. "Jema has pulled him out of school because the teacher was abusive. He's got to hide because his ID is still in the hands of the school principal and we haven't figured out a way to get it back."

Boatman whistled. "So you got an illegal on your hands. Not good."

They settled at the table for their meal. It was an oft-repeated regulation of the RAA that family meals should begin with a formula of gratitude to "Owr Preshus and Perfect Leeder uv de Glorius Noo Wrld Reepublik uv Azhu and de Amerikas," accompanied by the RAA's four-part salute: right hand to heart, to the temple, to the heavens, and back to heart.

In unspoken agreement, Elve and Boatman executed an abbreviated formula. "OPPL" they said, waving sarcastic hands at the heavens, and fell to.

As his fork clattered to his empty plate, Boatman shoved back his chair, pushing his soiled cap back from grizzled curls. "Wanna fuck?"

Elve was willing. They didn't shut the bedroom door, nor tell Hom he couldn't watch. The operation was no more private or intimate than hand-washing. It achieved its intended relief, and the participants, adjusting their clothing as they came, returned to the other room without embarrassment.

Hom paid little attention. He'd seen the procedure before, his grandmother a partner with a couple of men. He continued to play with his donkey and cart, pausing many times for necessary repairs to the outfit.

8

Though her own education had taken place in an age of ubiquitous digital devices and free information access, Elve had been a pen and paper person. As a teen, she filled workbooks with fragments gleaned from varied sources. Her preference for Trad led her into labyrinths of stored literature where her random wanderings gave her a shaky framework for millennia of natural history, anthropology, political activity, and stories, always stories. Imperfect though her world-view was, it inoculated her against the propaganda of the GNWRAA.

And then her sources vanished. First came the Great Cultural Cleansing of Decade 290 = 299, when sources not already rendered into Inglish were eliminated. Then Galaxy and Populopedia disappeared overnight, and with it access to the stored knowledge of humanity.

Before the digital disaster, it was well-known that the infrastructure supporting Galaxy and Populopedia had been bought up by an immensely powerful global conglomerate, Alpha-Populopdedia , under their CEO, the billion-billionaire, John Franklin. Franklin proceeded to consolidate this infrastructure in one location outside Paris. In the interests of efficiency, he claimed. Governments and other global parties had protested this consolidation feebly, because all had interests affected by Franklin's enterprises.

A massive attack melted the infrastructure, killing the Web and communication with it. Hundreds of technicians perished as well.

Who was the perpetrator? A rogue nuclear state? A resurgent ISIS? An extraterrestrial attacker? With no one better to blame, the disaster was dubbed Franklin's Folly.

Elve considered ways and means. How was she to educate her small great-grandson? The safest course would be to teach him to read Inglish and write in Uniscrip, concentrating on the glories of the GNWRAA and Hiz Superbnes, Owr Glorius and Preshus Onerabl Leeder. To coach him in interacting with authority. To make him as far as she could into a "Loyel Sitizen" who could melt unnoticed into the general population.

But she couldn't. To confine Hom's beautiful alertness and curiosity, to squeeze it into the mould of the obedient "loyel sitizen", to return him to the state of discouragement engendered by his first days at school—that was something Elve could not do.

"Hom," Elve said one rainy autumn afternoon, "I've got something to show you."

She went to the storeroom and brought back the dented tin box. She set it on the table. "Bring your chair around beside mine."

With much thumping and scraping, Hom brought a chair around the table and climbed up on his knees beside his Granny. He wrinkled his nose at her smell, a mixture of food and unwashed hair and clothes. Hom didn't seem to be fussy; he nuzzled into Elve's shoulder, watching her open the box.

"Aw-w-w, Granny. I thought it would be something to play with."

"It's better than toys. We'll start with this one." Elve lifted out the book of Mother Goose. It was in the best shape of all the books, only a little scorched at one corner and its binding almost intact.

Elve leafed through, watching Hom for any sign of interest. At "Sing a Song of Sixpence," he pointed to the black birds flying from the king's pie. "Like the peregrines," he said.

So Elve read the ditty. It was easy to liken the king to Hiz Superbnes, and the king's place high in his palace chimed with what Hom had learned of the elevated position of the Onerabl Leeder on the Holy Magic Mountain. Hom had seen blackbirds too, as well as the peregrines. After Elve's explanation of "four-and-twenty," Hom decided to count the birds. When he could find only twenty-three birds in the picture, they discussed adding one to make twenty-four.

Elve was loath to deface the page with a hand drawing, so she said, "I think one has flown away."

"No," said Hom, "He's behind the palace over here where we can't see him." Hom pointed to a second tower in the distance. They were both satisfied with this explanation.

Thus began the unpacking of the old rhymes, their exploitation for lessons in nature, of politics, of number, size, and orthography. Hom liked the rhyme and rhythm. He soon committed many of them to memory, and began to "read" them to Elve.

"Hey Granny, we never read this one Why didn't we read this one?" He went on to read:

Ring around the rosies,
Pocketful of posies,
Hush! Hush! Hush!
We all fall down.

"Maybe I just missed it," said Elve. She didn't explain that she understood the "Hushes" to be sneezes and the falling down to refer to death from the plague. She'd omitted it out of secret horror.

Hom began to search for other neglected verses and read them all joyfully. Not without Elve's help with "bough" and "sew", and other Trad puzzles.

"I can read the whole book," Hom claimed. And read it aloud he did, from cover to cover, while Elve made pickles and mended his pants and tended her houseplants.

Hom pondered the illustrations. He surmised that the people who wore colour were rich, and the people in brown and grey were not. He was familiar with a world where colour was reserved for the high and mighty. The variety of shoe styles amazed him. He had only seen the boots of the police and his teachers, while everyone else wore sleazy cloth running shoes, even in winter.

Hom needed something new to read. Elve turned to *Alice in Wonderland*. The volume included *Through the Looking Glass* and *The Hunting of the Snark*. Not very suitable fare for so young a child, but it was what she had.

Winter came on, sharp and bleak. The boats were ice-bound at the docks, and fishing was halted.

Children's coats (warm and very ugly) were available in the Emporium. Boots were unaccountably lacking. Elve herself had a pair of old boots, leaky when the footing was wet, but adequate as long as the ground was frozen. Hom had only thin canvas runners.

The winter days were so dark with cloud that the solar lantern couldn't be fully charged. Elve lit a candle and invited Hom to sit with her in her big chair, frayed and soiled with the years, but still serviceable.

Banking on Hom's affinity for rhyme, she turned to "The Walrus and the Carpenter" in *Through the Looking-Glass* and began to read:

> The sun was shining on the sea,
> Shining with all his might:
> He did his very best to make
> The billows smooth and bright—
> And this was odd because it was
> The middle of the night.

Hom laughed. Encouraged, Elve read the whole thing, all seventeen verses. At the end, the boy sat disconsolate, tears wet on his face.

"They *ate* them all. They *ate* the poor little oysters. It was all a big trick."

Elve gathered the child in her arms. "It's just a silly story, darling. Don't cry. It never really happened."

"Couldn't *some* of the oysters have got away? When they saw what the walrus and the carpenter were doing?"

"Maybe some of them did. They just didn't get into the story." Elve allowed Hom to reimagine the verse with a happier ending.

Elve pondered the horror and violence contained in the Lewis Carroll books. Tempered always with humour, yet a satirical humour at the expense of ridiculous characters. Still, the horror always passed off without hurting Alice herself. My poor little oyster, she thought. The monstrous crow hovers, and you have always to hide. How can I get you away? Where can we go?

Now that Hom's hands were better, it was time to teach him to write. Pencils and paper had long disappeared from the Emporium. How was it to be done?

A fragment from the blue schoolbook came to mind. *Life and Literature* had something about people devising a chalkboard. She found the passage: "They had made a slate of a slab of the native rock. . . They wrote upon it with softer rocks." And she recalled her sons, Max and Mungo, writing with soft rock on cement and other surfaces. Years ago. She had no suitable rock and no place to get it, but she had an area of plain wall. It could be a writing surface.

The Emporium was lacking in many commodities, but low quality paint was abundant. Elve bought a pail of flat black interior paint and a cheap roller. Hom helped her paint a section of the wall opposite the balcony door with two coats of the stuff. Elve didn't care that black drops dribbled from Hom's roller, he was so obviously happy.

She now had a writing surface. What could be used to write on it? Elve remembered the broken drywall in the ruin across the road. Perhaps small chunks could serve as writing instruments.

She had never returned to the ruin after the fall of the façade. The reputation of the site had become even more gruesome; people imagined the cats to be larger and fiercer than before; associated tales of suicide and murder sprouted and flourished.

Elve's terror on the night of the fall had eased. And she didn't believe any of the tales. She didn't see any reason why the cats would become more dangerous than before. As for suicide and murder, the activity of the RAA was sufficient to account for all cases of missing persons.

"Hubboo!" Hom shouted when Elve said they would go there to look for a special kind of rock. Something to write with. They would have to wait for a mild day when Hom could go out without risking frostbitten toes.

Every morning Hom pestered Elve. "Can we go today? Can't we go today?' Why can't we go today?"

But the bitter weather continued. Elve blamed herself for even suggesting the expedition to the ruin. She should've kept quiet. In desperation, she went down to see Ovid.

"This kid is driving me crazy," she said. "He has to stay inside because he hasn't any boots and he doesn't give me a moment's peace." Elve didn't mention that Hom's presence also precluded her regular visits to O's place. She daren't risk a daytime journey with him. Further, she doubted that she should entrust O's secrets to so young a child.

Ovid leaned on his workbench with its scattering of tools. "So-o-o?"

Elve felt that she was about to trespass on Ovid's goodwill. No doubt he approved of her in a general way, but the enormity of the favour she was about to ask might be overstepping his approval by quite a margin.

"I was wondering—could the boy spend an hour or so with you in the morning? Just to give me a break?"

Ovid was taken aback. "Me? and a kid? What makes you think that would work?"

"He's sturdy and smart. Not afraid of heights. Could help change lightbulbs."

"Haven't seen a lightbulb in the Emporium for months. Maybe a year." Ovid was obviously cool to the idea. Elve needed to sweeten the deal.

"I have some good tools," she said. "A hammer. A box of nails."

Ovid's head shot forward. "Where'd you get those?"

"Hom could bring them down. And stay a while just to try things out?"

An acquisitive leer closed one corner of Ovid's left eye. "Send the lad down. Around ten tomorrow."

"Oh, you dear man, what a gem you are!"

"Save your raves till I see how the boy works out. And how good that hammer is."

9

Elve left Hom in Ovid's care along with the hammer and nails. She kept the other tools in reserve should another bribe be necessary. She set off immediately for O's place. She hadn't been there since winter set in. She dressed in her down parka with its permanently dirty cuffs and put on the leaky boots.

She took potatoes and beets in a polybag, and two eggs she thought she could spare.

The road was slippery with ice and snow packed by the passing of many feet. Elve envied people she saw who had armed themselves with canes or improvised walking sticks—old broom handles, curtain rods—anything that could be commandeered. Snow masked the little-used paths by the creeks, but Elve found her way by judging the natural course of the hidden waterway.

O greeted her with a cry of joy. "Come in, come in, come in! I've been missing you."

Elve inspected her old friend. "You've been well?" for O looked thinner, though still sinewy and upright in posture.

"The food is very welcome," said O. Elve guessed that some of O's sources had diminished or disappeared.

O read Elve's thought. "Others have discovered that the ravine is a source of meat. My rabbit traps show signs of being robbed."

"Are other people laying traps too?"

"I don't think so. Just getting their meat the easy way."

"Bastards."

"Never mind. I hope she took the meat home to her children. The footprints looked female."

"We do what we hafta do. There's no meat in the Emp just now. Not even Sprem."

"There's still tea. Lots of tea. What will you have?"

O had fresh melt water in the boiler. They soon had hot cups of chicory brew on the table.

"Of Max and Mungo, there is no word today."

"Not today, but sometime soon." Elve sighed. She was weary of hoping, yet couldn't help herself. O touched her hand in sympathy.

"The radio has been useless," O said. "Two new propaganda stations have popped up. Their signals are so powerful they interfere with all other signals. Very late at night, I picked up a few words. A woman's accented voice calling 'Can you hear me? Can you hear me?' She said she was calling from NYVR."

"Please, O, try again. See if you can raise a signal."

O's shrug showed how little she hoped, but she moved to her primitive set in the corner. Elve shoved over a stool for her. O put on headphones and sent her identifier, 'OYYZ'. The radio buzzed and crackled. A strident voice declared a MNWRAA victory over dissident forces in . . . the voice died in an explosion of static.

"Nothing," said O. "Just a RAA news report."

Elve conceded defeat. But then she said, "Boatman has two-way radio on his boat. The fishermen use it for local communication. Could it be fixed up somehow to pull in more distant signals?"

"It's an idea. Not something I would know how to do, or any of my friends, though we're an ingenious lot." O scratched a dark brown patch on her cheek, and Elve noticed that there was another on her wrist.

"I've no time to think about anything just now, not even the writing project. I've got myself into a pickle, looking after a great-grandson, and I haven't a moment to myself."

So Elve told her friend about Hom. "He's a dear kid, but a terrible responsibility. He has no ID, so I hafta hide him from the authorities. I need to think about his education. How best to secure his survival."

"Is he smart?"

"Seems to be. He's learned to read Trad. One of my books. I got him into Mother Goose just to keep him busy."

"Protect him from the propaganda. It's getting worse all the time. It anaesthetizes the mind."

"Or should he just meld into the general population? Look and sound like all the other kids? Somehow keep from attracting attention?"

"I think you've already scuppered that possibility. If he's reading Trad."

"*Alice in Wonderland*. Great food for the imagination. The RAA has no truck with imagination."

"You have cooked your goose. No choice. Make him as clever as possible. He'll have to work out his own salvation."

Elve drained her blue-patterned mug. "That was good," she said, wiping her mouth with the back of her hand. "Are you having any luck with the ink?"

"Lem has made me pens out of goose feathers. I was thinking wood, but he says feathers are better. The chokecherry ink was good with a few drops of vinegar as a preservative. But chokecherries are frozen now, so I'm working on something with oak galls."

"Sacable! How do you know these things?"

"Observation, mostly. I've seen a dark liquid exude from the oaks. It looks very promising." O fetched a small bottle from her shelf. The oak gall floated in liquid. "Lem sent Reedwoman to me to talk about paper. Her right name is Lali. She's working on small sheets made with a sort of grass that grows plentifully near her home by the river. It's a half-day's walk from here. She's keen on the project because she has a collection of loose pages written in Estonian. She wants to preserve them too."

"There must be more literature hidden away," Elve said. "I think there were always people who loved physical books, even when the texts were all available on the web. But we've all we can do to preserve what we've got."

"One bit of good news. Lali has an immense sheet of polished granite. Was once a kitchen countertop. It makes a great surface for our work. Making the paper and for a scriptorium."

"A scriptorium?"

O laughed. "I just made that up. A place to write in."

Elve stood up. "Maybe by spring we'll be ready to start. Spring seems so far away. Poor Hom is housebound because he has no warm boots. I don't want to risk frostbite in this weather."

"I could make leggings of rabbit's fur if that would help. Though I haven't got a good needle for the work."

"Needles. I've got some. Specialized for working with tough materials, I think. They're in the bag I rescued from Statesfield. I'll bring them as soon as I can. Maybe Hom could have the leggings for his birthday."

"How soon?"

"He'll be six in May."

"Winter will be over by then. Get the needles to me right away and I will make the leggings expeditiously."

Elve nodded. "I'll try. I should be getting home. I left him with Ovid."

O went to her rustic cupboard. "Here is a treat for him." She handed Elve a small, sealed jar. "Jellied rabbit. It is very good."

Elve didn't doubt that the meat was very good, but felt that her friend could ill afford to give it away. Still, she knew what O would say if she refused the gift. 'What does it matter,' she would say, 'what does it matter if an old woman fails and dies? I've had my time.'

So Elve tucked the meat into her bag, clasped hands with her friend, and stepped up out of O's secret lair. As she walked home, she pictured Hom outfitted in warm fur leggings. She could take him outside. How he longed to go outside!

The cupboard was bare. A trip to the Emp was in order. Hom was spending the afternoon helping Ovid clean the halls, a chore the super rarely undertook.

Elve pulled on her down coat and a warm, red tuque of similar vintage. Thick socks and the leaky boots. Frosty snow at the back door crunched and squealed under her feet. Good. The boots wouldn't leak.

A few people trudged the frozen ruts of Miller's Lane. Grannies heading for the Emp. A young woman with her infant tied to her back. Workers with shovels looking for odd jobs.

Obligatory greetings were exchanged.

"Yo, Loyel Sitizen." "Enjoy and give thanks for this glorius Day uv de RAA."

This greeting was becoming worn at the edges by constant use and sounded more like, "Yo, Loytsn." Daring folks shortened the response to a basic "Glordyraw."

At the corner of Old Bloor, Elve looked up at the ever-changing electronic billboard depicting scenes of the Magic Mountain. Most featured lofty peaks and rivers flowing between verdant hills. But a vision of falling waters stopped Elve in her tracks. I've been there, she thought. That's no Magic Mountain. That's Niagara Falls.

Elve had been there as a child of ten or so on a rare school excursion. Her school's administrator happened to believe that, even though her students could experience the sight and sound of the falls by virtual means, the real had something to offer that the virtual did not. Elve could still feel the spray thrown up by the mighty cascade.

She wondered whether the RAA used the same photos worldwide for their billboards. Maybe someone in the Honoured Ministry of Government Self-Aggrandisement goofed in sending Niagara Falls to Urb 43.79. She couldn't be the only Loyel Sitizen of old Tranna who would recognise Niagara Falls.

Snowy pyramids stood in little parks along the way. A little taller than a man, they were irregular constructions, yet obviously monuments. Elve knew that the snow hid piles of skulls, all that was left of the thousands who had perished in an influenza epidemic in a long-gone time.

Grandma Atlanta had passed on the stories she'd been told as a child. Survivors were so weakened and their numbers so diminished that they couldn't provide proper burial for the dead. After a time of recovery and migration, the new people collected the skulls and built these cairns. Perhaps the other bones were buried, for the most part, but it was quite usual to find the odd skeletal remnant in the grass or by the creek.

"Yo, Loytsn." A younger woman caught up to Elve and began to walk beside her. Elve recognized Sor, the woman who lived in the rooms on the other side of her bedroom wall.

"Glordyraw, neighbour. You're not at work today?" Elve asked.

"My office closed very suddenly. Like overnight. I hope I'll get a new assignment. Like tomorrow."

"What office was that?"

"The local office of the Respected Ministry of Spirituality and Entertainment. We think the ministry is being abolished. But we don't know."

Cloud flew before the east wind, freeing the sun's brilliance. Frost glittered on every twig and branch of the roadside maples, drawing the women's eyes to the treetops.

"What's that?" Sor pointed to the patch of blue at the top of the sky.

A silent white shape moved at a great height, needle-nosed, streamlined, with wings like the aircraft of the olden days. Elve and Sor watched until it became a pale dot in the western sky.

"It's a whiteship. They told us on the Hour of Power. Can move at tremendous speed, they said. But they didn't say what it was for."

"Not likely a pleasure craft," said Sor, and Elve chuckled at the very idea.

More billboards dotted their way to the Emp. Some of them showed the first Preshus and Perfect Leeder, stern yet avuncular. The largest, though, projected on a high blank wall above the Emp's great doors, was a heroic portrait of his son, the present Preshus and Perfect Leeder. A young man with smooth pale brow and prominent black eyes. He wore the white, gold-braided uniform and the enormous officer's cap of his office.

At the entrance, Elve and Sor parted ways, Elve to look for chalk, and Sor to find a new tunic for her boy.

The Emp, a shopping centre which had escaped much damage in the Statist bombardments, was a dimly lit, cavernous space. Two levels of numbered divisions displayed all categories of goods; everything from turnips to tiaras. Voices and footsteps echoed from the warehouse-style furnishings.

Elve laboured up the stairs to Division 23 which she recalled as offering a few stationery items, all that was left of a once prosperous trade in home digitals. Wall screens of many sizes with boxes to receive *Noo Wrld Gloree*. Speakers. Desk lamps. Desk accessories too, though no paper clips, pens, or pencils to go in them.

A young woman in a black padded parka stood behind a metal counter. Her white cap numbered 23 designated her as the officiating clerk. She didn't acknowledge Elve in any way, but watched her scan the utilitarian shelving. Her scrutiny was unnecessary, Elve thought, since the area was well furnished with security cameras.

"Do you have chalk?" she asked. "Chalk. To write with."

The clerk appeared to take thought. "No."

The woman indicated several keyboard machines above and behind her. "Here's the writers," she said. "But they hafta have paper."

"And you have no paper."

"No."

"Where else might I look for chalk?"

"Dunno."

The conversation was apparently over. Elve betook herself to the grocery area where she bought a turnip and dark bread. Oleo and .25 kilo of brown sugar to encourage Hom to eat his morning porridge. Two Porgel packs of tofu.

Chalk, if there was any, would be a bit of old stock lying on a shelf somewhere, thought Elve, trudging home past the billboards.

Hom should get his wish. His new leggings covered his feet and legs to the knee. Adequate protection from frostbite if coupled with warm socks.

A visit to the ruin. The first decent day. Elve found herself looking forward to it.

10

Hom proved his worth. Ovid found him very useful, at first for sending and fetching and then for more refined tasks. Over the winter, Ovid welcomed him into the workshop whenever Elve asked, allowing her the chance to visit O and do other errands.

The boy had remarkable dexterity, and Ovid set him to work mending broken tools with bits of wire. Ovid suffered severe arthritis in his fingers, so such projects frustrated his clumsy efforts.

Hom, like his Great-uncle Max, could make things. His chief pleasure was in the varied chunks of wood stashed in one dark corner of the workshop. Of various sizes and shapes and coming from different trees, they challenged him to find ways to make use of them. He was able to fashion a sturdy stool from some of the hardwood. The softer kinds yielded to his knife in an altogether fascinating way.

"Can I take this one home with me? And the knife?" Hom held up a chunk of cedar that he'd started to carve.

"What're you makin'?"

"I don't know yet. The wood is showing me where to cut."

"Don't make any sense to carve if you don't know what it's gonna be."

"But can I have it anyway? To work on at home?"

"Y' can have the wood. It's not good for much. But not the knife."

"Aw-w-w." Hom stuck out his lower lip in a not altogether innocent expression of disappointment.

Ovid yielded. "Y'can borrow it for the day. But bring it back tomorrow."

Elve's table became a sculptor's workshop. Ovid's precious knife traveled between the two workshops in a belted sheath that Hom made out of a chunk of old carpeting. Ovid showed him how to sharpen it.

"It's finished. Ta-da!" Hom flourished a hand over his piece. "Granny, come and see."

Elve stopped washing carrots. She stood drying her hands, pondering what she should say. Somehow she felt that "What is it" would be a rude question. She walked around the table, inspecting the work from all sides.

The object was about the size of a small cat. It stood securely on its base, the wood grain clearly guiding its shape, which was organic, but not identifiable as any particular animal or plant. The excisions were crude yet powerful, lending an aura of fierceness to the piece.

"It's very scary," she said at last.

"Yay, Gran. I knew you would like it!" Hom exploded into a capering dance.

Ovid's response was less satisfactory. "Dunno why you want to spend time makin' something you don't know what it is," he said. "Now sharpen up the knife and use it on this plug for the front door lock. Can't find no new locks in the Emp so we just hafta plug the hole and hope nobody breaks in."

A brilliant, sunny day, cold but dry, filled both Elve and her charge with an urge to be outdoors. It was an ache, this need to be outside.

"This is the day," said Elve. "Our day to visit the ruin. See if old drywall can write on our black wall."

"Hubboo, hubboo!" chortled Hom. He pulled on his new rabbit fur leggings and black padded coat and was at the door before Elve could turn around.

"Hold your horses, young man. We need to think this through."

A spade to dig snow away. Some kind of tool to cut away chunks of the material. A polybag to carry it. A walking stick for the sake of her old legs. The terrain would be treacherous since the fall of the façade. Something to placate the cats. There was little she could spare for that.

"Here, you hafta help." Elve shoved the tin pot of food scraps into Hom's hands. Mostly vegetable peelings and eggshells but it would have to do.

There hadn't been fresh snow for some time. The banks were reduced to random heaps, frozen hard. There was no wind. They stood for a moment at the edge of the street, breathing the crisp air, exhilarated.

Across the road, Statesfield stood impressive, even in its ruination. The lowest storey of the fallen east wall still stood, crenellated by broken window openings. The wall appeared to have cracked along a fault line and tumbled inward. They might have to navigate a huge pile of debris. Elve and her charge crossed the road as soon as they could see no passers-by.

From their sun-warmed perches, wary felines watched them scramble into the ruin. Hom counted seven of them. He dumped the scraps in a sunny place and waited, but none of the cats came down to feed.

In the lee of fallen rubble, there were patches of bare ground. There was no need to dig. Chunks of drywall weren't hard to find. They were rotten and easily broken into manageable pieces. Hom charged about, picking up suitable pieces to put in Elve's bag.

"We don't hafta go home yet," he pleaded, when Elve said the polybag was full enough.

"I need to rest a bit anyway. Don't go near the cats." She sat down on a convenient slab to let the sun warm her face. She closed her eyes gratefully.

The cats were precisely the point of interest for the boy. A huge orange tom had approached the pile of scraps. He sniffed delicately. He poked experimentally. Unearthing an appetizing bit, he growled and took a bite. Hom crept to a vantage point behind a concrete bulwark, watching.

One by one the other cats approached. The tom snarled, warning them off. When he had snagged all the best bits, he moved off. The other cats, four females and two half-grown kittens, pawed through the food, looking for meat. Finding none, they settled for licking the leftover bits, finding the remnants of sauce or maybe a little gravy, a suspicion of egg left in the shell. It had been a hard winter for them. Their coats, though thick, were dull. Bony haunches jutted through their fur.

Hom longed to get closer, try to be friendly, maybe even stroke one of them. He inched around the concrete barrier, making soft noises in his throat. One young cat, a skinny grey tabby, eyed him steadily, still as rock. Hom extended a hand, still murmuring. The cat drew back, hissing. The others, alerted, yowled and fled to high ground. Hom withdrew his hand. He backed off, still making what he hoped were friendly sounds.

Elve was alerted too. "What did I tell you? Get away from those cats." Though she discounted the tales of their malevolence, Elve wasn't about to trust the good will of the Statesfield cats. She heaved herself to her feet, reaching for her stick. "We're going home."

She moved off towards a gap in the rubble, a little faster than she was wont to go. Hom hung back. The tabby had stopped hissing and seemed more curious than threatening. Avoiding eye contact, but still making soft sounds, the boy backed away. "I'll come back," he told the animal. "I'll come back and bring you better eats."

As she mounted the last barrier at the edge of the ruin, Elve saw the police bicycles coming down the snow-packed road, two of them. She knew she was clearly visible, so stood her ground as they approached.

Dismounting, they shouted from the road. "Huah there, Missus. We greet you in the name of Our Moest Respected Hie Cumishoner and Preshus Onerabl Leeder. We require your ID."

Elve froze. Hoping wildly that Hom wouldn't appear, she picked her way as quickly as she dared through the tumble of concrete in front of her. "Mae hiz Onerable Naem liv forever," she gibbered, fumbling with chilled fingers inside her coat for the card. What excuse could she manufacture for her load of broken plaster? But they didn't ask.

The officers took their time. They inspected both sides of the card. They asked where she lived and with some difficulty, corroborated her information against the digital record. Elve thought again how much they resembled Tweedledum and Tweedledee.

They were about to tuck away the tablet when an ear-rending howl arose from behind Elve's back. Hom!

"The cats! The cats are coming after us," she yelled, and began to hurry towards her building.

White-faced, the officers mounted their bikes. They pedalled with all their might, haunches working like bellows. They turned the next corner and were gone.

Elve watched them go. She breathed in great gulps to ease her panicking heart. But it would not ease. Was Hom all right?

As she turned to go back into the ruin, Hom stumbled into view, waving the tin pot.

"I got it, Gran. I didn't forget the pot."

"What happened? What made you yell?"

"I was running to catch up and I tripped on a rock. I think I hurt my hand." He displayed a wrist that was already red and swelling.

At home, Elve applied what she knew of first aid. An ice-pack using ice from a pail she kept on the balcony. A sling contrived from an old sheet. She pondered trying for some kind of cast or splint to immobilize the joint, but since she didn't know how to do it, or even if the wrist was broken, she decided to forgo such an attempt. Might do more harm than good.

Hom should be seen by a doctor.

If she took him to the hospital, his ID would be required as soon as they were in the door. Or maybe before. Without it, he wouldn't just be denied treatment, he would come to the authorities' attention, with consequences that Elve dared not contemplate.

Hom must have ID. It would have to be counterfeit. How was this to be accomplished?

11

Elve had to set aside the question of acquiring ID. Hom badgered her with pleas to complete their chalk experiment. The polybag of weathered drywall had to have attention.

To Hom's great disappointment, the pieces were useless in their present form. When he tried to mark the black-painted wall with them, they left only smudges and crumbled instantly into a mess on the floor.

Elve saw that the plaster would have to be reconstituted in some way. "Don't worry," she said, faking confidence, "I'll figure something out."

She thought the plaster should be dried out completely and reduced to powder. She would try mixing in some water and packing the mixture into some kind of mold. What kind, she had no idea. But inspiration might strike.

Elve cast about for some way to crush the drywall. Her eye fell on Hom's sculpture. It had a sturdy base and was about the right size to serve as a crushing instrument. Its rounded top looked friendly to her hand.

"Hom," she said, "do you mind if we use your sculpture to crush this stuff up?" She grasped the piece to show how it might be used.

Hom looked first dismayed and then joyful. "Hubboo," he cried. "Let me do it. Let me smash it up."

"But I think the chunks should dry out for a couple of days first," said Elve. Hom was anxious to press on with the smashing. Glumly, he helped his granny lay out the pieces on the floor to dry.

Elve turned her mind to the ID problem. She had no immediate resources to produce a convincing laminated card. No typewriter, no cardboard, no laminator.

Who among her trusted friends would have such resources? No one she knew. Not even O with her store of practical knowledge.

She'd been careful to limit personal contact to a very few people. The less others knew about you the better. It was a strategy for surviving in a society where anyone might become a government informer. Though being standoffish could generate suspicion even among friendly people. It was a balancing act.

Ovid. Ovid was the person most likely to have useful contacts for an illegal operation. Her trust in him was tempered by certain wariness. Ovid was a guy to keep on the right side of. Not necessarily the friend who would back you in time of trouble.

She was already beholden to him for his time with Hom. She decided to risk adding to her burden of debt. She took the staple gun from the zippered sports bag, noting how depleted its contents had become.

Elve went down after Hom was asleep. She daren't discuss the matter in his hearing. Hom must be kept completely innocent of incriminating knowledge.

She knocked on the door of Ovid's first floor suite.

She heard a chair scrape and shuffling feet. Ovid's face appeared in the slightly opened door. Elve sniffed a pungent odour, one that she remembered from her teen years. Pot.

"Oh, it's you," Ovid said. He opened the door a little wider, still barring her view with his body. "What can I do for you?"

"I need a fake ID. For Hom. The school is keeping his ID. Jema told them that Hom went to live with his mom in the Northern Tundra Region. They'll only release it to the mom."

"Why doesn't Jema get the mom to get it and send it back?"

"There's no mail service to Tundra. Jema's lost touch with Reba entirely. I need it right away. The new police are a touchy pair. Rude.

Not likely to make exceptions. Do you know how to make one? Or know someone who does?"

Ovid grinned. "You don't make 'em, lady. You buy one. They're available for a price." He was enjoying her ignorance.

A female voice called from within. The words were indistinguishable, but the tone was querulous.

"Gotta go. Come down to the shop tomorrow. We can talk then."

Elve left Hom curled in the big chair reading *Alice in Wonderland*. "I won't be long," she said, and he barely grunted. Hom could get lost in a book with an absorption that Elve noted with some envy. That kind of concentration was a thing of the past for her. He wouldn't miss her at all.

She found Ovid in the workshop sharpening his knives. He stopped and leaned on the workbench.

"So you need a fake ID." His expression was unreadable. He had willingly colluded in hiding Boat's visits from nosy people, especially the police, but he had never participated in anything blatantly illegal on her account. Elve tried to measure his attitude.

"I think so. Yes."

"There's lots of IDs. The RAA's offing people every day. Old people, sick people, kids that can't make it in school. You just hafta know how to make contact."

"And you know how?"

"Not for sure. Never had no need to deal with them. But I know where to find them."

"But surely the IDs are collected and destroyed?"

"Sure, they're sposta be. But IDs are worth money. To the right person. Like you."

Was Ovid going to shake her down for a king's ransom? Money she didn't have? How would he exact his pound of flesh? She drew the staple gun from her bag and set it wordlessly on the workbench.

Only a slight nod acknowledged the gift. "I don't go there myself. I got me own issues with the law and I prefer to lie low. But the woman you want runs the shebeen. The one in old Mimico. You might know the place. It was a church in the real old days. When the RAA outlawed alcohol, the Blue Goose shut down and quietly moved into the old church basement. Looks like a ruin from outside, but the basement's still pretty cozy."

Elve's heart sank. She knew of shebeens, of course. Outlawing alcohol was probably the silliest of the RAA's prohibitions. People had never forgotten how to make their own wine and liquor, and illicit operations (production, transport, and sales) went on constantly. They were also constantly raided, with dire consequences for the perpetrators unless they had greased the palms of the right officials.

A person like herself with no connections in officialdom took great risk in visiting a shebeen.

"I know the place," she said. "I lived with my Grandma Atlanta in that area of Tranna. The church was beyond old then. Had apartments built on the back. It was deserted even in my young days and had been as long as anyone could remember."

"The front doors are still there," said Ovid. You can get in, no problem. The left side's blocked off but you can go down the stairs on the right and through a wooden door. There's a wall looks solid, but it's hollow. A big painted crest on it. Something left from the church days. Knock there. Special rhythm" Ovid must have noticed Elve's pallor. "You up for this?"

"I hafta be. Hom can't stay inside forever."

"Sorry I can't go. Got me some irons in the fire and it's too dangerous just now."

"So what's the special knock?"

"Shaveannan'aircut—two bits." Ovid sang and knocked out the rhythm on the workbench. Elve tried it and managed a good imitation.

"What's it mean?"

"Don't know. Something from way back."

"Remember Populopedia? Where you could find out anything?"

"Yeah." They sighed in unison.

"Then you got to know the password. It keeps changing, but last I heard it was 'Shibboleth.'"

"Shibboleth? What's that?"

""No idea. Anyhow, they'll let you in. Sit down and buy a drink. Look for a woman with red hair. Lots of it. Y' can't miss 'er. You'll need to go a few times till she knows you. Tell 'er what you need and she'll make you a deal."

Elve felt she should be getting back upstairs. "Thanks," she said. "I'll think about it." Impulsively, she held out her hand. Ovid responded with a closed fist. So she fisted her hand and they connected.

Hom had changed his position to a sprawl, but was still reading. He looked up.

"Where'd you go?"

"Just down to see Ovid. We had business to do."

"What kinda business?"

"Business that's none of your business. You wouldn't understand." Elve didn't like to discourage Hom's curiosity. She thought, though, that in this case, his only safety lay in ignorance.

Hom jumped up. "This book is crazy, Gran. How can a girl keep growing huge and then getting little again?"

"You're not sposta believe it. It's a fantasy. You don't think you can really fall down a rabbit hole, do you?"

"I dunno. I never seed a rabbit hole."

"I guess you haven't. Well, they're much too small for anyone to fall down into." Elve reflected that she really needed to get Hom outside more.

"Hey, Gran. The plaster's dry. I tried it and it's all crumbly."

Hom was right. The plaster was ready for treatment.

So they enlisted Elve's wok as a vessel and employed Hom's sculpture as a crusher. Thus Elve and Hom reinvented the mortar and pestle of millennia ago.

Hom mashed and crunched. Elve removed the pieces of heavy paper from the mess. She took over the mashing to reduce the plaster to a powder. She put it through a sieve to remove the last of the stubborn lumps.

Careful addition of water to the powder produced a paste that Elve thought might work. She ladled the paste into a cake pan and smoothed it with a wooden spoon. She scored it deeply with a knife, hoping that she would be able to break the mass into sticks once it had dried.

In three days, the mix looked dry and hard.

"Let me. Let me do it," Hom yelled. He turned over the pan on the counter, but the stuff didn't fall out. He grabbed his sculpture and whacked the bottom of the pan. With a satisfying crunch, the mass yielded. It broke into two pieces on a diagonal line. But Elve's plan was good. The mass could be broken along the scored lines, and useable pieces resulted.

Hom took a piece of his homemade chalk. He ran to the black wall and chalked in proud upper case—HOM.

12

The draft in the stairwell was colder than usual, Elve thought, as she climbed to her floor. She locked her door, shivering. A windy blast shrieked across her balcony. She went to look out. A wall of swirling white blanked out the three spruce trees on her side of Miller's Lane. Nothing of Statesfield was visible. Elve was surprised and a little uneasy. Her sunny day in the ruins had lulled her into thinking that winter was over.

The blizzard continued through the night and all the next day. It paused in the evening, only to gain strength for another onslaught the following night. It subsided sullenly on the third night, still sending up whiteouts from the drifted banks when there was no new snow to play with.

Hom and Elve holed up. Elve couldn't risk her journey to the shebeen until other, younger citizens had broken paths through the hard-drifted banks. The rickety public transit wouldn't be operating for many days, she supposed. The tracks would have to be cleared by hand, an arduous and unpopular job. Not many would sign up to do the work, because the Urb officials had a reputation for cheating. Casual workers would be charged for the rental of their tools and might very well end up owing more than they earned.

Hom wouldn't keep his wrist in the sling. Elve watched and worried. The swelling subsided, and there seemed to be no damage beyond a bruise that turned a bilious green shade after its purple phase. Hom declared that it didn't hurt anymore and nailed his sling to the black wall as a sack to hold the chalk. He didn't ask permission for his little projects. He had them done before Elve noticed what he was up to. She realized ruefully that his agility, mental and physical, left her old eyes and bones vainly trying to catch up.

Imprisonment in the apartment with their new supply of chalk and the black wall provided the opportunity for a crash course in handwriting. Hom was used to the ornate fonts of the old books at his disposal and was trying to imitate them. Elve introduced the ABCs in unadorned Arial, six letters per day over four days (plus a day for y and z). She demanded twenty minutes of practice each day. After the drill, Hom wrote what he liked.

The chalk sticks were an awkward size, rough-edged, and messy. They hurt the fingers and crumbled into dust on the floor. Elve decreed that every writing session should conclude with the sweeping of the floor.

Hom found a light file in the bottom of the tool-bag. He set to work, filing the chalk sticks down to fat cylinders so that they were comfortable to use.

He liked to copy rhymes from Mother Goose. He stood on a chair reaching high to chalk the tales of Humpty Dumpty, the cat and the fiddle, and the pussycat who visited the queen. He didn't copy illustrations from the book, but drew his own representations around the text.

"Hey, look, Gran," he would call. "Come here and see what I writed."

Elve hid the intensity of her joy in Hom's aptitude for both writing and drawing. The lines were straight, unless he wanted them otherwise. The illustrations were lively and imaginative. But he shouldn't see how deeply she was moved nor discern the searing hope that threatened her composure. Hom would be all right, she thought. He would be too valuable to kill. Hom would survive.

"Waw-waw, what a lot of fun you're having!!" she said. "That queen is quite wonderful."

"Yeah, I made her really scared." And indeed the queen looked like she might jump right off the wall.

Hom developed an artistic hand, taking liberties with the font so that it flowed with easy connectedness. Elve required no standard beyond legibility and didn't correct his liberties.

A trip to the Emporium became necessary. By this time, the passage of many feet and carts had trampled wide paths in the snow. Elve thought she could manage the walk with the help of her stick.

"I wanna go too," said Hom.

"No, you can't go. The Emp police. . ."

"But I wouldn't do anything bad. Why would the police get me?"

"The Emp guards are very fussy about ID. Your ID is still at the school."

"Then we should go and get it."

How to explain to the child that he was supposed to be with his mother in the Northern Tundra Region. That his ID couldn't be retrieved without revealing the lie, and that the lie endangered his very life.

"Maybe someday," Elve extemporized. The lower lip thrust out again. "Let's go down now and see what Ovid's doing."

"Don't wanna stay with Ovid."

"But you always have a good time with Ovid."

"Don't wanna go down. Wanna go out."

"You can't go out. Not to the Emp." Elve's voice sharpened with her fear of Hom's intransigence. His safety depended upon obedience. Softening her tone—"I'll bring you something nice from the Emp. A sausage, maybe."

Hom stood with clenched fists, his face a mask of obduracy.

"Alright then. Stay here. I won't be long." She shrugged into her old coat, gathered her basket and walking stick. With a parting glare that she hoped would scare Hom into being good, she left the apartment.

Hom was not scared. First he raided the cupboard for something to eat. Alas, it was bereft of anything good. Not even a stale crust.

He decided to use the file to smooth rough edges on his sculpture. But the file wasn't suitable for use on wood, so he abandoned the project.

He read awhile in *Alice in Wonderland* but stopped because he felt so acutely the contrast between his own incarceration and Alice's freedom to wander about outdoors where there were rabbits and rose trees and caterpillars.

He picked out a new piece of chalk. A new piece that Elve would not have allowed, since there were some short ones in the sack.

When Elve came in, she found him still perfecting his work.

> **My name is HOM.**
> **I hav no ID.**
> **I am noebudy.**
> **The polies wil kil me**
> **if thae fiend me.**

Under the text, Hom had drawn a boy under the foot of a glowering uniformed man. The man held a huge hypodermic needle.

Elve cried out, "Oh, darling." She dropped her parcels and ran to enclose the child in a fierce hug.

How does he know this, she wondered. But of course he does. He's exposed to the RAA's Hour of Power every day.

The usual technique used by the RAA for informing all "Loyel Sitizenz" consisted of a uniformed official using a pointer to guide viewers while reading through a power-point script, an Inglish text rendered in large Arial. A functional, if boring, reading lesson.

The regulations, the threats, the homilies that would pass over most children's heads would be clear enough to a child as perceptive as Hom.

He knows, she thought. He can read and write. There will be no holding him back. To protect him and yet nurture a curious and absorbent mind, given her limited resources, was a daunting task. Elve wasn't daunted. She felt a surge of courage, a sense of power. Joy, unearned and undeserved. Grace.

13

Faced with the faded church crest, Elve had a frightening lapse of memory. Her mind was wiped clean of the code Ovid had sung for her. Although she had rehearsed it several times, it wouldn't come to mind. Why is it, she thought, that I can remember stuff from my childhood like our old telephone number, but I can't remember something important like this? All she could recall was Anna—Anna was part of it. She tapped the word on her chest, but the rest of the code escaped her.

Elve had learned a trick that sometimes helped when memory failed. Diverting her attention from the thing she wanted to remember could sometimes break the mental logjam.

So she controlled her breathing and concentrated on the emblem. Though it was cracked and peeling, Elve could make out its pointed oval shape. A strong red X crossed it. She discerned four icons in the resulting sections, all but one defaced and indecipherable. In the top quarter, transcendently clear, a white bird descending.

Her clenched mind unlocked. She heard Ovid singing the formula, heard it as if he were beside her ear. "Shaveanna'naircut—two bits."

Elve thumped the rhythm on her chest, murmuring the tune. She practised it again before tapping it on the crest. The thin panel swung back. A bearish, glowering man blocked her way.

"Password." It was a threat, not a question.

"Shibboleth," Elve whispered.

The man stood aside.

Under the feeble illumination of two solar lanterns, the low-ceilinged room held more shadows than light, more menace than merriment. Elve expected noise, but heard only sibilance. Heads in twos and threes, close together over the tables, no voice above a whisper. Behind the bar, a red-robed woman with a cloud of fine red-gold hair, watching. Behind the woman an extension of darkness.

When Elve sat down on the bench by the wall, the woman approached with a questioning look. Elve thought it likely that beer was still a standard request. She asked for a half-pint. The woman nodded and soon returned with a foaming glass. She scooped up the yuan Elve had laid on the table, and waited, hand on hip, outstretched hand signaling for more money. Elve laid down another rael and the woman left, satisfied.

Elve nursed her beer, a vile brew of extraordinary bitterness. But the alcohol spread its warmth in her belly as it had in long-gone days. It also warmed her view of the shebeen's scruffy denizens, twelve customers, thirteen counting the leathery man guarding the door. Elve looked for someone she might trust. With the dim light and the lowered heads, there was little profit in such an exercise. Besides, Elve knew, the red-haired woman was key to her enterprise. So, trying not to stare, she kept a close eye on the barkeeper's activity.

Nothing but beer sales seemed to be on the woman's mind. She spotted empty glasses, refilling them promptly from a ewer, unless the customer unequivocally indicated "no more". She collected the coins in some kind of purse inside her robe.

After a time, a customer who was becoming noisy was visited by the guard, who tapped him on the shoulder. The man looked up, protesting. But his protests did him no good. He was escorted out by a back way behind the bar, and the voices fell back into whispers.

The couple on the bench beside Elve proceeded to fuck even though the table was very much in their way. Elve was used to public sex, as it was practised freely in many venues, especially by newly privileged eighteen-year-olds. Elve looked about and spotted in a dim corner the green government-issue condom dispenser, a feature of most public buildings and many street corners.

Still, she found herself reminded that she'd hardly had any sex all winter and felt vaguely sad. She thought she would leave then, but the red-haired woman was approaching her. She motioned to Elve to follow her to the bar, at the time vacant of customers.

"Tell me your contact." Elve couldn't read her face, which seemed neither hostile nor friendly. But the imperative in her voice was unmistakable.

"Ovid 10.75.43.75"

"From 403?"

Elve nodded.

"Haven't seen him for a while."

"He's laying low."

"And?"

What did she want? More info on Ovid? Elve hadn't any of that, so she decided to state her business.

"I need ID. For a kid."

Elve shrank under the woman's appraising glare, but kept her composure stoically. For Hom. She had to do this for Hom.

"A thousand yuan. Up front. Then we talk business."

"How much time do I have?"

"As much as you want, granny." The woman's face was transformed by a smile so broad and friendly that Elve felt she must have totally misread her. Then the woman said, "By the looks of you, you're headed for the funeral celebration right soon."

Elve withheld the rude reply that came to mind. "My name is Elve 29.07.-40.43.79. And yours?"

"Call me Meemee. Short for Meemeeco."

Elve felt that she had passed some kind of test. Meemee was willing to help her. For a price.

14

Early morning sunshine bounced off Statesfield's south tower, which rose in brooding splendour from the tumble of concrete at its base. From her balcony, Elve remembered its glory before the fall of the façade. For a moment, she could still see it, its glowing planes and soft shadows. But even then, she thought, it was only beautiful in the sun. In itself, it was glowering and brutal, especially when rain darkened its stony face.

Hom ran out to stand beside her. "Granny, I wanna go over there. Over to the roons. Can't we go over there again?"

Elve hesitated, looking down at Hom's eager face. A west wind softly lifted his straight, black hair.

It was Washingtonday, designated by the GNWRAA as a day devoted to public ceremony glorifying the regime. The Emp was closed, and local officials made speeches from a stage erected in front of the great doors. Schoolchildren paraded to the square, accompanied by brass bands. Hundreds of children stood in close formation on either side of the stage, singing patriotic songs and reciting the prescribed motto of the week. And every week, all those gathered recited the Sitizen's Plej:

I plej alejuns too de flag and too de Glorius Noo Wrld Reepublic uv Azhu and de Amerikas. Wun wrld uenieted in loyaltee and in luv for His Superbnes, owr Preshus and Onerabl, Wiez and Hoely Supreem Leeder.

Everyone was expected to attend the ceremonies. Virtually all the police force would be mustered to monitor the crowd. But Elve quietly resisted. She would not go.

"We need more chalk," Hom pleaded.

Indeed they did. Only screechy stubs remained in the chalk bag.

"We'll go," Elve said. "After everyone else has left for the square."

Hom rewarded her with an impulsive hug around her hips. Elve couldn't bring herself to discourage his spontaneous gestures of affection. She loved them too much and Hom as well. Among the other harms that might befall, official punishment for such gestures seemed a minor threat.

Hom insisted on saving his breakfast of oat porridge and soy milk for the cats. Elve added some scraps she'd intended to use up in the soup pot. They collected their gear and waited behind the curtain, watching the gathering parade of citizens headed for the square. Though the road was muddy, the crowd moved quickly with a cheerful air. A pregnant woman carrying one youngster and taking another by the hand straggled behind all the others. When she had passed, Elve and Hom set out.

Among the ruins, life defied destruction. The bare patches were already greening; scrubby bushes held up yellow buds like tiny candles. To Hom's delight, a grazing rabbit, surprised, rose on its haunches to look at him and then hopped away into a crevice among the debris. Snow was melting on sun-warmed slabs, and the trickling of water mingled with the twittering of a pair of small brown birds.

The cats lazed about in sunny spots, their sides still gaunt but sleeker than before. Elve surmised that mice had become available and other prey as well. The felines kept their distance, watching.

Hom scrambled through the rubble to the slab he'd used before as a feeding station. "Hi, pussy cats," he called, dumping the food. "Come and get it."

He backed off. He waited. He made the rising sound in his throat that he hoped was encouraging, a sort of coaxing cat-sound he'd heard from a mother cat.

The orange tom looked on. Then he moved with supreme dignity to the slab, and began to nose out the best bits. In spite of his growls, the young tabby joined him. But the others waited until the tom had finished before they came down from their perches.

As the cats moved off, Hom, crouching, edged towards the young tabby, a morsel in his hand—a bit of sausage he had snitched from the balcony cooler. He held it out, making his encouraging murmur. The animal stared into Hom's eyes, unmoving. The boy averted his gaze, but maintained his vocal coaxing. He inched forward. The cat recoiled just a little, but held his ground. Hom, judging that he dared advance no farther, laid the morsel on the grass and backed off slightly.

The tabby padded to the food. He sniffed it. He devoured it. He bounded away to a high perch and sat there licking his paws in the sunshine.

Hom clapped his hands. "Youpee! It worked. He's my cat now. I'll call him Roon because he came to me in the roons."

Elve had stood watching from a little distance. Her displeasure at the stolen meat was overshadowed by her wonder at Hom's patience with the animal.

They went to work, collecting two bagfuls of drywall pieces. Elve sat down to rest, while Hom went in search of more rabbits.

They could hear from the square the sound of the brass band and the children's voices rising in the raucous, atonal shouting that was their instructors' version of song. The words were indistinguishable from this distance, but Elve knew them. Jema, especially, had sung them with enthusiasm.

> Onward, loyal children
> Sons of brave new world
> Daughters of the Glory
> With your flags unfurled;
> We are never downcast
> Always glad are we

> One in loyal spirit
> Cheerful, glad and free.
>
> Onward, loyal children
> Onward to the light,
> As our starry banner
> Leads us through the night.

Hom paused in his play. His face darkened. He clenched his hands and stuffed them in his pockets.

The song probably marked the ending of the ceremonies. They should go home immediately. Elve picked up her walking stick and called to Hom, who came unwillingly, his joy extinguished. Their path through the ruins seemed more tortuous than before as if the very stones conspired against them.

They were laying the drywall out on the floor when they heard the returning multitude. Their jubilance seemed to Elve to have a hostile edge. Filled with zeal for the RAA, they were primed to spot the smallest infraction of the regulations and report same to the police. Who among them could be trusted?

But Hom with a child's resilience laid out the chunks with good cheer, chattering about how soon they could make the chalk and his plans to write "something really big" with it.

16

The sudden onset of warmer weather soon made gardening possible. Elve had seedlings ready to plant as soon as the danger of frost was minimal. The weather was always uncertain; some risk must be taken or nothing could get done.

She worked very early in the mornings when she deemed the police were unlikely to be on patrol. They were on foot these days because the muddy road had dried with deep ruts that made cycling impossibly bone-rattling. Hom helped, setting the tiny plants with the gentle yet firm hands of a gardener. Peas, tomatoes, cabbage, and three kinds of beans.

Elve was grateful for the help. Squatting and bending were a little more difficult for her this year. She saw the gift in Hom's fingers and reflected on the abuse they had suffered. The miracle of their healing, surely a blessing, in spite of the loss of two fingers.

They went inside as soon as the parents with schoolchildren began to pass. Dum and Dee would likely follow them in a short time, plodding cantankerously in the unfriendly road. They had no reputation as enforcers, and were felt to be arbitrary and unpredictable.

Boat made a welcome visit, bearing a sample of his first spring catch. Elve nearly fell into his arms, she was so glad to see him.

"Boat," she cried, "it's been such a long winter!"

"I spent most of it sleeping," said Boatman. He settled in a chair by the table. "I was planning to come one day. Had no fish, but I was gonna come anyway but then the storm got in my way."

"We were holed up for days. But we're getting a start on the garden now."

"This guy any good to you?" Boat jerked a thumb towards Hom, who stood close to Elve, looking slightly wary.

"Like another right hand. Hom, you remember Boat?"

"Yup. He's the guy you fuck with. And he brings the fish."

"Speaking of fish, let's fry this up right away while the power's on. It won't last more than an hour. I'll rustle up something to go with it." Elve lifted down the wok from its hook above the cooker.

She had potatoes, wizzled and sprouted but still edible. An onion desperately growing a yellow spear. Two respectable carrots that she dug from the bin on the balcony. She stir-fried the lot in sunflower oil, added the two brown trout that Boatman had filleted in the meantime.

Hom claimed the offal for the cats. "We hafta go see the cats, Gran."

Boatman sat up. "Not the Statesfield cats!"

"They're OK," said Hom. "I even got close to one. I named him Roon."

"We just had to get out of this apartment," Elve said. "We went over on a sunny day before the storm. Nothing bad happened. Except Dum and Dee came by."

Elve and Boat made the obligatory gesture towards OPPL and the sky. As they laid into their food, Elve explained who Dum and Dee were, and why ID for Hom had become an immediate necessity. "I need a thousand yuan for a bootlegged ID."

Boatman whistled. "Where can you get that kind of money? Nobody but bootleggers and pirates have that kind of money."

Elve lived on a generous government senior's pension. Generous when it arrived, but sporadic in its appearances. It came, when it came, to her account in the Guverment Bank of Owr Astute and All-wise Guvrner, Mistrlaw Gowd. The GBOAAGMG. She could access the account at a machine in the Emp.

Gowd was the first RAA leader to append his own name to that of any government institution. He had assumed the position of SEEOE (CEO) of the bank and taken direct control of its operations. People knew little of his managerial style, but the GBOAAGMG seemed to be in a constant state of disorganization and terror.

Since GBOAAGMG is unpronounceable, the people resorted to calling the bank "BOAG". But not in the presence of the authorities.

"I have some cash stashed away and some in my BOAG account. But I don't think it would amount to more than 500 yuan." Elve sighed.

"'Fraid I can't help you much. Takes all I've got to eat and maintain the boat. But give me a bit of time. I might come up with something."

Elve appreciated Boat's willingness to help, but as for time, she felt they didn't have any. Hom was a prisoner until they got him an ID card.

Hom had left the table and gone to his chalkboard. He was working on a story. Elve had helped him divide the wall into three even sections by scoring the black paint with a knife. Two sections were covered with his small, neat script. He finished up his work, adding tabby stripes to a kitten in one corner.

"Lookit," he said, "It's about Roon and his family."

Boatman inspected Hom's work with more interest in the script than in the story, though both amazed him. Elve was sad to see that Hom had given Roon a mother and two brothers. She sensed his terrible loneliness and deprivation. But what could she do?

"Where'd you learn this?" said Boat, touching Roon's name in serifed capitals.

"Granny teached me. And I made up the fancy bits. It's like Arial only with feet and roofs."

"More like Times New Roman," said Boatman. "When I used to paint signs, we changed all the Times New Roman to Arial. All the other pretty letters too. They just threw out the old signs, so I kept a couple. Still have them in the boat. I'll show you some day."

Boatman took the chalk. With a sure hand, he chalked **"Antigonish"** and "**Moosejaw**" on the board.

"What are Antigonish and Moosejaw?" Hom wanted to know.

"Places that used to be in Canada. Before the RAA."

Hom was indignant. "There is no 'before the RAA'. The RAA is the beginning. The beginning of everything."

Elve saw with despair that in his brief time at school, Hom had taken into his heart the first, essential lesson. Time begins with the RAA.

Boat's eyes met Elve's. They exchanged quick nods. They moved to the bedroom, leaving Hom copying Boat's calligraphy. This time they shut the door.

They talked. They felt that Hom needed to know the RAA's rules and regulations or he wouldn't last a week in public society. The songs too and the proper salutes. But they agreed that killing his intellect with the lies that spewed from the Hoely Mownten of the Glorius Noo Wrld Reepublik uv Azhu and de Amerikus was unthinkable. Hom should know what they remembered. What they knew of history and geography and literature.

He should know about freedom. Boat and Elve had known only a little freedom. But they knew it was possible.

17

Except for deaths and holidays of political significance, the only occasions of celebration in the GNWRAA were birthdays. The Reespected Ministree uv Soeshel and Paetreeotik Culcher had stripped from the world calendar all commemorations of a national or religious origin. They co-opted the dates of traditional holidays, using them for celebrations of GNWRAA victories, and the birthdays of the two Preshus Leeders who had come to power since the inaugural year (MNA One) of the Magnifesent Noo Aej uv de Glorius Noo Werld Reepublik uv Azhu and de Amerikas.

The closing days of the year, long known as The Holiday Season was proclaimed as the time of the establishment of the RAA (though the actual ratification by Azhu and the Amerikas had taken place in June), and Loyel Sitizenz were encouraged to enjoy a solid week of festivities honouring world unification under the RAA. This period was christened "Aech" for Holiday.

The RAA deemed that everyone, but especially every child up to the age of twelve, deserved a party on their birthday. The birthday was, after all, the day of initiation into Loyel Sitizenship and the birthdate a part of the child's name, given to them by the generosity and beneficent power of the RAA. Within one week of birth, the parent was required to bring the baby to the Nobel Ofis uv Sitizenship and Dokuementaeshun to receive the baby's ID, which was hung around the child's neck by a ceremonious official. A day of celebration followed.

Hom's sixth birthday fell on May 1, MNA 41. Or by Elve's reckoning, 3016 of the old calendar. Elve wondered what sort of celebration she could devise for a kid with no ID. Clearly impossible would be the customary parade with banners, the birthday kid borne on the shoulders of a proud father or other male relative. Equally impossible was a lavish dinner in the Emporium Dining Hall with all possible friends and relatives attending. Elve had neither money for that, nor any willingness to go into debt as many families thought it necessary to do. Even if Hom dared appear in public.

The dinner would have to be at home. Grandma Jema would come, of course. Uncle Odro, if he was at home, with Doro, his partner and the babies, Bez and Boz. Aunt Nura. Boat. Ovid? Yes, if he could leave his post for a while.

There would be food. Everyone would bring something.

The present. Quite recently, it had become customary (very nearly mandatory, Elve thought) to give the birthday child a ring or pendant engraved with the RAA logo. Sometimes the logo would be artfully entwined with the child's name. Even better would be a wide gold cuff, similarly engraved.

Hom was not a child of the RAA. Abandoned by a mother who embraced the government fucking policy, cast out and maimed by its education policy, he was a child apart. Elve couldn't think of hanging that logo around his neck. Hom's present had to be something different.

In a recess behind the headboard of her bed, Elve kept a pottery jar filled with odds and ends, mementoes of times long gone. If the police had searched her home, as they were entitled to do at will, they would have confiscated it as an illegal and evil remnant of the time before the RAA. So far, she'd been lucky.

She called Hom to her room. "This is a secret," she said. "You mustn't tell anyone about it. Not Grandma Jema or anybody else. Look."

The lidded jar was a delicate blue, painted with ferns and creamy peonies. A network of fine cracks marked the surface, and the lid had been broken and mended.

Hom pointed to the unusual character on the bottom. "What's that?"

"It's the potter's name. Japanese writing. There used to be a country called Japan."

"Funny writing. I can't read it."

"Nobody can anymore. This was Grandma Kumi's. She got it from her grandmother. And she got it from her grandmother too who had it from long ago grandmothers. Grandma Kumi told me that it is filled with the tears of the people who were forced to leave their boats and their stores and their homes and their gardens and go to live far away in the mountains. They were allowed to take only what they could carry. This jar was wrapped in blankets and carried in a big bundle on an old woman's back."

Elve, shaking out the contents of the jar, let her tears fall where they would. Hom, seeing them, was silent and afraid.

There were several scraps of paper also marked with mysterious characters. A length of rose silk ribbon. A quartz crystal that Max had found in the ruined museum. A baby tooth in a tiny box, Mungo's first. Two very old coins.

Hom seized upon the coins. "It's like the goose. The one in the Mother Goose book. I didn't know they could swim."

"Oh yes, they're great swimmers. The bird is a loon. There were lots of them once."

"And what's this one?" Hom held up a coin with a golden centre encircled by a silver ring.

"Those are polar bears. They're extinct now. Years ago, when I was a girl, the last one died in captivity. There were once lots of them too."

"It's a big bear and two little ones."

"Yes, a mother with two cubs."

"Oh." Hom became thoughtful. He bit his lip.

He examined the coins again. "Ca-na-da. It's money from Canada?"

Elve was surprised at the grip of childhood patriotism around her heart. "Yes. Before Canada became the sixtieth state of the United

States of America. After Guatemala and Peru. And now it's part of the RAA. We live in the Greater and Lesser Bay Region of the RAA."

Hom was fingering the polar bear coin, trying to rub away the tarnish on the silver.

"Would you like the bears for your birthday gift?"

Hom nodded. "That would be galubrious," he said solemnly.

Ovid drilled a small hole in the border of the polar bear coin. Elve strung it on an old leather bootlace from the junk drawer.

The morning of his birthday, Hom accepted it and put it on with sober grace.

The guests arrived at sundown. There were too many to be seated at Elve's modest table, so Hom's Aunt Nura spread a blanket on the floor. There she sat cross-legged, feeding Odro's babies, who sat with gaping mouths like little birds. By common consent, Hom had the seat of honour at the head of the table.

Since Jema was present, it was necessary to recite the complete, authorized version of the ceremony of gratitude to Owr Preshus and Perfect Leeder. Elve hoped Jema wouldn't notice that Hom was quite bewildered by the procedure. It was well that she gazed upward in a transport of reverence during the recitation. Elve resolved to remedy this gap in Hom's civic education.

The meal proceeded in leisurely fashion. Boat's fish were shared in a hearty chowder mildly flavoured with curry. Then everyone scooped a mixture of rice, tofu, beans, peppers, and tomatoes from a common pot, using wedges of flatbread.

Elve, at the counter, had just lit six candles on an eggless raisin cake when there was a knock on the door. Boat went to answer it. Ovid stood in the doorway, breathing heavily.

"They're in the building," he said. "Better get your shit together." He was gone.

Jema moved immediately to turn on the TV. It was the RAA Hour of Power, which they'd been joyfully ignoring. She stood watching, favouring her sore knee just a little.

Hom. Where to hide him? If this was just an Hour of Power TV check, he could stay in the bedroom. But a thorough search might be on the police agenda. Elve dithered, but only briefly. She seized Hom by the arm and pushed him under the table. She motioned Nura to take Hom's chair. Hom was hidden by the tablecloth and the adults' bodies.

Elve yelled, "Shtup. Watch," All turned their eyes to the TV. The babies, deserted, began to howl.

Boat opened the door. He sat down quickly to shield Hom's hiding place.

The two night police were unfamiliar to Elve. She couldn't guess their intention.

Apparently the studious attitude toward the TV passed muster, as the taller of the officers grunted to the other, who made a notation on his Apsam.

"IDs, you guys."

Elve felt Hom's head pressed against her legs. If he can just keep quiet, she prayed. She and the others produced their ID cards, which the officers duly noted.

The candles on the raisin cake were beginning to gutter.

"And the authorization for this gathering of more than two people from different households?"

"We're all family," said Elve. "We're celebrating the birthday of our uncle. It's Boatman's sixtieth." She hoped neither officer had noted Boatman's date of birth or had the wit to calculate his actual age.

"Immaterial. You should have obtained proper authorization for the meeting."

"I'm very sorry, sir. Is it a new regulation?"

"New reg yesterday. It was on TV." The tall officer seemed to be reaching for his peremptory tone. The shorter one looked apologetic.

Elve caught Boatman's eye and jerked her head toward the cake. The corner of his mouth twitched. His picked up the cake.

"Allow me," he said, "to offer this fine cake as a token of our respect for the new reg. Please enjoy to the utmost."

The officers exchanged glances. One raised an eyebrow. The other nodded. They both reached for the cake.

"You should blow out your candles and make your wish for the eternal prosperity of the RAA," said the tall one.

So Boat did as he was told. His rendition of the wish was quite beautiful, if not exactly sincere.

The policemen departed, pleased with their transaction.

The door slammed shut. "Can I come out now?" Hom whispered, peering up between adult knees. Odro pulled him out and ruffled his hair.

"Sorry, kid, you lost your cake. But it was in a good cause," Boat said.

Hom's lower lip trembled. What six-year-old can accommodate the loss of his birthday cake without tears?

"Never mind. As soon as I get some eggs, I'll make you another, an even better one." Elve squeezed Hom's body into her warm side.

The TV continued to preach, but no one watched. Nura produced her special treat, sweets in the shape of rabbits. These rabbit candies were always available in the spring, a tradition left from a long-forgotten holiday. Nura divided them up, one each for the adults and the babies and all the rest for Hom. This almost compensated for the loss of the cake.

Hom got down on the blanket to help Nura amuse the babies, who were now placated by the sweets. He had a repertoire of funny faces that the little ones found hilarious.

Boat, Odro, and Doro entered into discussion of the new reg—whether it was of any real importance. Boat maintained that it was a serious incursion on natural freedom. "Like we oughtta be able to get together when we want without asking the RAA about it."

Odro agreed, but Doro shrugged and said, "What difference? Just one more thing they get onto us about. I had my grocery bags searched last week to make sure I had bought at least four officially recommended items."

Jema said, "It's part of the plan, don't you see. The Awesome and All-encompassing Plan for the Perfect Health and Happiness of all

Loyel Sitizenz. The AAPPHHLS. It's been on TV. A truly amazing plan. I can't say enough about it."

The others hadn't been diligent in watching the Hour of Power, so they were ignorant of the Awesome Plan. They kept quiet though, because ardent believers like Jema could be dangerous. They might tell.

Seeing that her companions were unimpressed with the Awesome Plan, Jema moved away to inspect Hom's chalkboard. She turned from it, her face contorted and red. "What's this?" she asked Elve.

"It's my new story," said Hom, bounding up from his spot on the blanket. "I'll read it for you."

"You will not. It's an abomination." Jema turned to Elve. "Why are you teaching him this unauthorized writing?"

So it was the script, not the text that aroused Jema's ire. Elve replied mildly, "Oh, I did teach him Arial. He's been experimenting with it ever since. He likes this way because it's faster."

"In the RAA, all over the world, the official written language is Inglish Arial. It is an essential pillar of unity and peace."

"Hom isn't writing official documents," objected Odro.

"That is immaterial. No one is allowed to deviate. Hom must not be allowed to deviate. Deviations and irregularities are harmful to the RAA. They are deleterious to the realization of the Awesome and Encompassing Plans for the benefit of Loyel Sitizenz."

Elve briefly regretted Jema's eidetic memory, which enabled the recall of RAA pronouncements, word for word. It could be put to so much better uses, she thought. But she said, "Even the RAA won't concern themselves with a six-year-old's scratchings."

Even as she said this, she knew it wasn't true. The police were charged with enforcing the slightest infringement of the regulations. Though their actual performance fell far short, they might indeed take a child into custody for wrong writing.

The RAA had multiplied laws, rules, and regulations far beyond most people's ability to remember them. But they had simplified the justice system by decreeing two and only two sentences for offences of all kinds: hard labour and death. Even for children. Indeed, a recent

TV presentation had been a speech by the Most Respected High Court Magistrate in which he extolled removal of "bad apples" from society at the earliest possible stage of their recalcitrance.

Jema subsided, shaking her head. Elve wondered if Jema was bothered about her own action in protecting Hom from the teachers. If she might feel that she needed to make up for this disloyalty.

Hom had sought Elve's side, downcast by his grandmother's rejection of his story. He stayed there as the guests collected their sweaters and babies and babies' accoutrements. All but Boat were gone in a few minutes.

He pushed Elve aside as she moved to clean up the dishes and pots. "Siddown. You been cooking all night."

But she wouldn't, so they worked together, with Hom putting the things away as much as he could reach. "Never mind the wok," Elve told him. "I'll hang it up in the morning."

Boat and Elve left Hom to his chalkboard, where he started to copy the polar bears from his gift coin. In the bedroom, they stood together a moment, aware that each was drawing relieved sighs.

"I don't know. I just don't know."

"It doesn't look good for the boy. His grandma is loose cannon."

"My own daughter. I don't know how the RAA got her soul. But she's fond of Hom. I hope she'll keep her mouth shut. We hafta get that ID."

Hearing "we", Boat bridled, but recovered. He pulled her to sit on the bed. "Maybe that woman at the shebeen is open to negotiation. Wouldn't hurt to try again."

"Will you go with me?"

"Whenever you say."

"I love you, Boat."

"The RAA don't approve of love."

"May earwigs and weevils rain on the RAA."

That night, Elve and Boat reinvented the kiss.

18

The shebeen was more crowded and much noisier than before. Meemee circulated, trying to induce her customers to pipe down with little success. No one was egregiously loud, so she didn't call upon the bouncer, who hovered at the doorway shifting uneasily on his feet.

The place sounded like the pubs of old, Elve thought. Yarning, giggling, and guffaws hung in air muzzy with the odour of weed. She and Luky, her joog, dead now for thirty-six years, had once been regulars at a cheerful pub in the old time before the RAA.

Boat steered her to the bench at the back wall. There they could keep an eye on all the proceedings without attracting much attention. Meemee approached them immediately, questioning Boat's presence. "He's my friend," Elve said quickly. "We're here about the ID deal."

The woman nodded. "Talk to me later. What'll you have?"

When the glass mugs of beer arrived, served by a lad who was clearly underage, Elve knew right away the reason for the joviality. This beer was good. Nothing like the evil brew of her first visit. Everyone was relishing it and ordering more. No telling when there would be another batch like this.

A tableful of young people began to sing. Their song was one of the patriotic songs of the RAA because those were the only songs they knew. They sang with the same shouting tone they'd learned at school, but Elve thought there was an edge to the voices. Something not quite in tune with the words.

We have heard the joyful cry:

> Praise the RAA,
> Praise the RAA
> Loyel Sitizenz reply
> Praise the RAA,
> Praise. . .

Splintering wood. Thundering boots. Armoured cops, waving their armaces. Elve and Boat dived under their table. The patrol fanned out in the confined space driving the screaming patrons before them. They fled into the dark area behind the bar, knowing there must be an exit, having seen noisy patrons escorted out that way. Some, shot in the back, fell as they ran.

Someone leaped up on the table where Elve and Boat crouched. It overturned, leaving them exposed and effectively blocked from escape.

It became evident that the true purpose of the raid was the capture of Meemee. Three cops encircled and handcuffed her. One grasped her red hair, pulling her head back viciously, while the other two marched her away into the darkness. A couple of cops yanked the two solar lanterns from the ceiling to light the way. The others chased the fleeing found-ins, shooting randomly.

Elve and Boat were left in the dark. They heard a departing siren. "You OK?"

Elve tried to breathe. "I think so," she said. But she felt a warm trickle down her temple. She touched it and knew it was blood. "Something grazed my scalp," she said, "maybe a piece of glass."

"Not good," said Boat. "Here take my sweater to bandage it."

"Yours is too big. I'll use mine." She made a turban of her own sweater to staunch the wound. "Which way should we go?"

"Let's try for the door we came in."

They felt their way along the wall. The cops had broken down both doors, allowing a shaft of light to enter. The crest lay shattered, but a fragment bore the dove's wing still. On an impulse, Elve picked it up, tucking it in the pocket of her pants.

It was late, how late they didn't know. They surveyed the lakeshore road, but saw no sign of a velotram, nor anyone waiting at the stop. There would be no other vehicles, not even a cop car, the dearth of batteries being an effective deterrent to random cruising.

"We'll hafta walk. Can you make it to the hospital?"

"Home. I left Hom sleeping, and I don't want to leave him too long. They ask too many questions at the hospital anyway." Elve knew that scalp wounds bleed profusely, but not dangerously.

"If you're sure."

"Let's go."

A distinct rise in their road marked the location of a long disused and disabled subway station. The Octotrans had been the finest underground transit system in the world. Superior in speed and extent to the systems of London, Paris, and many newer cities.

"Where's the Octo, now that we need it," grumbled Boat.

Their progress, brisk at first, became more laboured as Elve began to feel light-headed. She leaned on Boat, scuffling her heavy feet. The eastern sky was beginning to grey when they reached her building.

Ovid roused from his place by the workbench when they came in. He raised a questioning brow.

"Tell you later," said Boat. Ovid opened the inner door. He activated the elevator, which he now only used for freight, since its state of repair was dubious.

Boat helped Elve to lie down. Blessed unconsciousness swept over her.

As Boat removed the sodden turban to assess Elve's wound, he felt Hom's watchful presence. He turned to find the child standing at the foot of the bed, his face bloodless with terror.

Hom pointed to the sweater. He tried to speak, but couldn't.

"It's OK," said Boat. "Just a scalp wound. It bleeds a lot though."

"Is Granny—dead?"

"Like I tell you, she just got hurt a bit. She'll be OK."

"Who did it? Who hurt my granny?"

Boat hedged. "I'll let her tell you about it when she's better. Right now, can you bring me some water and a clean towel?"

Hom left. Boat examined the wound. A bloody swath cut through Elve's thick, crinkly hair from hairline to crown. It should be stitched, Boat thought.

Hom returned with warm water and a towel. Boat washed away the blood as well as he could. The wound gaped, still bleeding.

"Go down to Ovid," said Boat. "Ask him for a staple gun and the shortest staples, if he has them."

Hom ran to do as Boat asked. Boat continued to staunch the wound, now making use of the bed sheet, since the towel was no more use.

Hom returned in a few minutes with both Ovid and the staple gun. Ovid took a look at Elve's head and turned white. "I gotta get out of here," he said, ashamed. "Blood makes me seriously queasy."

"I need you to give me a hand," said Boat.

"Sorry," said Ovid, retreating. But he waited by the door.

"I can help," said Hom.

With his strong but gentle fingers, Hom held together the edges of the gash while Boat operated the gun. With each staple, Elve flinched, but remained unconscious.

Together Boat and Hom applied a neat row of staples the length of the wound. The flow of blood reduced to a slight ooze. Boat sponged it up, surveying their work with satisfaction.

"Now, if she doesn't get infected, we've done a great job." He stood up and clapped Hom on the shoulder.

"What do you do for someone who's lost a lot of blood?" he asked Ovid.

"Get her to the hospital, dontcha think?"

"In this case, I don't think so. Too many questions. We were at the shebeen and it got raided."

"Well, yeah." Ovid scratched his nose. "I'm no doctor. Who do you know that knows this kind of stuff?"

"There's O, Elve's friend. Knows plants and things. But I don't know how to get hold of her. She lives in a hideout somewhere."

Hom spoke up. "She gave Granny rabbit meat for me. She traps them in the ravine."

"I think Lali the Reedwoman knows her," said Boat. "The one that lives by the river flats and makes baskets. Maybe she knows where to find O and send her over. Or some medicine maybe."

"I know the woman. I got a summer hat from 'er," said Ovid. "It's still early. I'll go find 'er."

After Ovid left, Boat and Hom did what they could to clean up the mess. Hom brought the sheet from his own bed to cover his granny because he couldn't find an extra one in the linen closet.

They brought the folding chairs from the other room and sat, waiting for Elve to wake up.

They talked softly about the coming summer. Hom hoped he could go outside, because other kids would be out having holidays from school and he could blend in. Boat said maybe he could use a good boy on his boat. "There's lots to do on a boat," he said. Hom responded so ecstatically that Boat suspected he would have to make good on the suggestion.

Elve stirred and groaned. Then her eyes opened. She studied the ceiling and walls.

"Where—where...?" she said weakly.

"At home. We made it." Boat stroked her sticky hair.

She touched the staples and recoiled. "What's that?"

"Hom and I, we stapled you up. Just like the doctor would."

"I'm not in hospital? Where are the cops?"

"No cops. We're safe. You better rest. Ovid's trying to get in touch with O. She should have some idea about medicine and such."

Elve cried out, "She can't come here. She has no ID."

The word "ID" reminded Elve. "Meemee is gone and we're nowhere nearer getting ID for Hom."

Even through her disorientation and pain, Elve determined that as soon as she was able, she would make a bold move to get Hom's ID.

19

It was two days before Lali came.

Reluctantly, but mindful of the need to keep his fish contract with the army in good order, Boat left Hom watching Elve toss on her bed, ravaged by periods of searing pain alternating with hallucinatory semi-consciousness. She would eat nothing.

Hom got by on canned beans, which he ate with the stale flatbread remaining in the cupboard. He sat by Elve's bed, watching sadly.

He got out the tin book box. He chose the comfort of Mother Goose. He studied the illustrations again, looking for familiar objects—things that had maybe been the same for a very long time. He found a blue jug like the one in Granny's headboard, Wee Willie Winkie's lantern, old Mother Hubbard's teapot, a wooden stool. But there were strange objects, too—the clock with its pendulum, Jack Horner's Christmas tree. Oddest of all, a ball, kites, a hobbyhorse and a seesaw. Hom had never seen any of these. The RAA frowned on toys, and none were available in the Emp.

Birds, cats, mice, and spiders were familiar. But not dogs, sheep, cows, or horses. He had never seen pigs, but he knew that Sprem came from pigs, as well as Porgel, the common pig's gut packaging material. It was odd, he thought, that Mother Hubbard's dog seemed to live in the house with her.

Still on his chair, he slept.

Ovid conducted Lali to their apartment. She entered, a heavy woman of dark complexion, carrying two polybags and puffing from the effort of climbing the stairs.

"Eats first," she said, plonking one bag on the counter, "then medicine."

Lali proceeded to make soup from the vegetables she'd brought. She added a cubed yeast product that gave the mix a beef flavour. While the soup simmered, she went in to see Elve, taking the second bag with her.

"O sends her greetings," Lali said, heaving herself on to the folding chair by the bed. "She isn't really well, you know. Looks terribly thin."

"You must be Lali. You've been making paper for the project," Elve whispered hoarsely. With a groan, she sat up to see her visitor better.

"Never mind the project just now. You need to get better. What happened anyway?"

Elve hedged. She hadn't yet told Hom, who now stood at the foot of the bed, how she came to be injured. She didn't want him to know why she'd been at the shebeen and wasn't ready to confide in Lali either. "A piece of glass cut me," she said to Lali, with a meaningful cock of her head towards the boy.

Lali understood. "This is from O," she said, pulling a small earthenware jar from her bag. It was covered with a square of red cloth tied with string. "It will cleanse the wound."

The jar contained a pungent yellowish paste. Neither Elve nor Lali could guess its ingredients. Lali spread it on Elve's crown to forehead gash. It stung viciously, bringing tears to Elve's eyes. She clutched the sheet to keep from yelling.

"Stop it. You're hurting Granny," Hom cried.

"Antiseptics always sting," said Lali. "It's the germs doing their death dance on the sore place. The stinging will stop in a minute."

"What're germs?"

As Elve lay back to deal with the pain, Lali did her best to explain microscopic organisms. "Do you have a magnifying glass?"

"I think so." Hom went to Elve's junk drawer and came back with a very old, much scratched round magnifier with a metal handle. Lali rubbed it clean on her thigh. "See, when you hold it here, you can see the hairs on your arm." Hom looked at his arm with interest. The short dark hairs seemed alive and wiry.

"Now look at your thumb."

"Hey, it's got a pattern on it. I never seed that before."

"So it you have a really powerful glass to magnify things, you will discover germs. We're crawling with them. Most of them are fine, but some can make us sick. So we kill them with antiseptic stuff."

Hom looked thoughtful. Lali stood up. "That soup has cooked enough. Let's eat."

Elve held out shaky hands to receive the warm bowl. Lali laughed at her. "Not so fast. You're a bloody invalid, you know." She spooned the soup into Elve's mouth. The patient seemed to relish it.

Elve fell into a light sleep. Hom and Lali stored the remaining food in the fridge, hoping that the electricity would function well enough to prevent spoilage. Sometimes it did.

"Put the antiseptic cream on your granny's wound tonight and twice a day until it's all gone. I'll come back in a couple of days," Lali said. She gathered her bags and left Hom gaping at this unusual responsibility.

O's ointment proved effective. The wound began to heal around the staples, incorporating them into Elve's flesh. Boat and Lali and Hom saw this happening, but not one of them could see how to remove the staples without ripping the gash open again. Elve was forever marked by a broad white track through her hair, very like a miniature train track.

As Elve waited for her strength to return, she lay in her bed, thinking. She needed a strategy. To simply walk into the school and ask the RHA Garg to fork over Hom's ID wasn't going to work.

School would be closed soon. The students aged ten and older would all be shipped out to the camps. Camps with names like

"Glorious Shining Waters" and "Transcendent Heavenly Peaks". Not that these camps were anywhere near any lakes or mountains. The glory and transcendence was supposed to be derived from the nightly inspirational talks imposed on youngsters exhausted from their day of labour in the government agricultural compounds.

Though exhausted, they needed to listen. They would be tested weekly and their progress toward Knowledge of and Devotion to the RAA measured. Failure to improve resulted in transfer to camps with utilitarian names: "Swine Barns" and "Oil Sands." With nightly lectures on "Correct Thinking."

The RAA had at first sent all the school-age children to camps. But the little ones cried too much. They were of no use to anyone, not even the RAA.

The younger children would enjoy extraordinary freedom, as their parents were always working and their teachers all flocked to real shining waters and heavenly peaks. They congregated in the streets and vacant lots. They played in the creeks and ravines and on the lakeshore. They only came home when they were hungry.

The administrators complained that the kids were calamitously unruly when they returned to school after the summer break. The Office of Education, Training, and Occupations (a division of the Respected Ministry of Social and Patriotic Culture), introduced the Daily Practice of Motionless Quietude to rectify this.

Elve questioned Jema about the disposition of RHA Garg, the Respected and Honoured Administrator. Carefully, because Jema mustn't know of her intention to retrieve Hom's ID. Jema might lose her position if she were implicated in any way.

Jema sat on the folding chair by Elve's bed. "Garg is tall—really tall," she said. "She towers over everyone."

"Hmm."

"She's. . .scary. Like nobody dares complain to her or tell her about stuff that's happening."

"Stuff?"

"The way the teachers, especially the guys, make things hard for the office and maintenance workers. There's always groping and remarks. And practical jokes. The female teachers laugh. They like to see us humiliated."

"Hm-hm?"

"The Honourable Keeper of Records tried to complain and somehow Garg made it all her fault." Jema had been looking down at her hands and picking at bits of rough skin on her fingertips. Now she sat up, remembering her duty as a Loyel Sitizen. She proclaimed, "RHA Garg is a fine administrator, and our school is the best in District 79."

"So she's a no-nonsense boss. Runs a tight ship?"

"You bet. You should see how the kids stop squirming when she comes into the room. They stand up like little soldiers. Not an eyelash out of place."

Elve wanted to return to Jema's unusual admission of trouble. "The guys shouldn't be giving you a hard time. They're sposta get all the sex they want under the RAA Fucking Rules."

"Mom, it's not about sex. They're jealous. The teachers have a rotten job, you know. They just ride herd on the kids while the television does all the teaching. Some of them actually trained to be teachers, so they're pretty frustrated. But if anyone deviates from the plan. . ." Jema stopped, perhaps realizing that she was about to commit heresy again.

Elve noted these small cracks in Jema's armour of absolute loyalty to the authority of the RAA and all its offshoots. It gave her a little hope that someday Jema would abandon it.

Elve felt that she would gain little from further questioning. She changed the subject. "Would you take a look at my garden? The weeds must be taking over while I lie around here."

"Sure. After supper. I brought lovely asparagus from the market."

Elve knew that the "market" was a black market. Even Jema shopped at the black market. Growers kept back a portion of their produce from the Respected Department of Goods and Services, under whose authority the Emporium was the sole official source of absolutely everything.

The black markets had no fixed location. The growers set them up at dawn and planted flags to indicate their whereabouts. Word of mouth spread the news. By the time the police began their rounds, the markets had disappeared, though birds and squirrels gleaning the leftovers marked the spots for any observant person.

As Jema made supper, Hom came into Elve's room. She had sent him down to Ovid after he tired of reading and writing.

"Hey, Granny. Are you better now?"

"I'm getting better all the time. What's that?" She pointed to a wood fragment strung on the leather thong with his birthday coin.

"It's a bird's wing. A white bird's wing. It was in your pocket. Ovid bored this little hole for me."

Hom had done his best to launder Elve's blood-soaked garments. He had no idea how to treat bloodstains and assumed that very hot water was the answer to that problem. Rather than take the clothes to the laundry room, where the one machine still in working order used only cold water, he'd boiled water in a pot on the cooker and soaked the clothes in that.

"It came from the dove. The bird that helped me remember." Elve didn't want to explain her trips to the shebeen and the origin of the white wing. She was saved from Hom's questions by the appearance of Jema with bowls of savoury foods: the asparagus with butter (where did she manage to get butter?) an egg, and good bread.

They ate together by Elve's bed. Elve felt a surge of gratitude, but she didn't attribute any of the goodness to the RAA. She was thankful for Jema's good heart and courage. Black market shopping was never safe.

Days passed. Elve lost track. She asked Hom every day what day it was but she couldn't keep it in mind. She hadn't quite mastered the ten-day week, and now the extra days confused her. She was distressed by this and worried that she was having the first symptoms of dementia.

Her projected mission to see RHA Garg tormented her. She rehearsed the dialogue mentally, but couldn't arrive at an ultimatum that would force the woman to give up Hom's ID. What could she use as a threat?

She decided that she would threaten to expose Garg's policy of collecting the IDs. She would go to the police. A weak threat, but it would have to do.

A morning came when she decided it had to be the day. She had to get it done before school closed. She dressed as well as regulation allowed, and covered her scar with a polycloth wrap. She made her way to the balcony. The usual morning procession of schoolchildren and mothers with burdens and babies was passing by. Good.

But as she stood, her field of vision began to swim and she felt in the centre of a whirlpool. Nausea gripped her stomach. She seized the rail for support, but fell heavily.

Hom heard her fall and came running. "Are you OK? Granny, are you OK?" He tried to help Elve stand, but she slumped stupidly against his body. He ran for Ovid.

Ovid slung Elve over his shoulder like a sack of potatoes and carried her to the bed. The room continued to turn in a lazy whorl, even when she closed her eyes. Through the confusion, she saw that her mission would have to wait. How long, she wondered.

Elve continued to be afflicted with vertigo, for how many days or weeks she didn't know.

Eventually, when the vertigo eased, and she felt well enough to come to the table, the RAA's evening show dealt a further blow to Elve's construction of time. A glum official—a Respected and Honoured something-or-other--made the announcement:

"The commemorative names of the days are henceforth eliminated. They will be replaced by numbers, starting tomorrow, which will be Day One of the ten-day sequence. Loyel Sitizenz will not allow any use of the old names for any purpose whatsoever. The beneficence and empathy of the GNWRAA allows ten days of grace after which use of the commemorative names will be punishable."

Elve groaned. "I'd just got used to the names we had. How am I gonna deal with this?"

Hom solved the problem. Every morning, he wrote at the top of his wall, "Day One" or "Day Six", or whatever the case required. Since Elve's days were very like each other now that she was virtually an invalid, she wallowed in a timeless void, clinging to Hom's sign as if she were drowning.

It was on one of those formless days that she woke from a deep sleep. She judged from the sunlight that it must be afternoon. The apartment seemed too quiet.

The door slammed. Hom raced in, breathless, laughing, the bear coin and the bird's wing flying across his naked chest. He stood at the foot of her bed, suddenly tall, his skin a burnished copper. But comical too, his lost incisors marking his grin.

"Where've *you* been?"

"Outside. There's lots of kids out there. We play a hiding game. I'm real good at hiding. No one could find me and they all went over to another street. I'm hungry so I came home."

Hom spoke without shame or fear. He seemed to have no sense that he had broken any rules or flouted any authority. His black eyes shone and his springing hair seemed alive with power.

Elve realized two things: Hom was unaware of the true risk he ran. He had also slipped out of her control.

20

Lali appeared at Elve's door early one summer evening. To be accurate, 7.07.41 MNA. (The RAA had soon followed up its abolition of names for the days of the week with the institution of a ten-month year: Ten numbered months.)

"Look who's here," Lali crowed, and stood aside to present O.

Elve stretched joyful arms toward her old friend. "But you shouldn't have come, you really shouldn't have."

"What difference if they arrest me now," said O. "I'm going die shortly anyway. So I'm doing what I please for whatever time I have. And it pleases me to come and see you. And I brought some tea. It will help build you up."

O did indeed look dangerously thin. But her grey-streaked hair crinkled thick from her brow to a large bun at the nape. Her voice was still strong and low and her posture upright.

"We pulled these out of your garden," said Lali, laying a bunch of tiny carrots on the counter. "They needed to be thinned anyway." She went to work to clean the carrots, stripping off the bits of soil and wiping the roots with a cloth dipped in boiled water.

"Where's your boy?" O asked. "I want to see him."

"He's—outside." Elve looked ashamed.

"Still without ID?"

"Yes." Elve sat at the table and gestured to O to do the same. "I've lost him, O. He goes where he pleases. He's still a beautiful kid—affectionate and helpful—but he makes up his own mind."

"You know the risks, don't you?"

"Of course. But he's not scared. He says he's very good at hiding. And the kids have a system. As soon as anyone spots a cop, they yell 'Oyster shells'. Everyone disappears until the cops have passed by. They hate having to wait around while the cops check everyone's ID."

Lali brought the carrots to the table. "Oyster shells?"

Elve shrugged. "Something kids know that adults have forgotten, I think. Anyhow, it's good, because it doesn't sound like a warning. The cops must be turning a blind eye as well. ID-ing a crowd of kids interrupts their day."

"Yeah, they gotta catch all them bad guys for the RAA." Lali sampled a delicate root. "These are good. Try one."

They did, and finished off the carrots with no thought of returning thanks to Owr Preshus Leeder.

"Look what we've brought you," said O, placing a hemp bag on the table. Elve fished inside and drew out a small stack of paper, maybe twenty sheets. There was also an earthenware bottle and three feather pens wrapped in faded cotton.

"Ink! It's the ink you were making. This is wonderful." Elve's cheeks flushed with joy.

"We thought, since you can't get out these days, you could make a start on the writing project," Lali said.

"And we want to see the books. Please let us see the books."

"Yo, Gran." The shout preceded the noise of the opening door and the entrance of a laughing, exuberant boy. "What've you got to eat?"

Seeing the visitors, Hom stopped short. "Oh. Yo, Lali."

"And this is O. She made you the rabbit-fur leggings."

"Best leggings ever. Slootly glor."

O replied, "It was my pleasure to make them. I'm glad you were able to go outside."

"Before you eat, do us a favour," said Elve. "Bring out the book box."

"OK." Hom went to the storeroom. They could hear him shifting things, because Elve still kept the books well hidden. He came out bearing the metal box and placed it on the table in front of Elve.

"Now go find something to eat. Grandma Jema left fresh bread and new peanut butter."

There had been words with Jema over Hom's being outside alone. Elve was meekly defensive. "He's too agile for me. He's beyond physical restraint. How can I keep him inside?"

While Jema remonstrated at some length, Hom charged in. "Why are you guys all worried and scared?" he said. "Dontcha know I have things to do out there?" Without explanation, he'd taken the magnifying glass from the drawer and left.

Now Hom foraged in the cupboards for his snack.

Elve slid back the lid of the box and lifted out the precious volumes: *Anne of Green Gables, Life and Literature, Alice in Wonderland, The Rhymes of Mother Goose,* and, tied with Elve's ribbon, the fragmented Holy Bible.

Lali and O were awestruck. Lali had never seen an actual paper book. They had seen pictures of ancient books and manuscripts on museum websites: the Dead Sea Scrolls, Sanskrit writings, a fragment of Euripides, runes. That was before the annihilation of Populopedia and Galaxy. Ordinary paper books, rendered completely obsolete in previous centuries, had simply disappeared, being used as fuel or recycled as cheap paper packaging many times over.

Lali picked up one of the singed volumes reverently. It was *Life and Literature*. She opened it randomly and gave a shout. "John Buchan! He wrote *The Thirty-nine Steps*. I read all the Buchan I could find on Galaxy."

The others hadn't read Buchan. Lali leafed through the book, finding authors she'd heard of: Charles Dickens, Keats and Wordsworth, John McRae. "What kind of book is this anyway?"

"It's definitely a school book. Authorized by the Minister of Education for Ontario. Printed in Toronto," said Elve. "But it doesn't say when."

"What's literature?" Hom had come to the table with his bread and peanut butter.

The women looked at each other, unsure how to answer him.

"First, stand back with that peanut butter. These books are in rough enough shape without adding grease marks," said Elve.

"Literature is what people write to. . ." Elve searched for words. In her own time, "Literature" was a word uttered with a sneer. The "Literature" category of public domains was, as long as she could remember, a vast morass of uncatalogued works, many of dubious quality. For centuries, writers had been self-publishing digitally, adding to the immensity of the literary list. No one was authorized to cull the collection, and nothing, not even the worst twaddle, was ever deleted. Elve, herself, had explored only a few of the authors of recent centuries. The good ones were hard to find. Then it had all come to an end with Franklin's Folly followed soon after by the government confiscation of digital devices.

"Literature is our written heritage of stories and poems," said O.

"To tell about adventures and heroes," said Lali.

"And how the writers feel about it all—the adventures and the tragedies and the funny things too," said Elve.

"I write stories," said Hom.

Elve looked at the boy, surprised that she hadn't attached any importance to his writing. To her, it was simply a nice, quiet activity that gave her no trouble.

It surprised her, too, to realize that her present life didn't include any writing. As a student and in her working life, she had written things. Reports, instruction manuals, lists, charts, blurbs, but a few personal things too. She had never saved them, feeling embarrassed for their amateurishness.

But now, she told herself stories in her head, working out her desperate hopes for Max and Mungo, and for Jema too. Imagining a suitable end for Owr Preshus Leeder, whom she saw as a despicable charlatan. But she'd never thought of writing these stories. The means of writing had been taken away.

Besides, she knew, displaying such stories and any way would be extremely risky.

Hom ran to his chalkboard. "This is a good one," he said, and began to read:

> When I am big, I'll journey to the Magic Mountain of the RAA. I will fly on the back of the peregrine that circles the Roons. My peregrine will protect me from the cops who will try to shoot us down from the sky. We will fly so high that the armace and the laser will be useless.
>
> At the RAA, I will march into the high place of Owr Preshus Leeder and say to him. "Free the kids. Don't make them sit on their hands. Our hands are ours, not yours."

Beside his first draft, he had written his story in Uniscrip.

> When ie am big, iel jerny too de Majic Mownten uv de RAA. Ie wil flie on de bak uv de peregreen dat serklz de Roons. Mie peregreen wil proetekt mee frum de cops hoo wil trie too shoot mee down frum de skie. Wee wil flie soe hie dat de armace and de lazer wil bee uesles agenst us.
>
> At de RAA, ie wil march intoo de hie plaes uv Owr Preshus Leeder and sae too him, Free de kids. Doent make dem sit on der hands. Owr hands ar owrs, not yors.

After Hom's reading, the women were silent for a moment. His ambition was at once both completely childish and profound. He expressed a yearning for freedom that they all felt.

Finally, O spoke. "It's a beautiful story, Hom. I think you really will fly someday."

It was almost dark, and time for the guests to make their way home. They'd had the foresight to bring solar handlights. Stout walking sticks provided a little protection from casual miscreants, though not from determined criminals if they should be so unfortunate as to meet any.

"You know," said Lali, "I'd really like to take home the blue book. *Life and Literature.*"

Elve hesitated. She'd treasured and hidden the books for such a long time. But if they were to be disseminated, she had to trust her companions in the project.

"Of course," she managed to say. Then, "Which one would you like?" she asked O.

O laughed a little. "Mother Goose, please. My mother told me some of those old rhymes when I was very little. They helped me to learn English. I'd love to see them in print."

The women packed the books in clean rags that Elve provided and tucked them in their bags. When they embraced at the door, Hom came to collect a hug as well. They stood silent, seeming to understand how precious their gesture was.

Elve still felt mildly dizzy as she moved about the condo. But sitting down steadied her vision, and she decided to embark on using the paper, pens, and ink her friends had brought. She laid them out on her precious old table, sat before them and clasped her hands in what can only be called prayer. "Oh please, let this work. Let this work. . . work."

She was not at all clear about the work she hoped this effort would accomplish. Something that needed to be done in the stiflingly ignorant world the RAA was creating. To open a window. Create a current of fresh air. Let in the light.

She was totally inexperienced in the use of a quill pen and liquid ink. Stick pens had been the writing instruments of her youth. At the time, they were only used by children in their first two years of schooling, when handwriting was taught in a cursory way. If the kids learned it, fine. If not, it didn't matter because by this time they were proficient in the use of a variety of keyboard devices as well as spoken-word transcribers. Spoken-word works were taking the place of text everywhere. It was so much easier.

Elve had liked pen and paper, and continued to use them as long as they were available. Teaching Hom had sharpened up her handwriting skills. She placed a sheet of precious paper before her and dipped the pen. She would write a title page for *Alice in Wonderland.*

Elve was left-handed. As soon as she wrote *Alis* at the top of the page, the side of her hand smeared the ink into a barely legible mess. She persevered, but *in Wunderland* wasn't any better. The pen point had caught on tiny imperfections in Lali's hand-made paper, sending showers of black droplets over the page.

She stopped and waited for the ink to dry. It didn't dry quickly. She wrote *Looes Carel* with no better results.

She looked on the volume for a date of publication. Finding none, she took a guess and wrote *sirca 1900.* The smearing was even worse and the ink spattered like rain.

Since her paper supply was so limited, Elve decided to waste no more of it on preliminaries. She launched into the story. She was scarcely able to squeeze the first paragraph onto the page. She saw that her twenty pages of paper written on both sides would make a small dent in transcribing the whole book.

Elve surveyed her smeared and blotted page. It wasn't going to work. It couldn't work. Even if people *could* read it, they wouldn't. Overwhelmed with her disappointment, Elve laid her head on her arms, utterly disheartened.

Then she straightened. She swiped at the tear on her cheek. Another way. There had to be another way.

BOOK II
Hom

21

I go outside real early while Gran is still sleeping. She sleeps a lot cuz she's still kinda sick. I go across the road to the Roons to see the cats before the other guys come. Gran says the right name is Statesfield, but we just call it The Roons.

Roon, he's my special cat, comes to me and I give him his treat. I hafta save it out of my supper every night because we have hardly any scraps. Gran uses them all for soup. Roon will come if I put a bit down and back off. I never chase him. That would spoil everything.

After a while, the other guys will show up—Jog and his brother, Bim, and Hara and Rafu. Jog and Bim are eight. Hara, she is nine, and Rafu is just six like me and very smart. He is the best climber and rock jumper. Jog and Bim aren't scared of anything and Hara brings the best food. She's the oldest and sometimes we listen to her.

Hom wrote in Inglish:

Ie goe owtsied reel erlee wiel Gran iz stil sleeping. Shee sleeps a lot beecuz sheez stil kienda sik. Ie goe akros de roed to De Roons too see de cats beefor de udr gies cum. Gran

At this point, Hom ran out of chalkboard space, so he couldn't complete the Inglish version. It doesn't matter, he thought, with a shrug.

The sun hadn't yet cleared Elve's building on the east side of the road when Hara picked her way through the rubble at the north end of the Roons. The children had piled even more rubble at their entrance to hide their point of entry. Only they knew which of the rocks provided solid footing and which were dangerously tippy. Hara, who was strong and sturdily built, negotiated the passage with agility, holding her basket of food on her head.

"What did you bring us today?" Hom was squatted on his special rock.

"Never mind," said Hara. "I'll get it out when the others come. How's your granny?"

"She's still dizzy when she tries to walk around. But she eats at the table now. Lali is always bringing her good stuff to eat, so she doesn't hafta cook much."

Soon Bim and Jog joined them, but Hara still refused to open her basket.

Rafu came leaping from stone to stone. He grasped the slender trunk of the young birch tree, swung round it and landed near the others squatting near Hom's stone. Rafu was tiny, dark, and wiry, with the same wise dark eyes as Hom.

"Now, Hara, now!" The boys clamoured for Hara to open her basket.

She folded back a clean white cloth to reveal her offering—a solid yellow loaf of corn bread, seeded with tiny pale green crescents.

"What're those?" said Bim with a suspicious eye.

Hara laughed. "You think I would poison you? They're the seeds of a weed that grows behind our house. If you pick them when they're green, they're like little nuts. But when they're old they turn brown and hard and aren't good anymore."

The other children no longer marveled that Hara knew these things or that she was an able cook. They simply expected that she would turn up with something good, and she seldom failed.

Hara had heavy responsibility at home, as her father, Respected Health Team Inspector Dag, was frequently away, and her mother suffered a debilitating mental disorder. The disorder, which kept her mother anxious and disoriented for days at a time, left Hara to care for herself, the house, and a demanding older brother.

This summer, the brother had been sent to the Glorious Shining Waters Camp. The mother entered a period of calm that allowed Hara an unaccustomed freedom. Still, she would go home early in the afternoon while the boys still talked and worked and played.

Their project just now was to clear away loose chunks of masonry from the fallen façade. The boys worked enthusiastically. They wanted to use the pieces to construct a fortification.

By a process of trial and error, Hom developed a sense of the way the chunks should be laid to make a durable wall.

"Here," said Hom, pointing from a commanding stance on a rock at the end of their nascent wall. He pointed to a likely spot.

Bim and Jog deposited the rock they were lugging on the designated spot. Rafu found them another manageable slab and the bigger boys did the heavy work. This process continued, marked only by curt words and the heavy lifters' grunts.

Jog and Bim stopped, mid-lift. They looked at each other. They dropped the slab. It cracked in two.

"You carry it," said Jog to Hom. "And you too," said Bim to Rafu.

An expression of hurt crossed Hom's face. A hint of anger. Then a grin broke through and he said, "Sure, guys," and came down from his perch.

Jog and Hom lugged one piece, Bim and Rafu the other. Hom picked the placement with a jerk of his head and the work proceeded.

Hara was eager to help, because she had another purpose in mind. She knew, because of the presence of the birch tree, that there must be earth beneath the recently fallen rubble. When a nice patch of bare earth was opened up, she would plant fruit trees. There was already a good deal of low vegetation in the Roons, its fallen leaves having contributed year by year to an adequate depth of soil. Hara pictured a garden. Peach trees and grapevines and fat, red peppers. Hibiscus and asters and daffodils.

The RAA forbade the growing of flowers by ordinary citizens. Sumptuous blooms decorated the platforms and pulpits from which honoured government officials made their announcements. They were a common feature of the H of P. Hara's garden would have to be a secret.

Hara took her basket and shook the crumbs onto the cats' feeding slab. She left the Roons while the sun was still high. The boys continued to work, more slowly now in the blazing heat.

After a time they took a break, and sprawling in the birch tree's lacy shade, drank the last of their water supply from their bottles. The cats, uninterested in Hara's mingy offering, napped on.

"Hubboo, lookit how much we got done today," Hom said, waving to the three-metre base along which they were beginning to build.

"Don't look like a lot to me," said Jog. "We'll never get it done before school starts."

At the mention of school, all the faces turned sombre.

"I'm not going," said Hom. "I won't go there. Gran can teach me and she doesn't make me sit on my hands."

"You'll hafta," said the others, and Hom let it rest.

"It's so boring," said Jog. "You don't learn nothin'. Just how stoopendous the RAA is." He sighed.

Rafu looked from one to the other, alert to this implied criticism of the RAA. "I got a good teacher," he said. "Instructor Lam knows songs and fun stuff." Then, with wrinkled brow, "We should've saved some corn bread for now."

Reminded of their empty stomachs, the others nodded.

"Hey, look!" Rafu was pointing to the feeding slab where Hara had dumped the crumbs.

Feeding on the slab was a pair of small birds with black caps and black triangles like little bibs below their beaks. There was a chipmunk too, stuffing his cheeks with the morsels. Roon watched from his perch, ears pricked, tail switching.

A long, lean streak of grey fur. A lift of wings. A scamper to a rocky crevice.

"Chickadee, chickadee," came the taunt from the twisted pine at the top of the rock pile.

On the feeding slab, Roon adopted a haughty pose. "Oh well," his posture said, "I didn't want to catch them anyway."

They boys laughed. As one, they stood and stretched. Hunger was driving them home. They could not have been happier.

22

I have a dream. It comes when I lie on my rock in the Roons watching the sky. I keep my eyes open and I hear a voice, but I can't see anybody. The voice is low and loud like a giant humming. It hums my name. HOM-M-M-M. It makes my body tingle all over. And then the sound dies and the wind brushes my face and I am glad.

Hom rewrote his dream in Uniscrip. "...**and de wind brushes mie faes and Ie am glad.**"

On the first day of what was once October, Hara and Bim and Jog and Rafu returned to their classes, doggedly accepting the routine of televised lessons and daily marches around the school field.

As he'd vowed, Hom didn't return to school. He was prepared to mount a serious rebellion against any pressure to do so, even promising himself that if he were forced out the door, he would simply go across the road to the Roons and spend the day there.

He was surprised, even a little let down, to find that Elve had no intention of sending him to school. Instead, she declared that three hours every day would be devoted to study, two in the morning and another in the evening

Hom had grown strong and tall over the summer. His face and body were bronzed by the sun. His black hair sprang thick and straight from a broad, high brow. He moved with the quickness and grace of his beloved cats.

His work with the concrete slabs had made his hands muscular and sure. Even the left, with its permanently deformed fingers, was of little hindrance to him. Nerve damage had rendered those fingers insensitive, and he could use his fist like a hammer.

Hom made a list of things he wanted to study:

>Olden days in Canada and Tranna
>Animals and plants
>Stories about adventures
>The wind
>How to cook
>How to make stuff
>The world

Elve inspected his list and added:

>Mathematics
>Logic—how to know what is true

"Gran, I wanna make more sculptures. We've kinda spoiled the first one I made."

Indeed the crunching of several batches of wallboard for chalk had obliterated the details of his first work. They added carving, writing, and making himself useful to his afternoon schedule. Elve agreed that before the schoolchildren began to fill the street after dismissal, Hom could venture across to meet his friends in the Roons.

Rafu was already in the Roons when Hom arrived one cool, damp day shortly after school had begun. Rafu was half-way up the face of the south-end shell of the building, climbing with gravity-defying agility.

"What're you doing up there?" yelled Hom.

"I wanna see how high I can get."

"Me too. I'm coming up."

Hom climbed, sure-footed, but more cautious than his friend. Soon they were together on a ledge high up on the ruin's face. A jutting ledge above them prevented further climbing.

"Waw-aw-aw," they breathed. "This. Is. Amazing."

The full extent of the ruin lay before them. Its structure, obscured at ground level by debris, showed clearly that the building had risen on three sides around a walled space—a courtyard or perhaps a garden. The latter seemed the most likely possibility, because from their vantage point, the boys could see that the vegetation was thicker in a rectangular area with their birch tree just outside its corner.

"Hara's right. There's dirt under there," said Hom. "She can make a big garden."

"She'll hafta move an awful lotta stones."

"Well, I guess we could help."

"But I wanna build our wall," Rafu said.

"We gotta do them both." Hom paused. "What's the good of the wall anyway? A garden would give us something to eat."

"I dunno. I just like it, that's all."

"Yeah."

The two considered why they needed a wall.

"If the police came into the Roons we could hide behind it and throw stones at them," Rafu said finally.

"It's good for hiding. I don't know about throwing stones. I think we should plant things in front of it to camouflage it. Then it would make a better hideout."

At that point, they saw Bim and Jog picking their way in at their north-end entrance.

"Shtup." Rafu punched Hom's arm. "Don't say anything. See if they see us." They watched, smothering snickers.

"Hey, nobody here," said Bim. "Hom's late."

"Maybe his gran wouldn't let him come."

"I think his gran lets him do what he likes. Anyhow, let's build some more."

The brothers began to look for slabs of a manageable size.

High above them, Rafu and Hom could no longer suppress their glee. They shouted, laughing. "Hubboo, hubboo, we fooled you."

Bim and Jog looked up. "Waw-aw-aw! How did you get up there?"

"Like cats. We climbed. Come on up."

Bim attempted the climb. Several times he clutched frail handholds and trusted uncertain footing. But he persisted, and was able to join Hom and Rafu on the ledge. Jog, discouraged by similar setbacks, chose to back down. "I'm not breakin' my neck gettin' up there." He went back to building the wall.

Soon the three climbers came down to help. They worked until the sun disappeared below the line of dead spruces beyond the west wall of the ruin.

"Last one out's policeman's piss," yelled Bim, taking off for the entrance. Jog, Hom, and Rafu followed, leaping from rock to rock in crazy zigzags. They paused behind a concrete abutment to peek out, checking for police or other dangerous persons. Bim left first. Jog counted to twenty before he checked again and moved out. Rafu did the same. Hom made doubly sure that passage to his building would be unnoticed.

Hara had been absent from the Roons for several days now. The boys missed her, and not just because she always brought food. Hom began to feel uneasy about her.

23

Hom wrote: **Our wall is progressing galubriously. It's almost as high as Rafu already. Bim and Jog are strong as tanks and can lift the heaviest slabs. I show them the best place to put them and help lift. Rafu searches for the pieces that aren't too big to carry. They're getting harder to find. But I miss Hara. Hara is strong and beautiful.**

Owr wal iz proegresing galuebreeusly. . .

The boys were heaving a lichen-covered grey slab half buried in turf. Jog had brought a length of rusted angle iron to use as a lever. He inserted it at the side of the slab and all three applied their weight to the bar. Grudgingly, the slab shifted from its bed. The boys renewed their effort and the stone lifted and tumbled out, a substantial chunk of masonry.

Hom yelled, "Hey, this thing is great. Where did you get it?"

"Out of a junk pile beside the old machine shop by the creek," said Jog.

Bim, Jog, and Hom joined forces to lift the slab and carry it to the wall.

"I can't hold it!"

"Rafu. Get over here."

"It's gonna fall!"

"Pissing shit!"

Miraculously missing their toes, the slab crashed on a protruding point of concrete and broke in pieces.

Rafu was on his knees, examining the disturbed earth where the slab had lain. It was alive with crawling things—shiny beetles and brown-dappled flat bugs crazily trying to escape the sudden light.

"Slooty glor!" said Rafu. "A whole city of bugs." And he knelt for a long time, counting legs and wings, observing how they moved.

Hom chose the best placement on the wall and they lifted the fortuitously broken pieces into place.

"Halloo!" They turned to see Hara hurrying along the path they had worn among the projecting rocks.

"Where've you been?" "What happened?" "Did you bring something good?"

The boys rubbed grubby hands on their pants and gathered under the birch tree, still hung with a filigree of golden leaves. They put on the jackets they'd abandoned as they warmed up to their work. They squatted in a circle, eyeing Hara's basket with greedy eyes.

Hara sat on a flat rock, tears brimming in her eyes. "It's been so long. So many horrible days. I'm so glad to see you guys."

Hom saw the purpled bruise on Hara's cheekbone. "What happened? Who hit you?"

Hara's eyes flashed. "Urgo, my brother, that's who. He's not my real brother anyhow."

"Yeah?"

"Only step. We fight, and it makes Ma sick and then I feel awful."

Jog and Bim moved closer together, touching knees. Rafu's lower lip projected and his eyes narrowed fiercely.

Hom touched Hara's arm. "I'm your brother," he said. "You don't need him."

The others made agreeing noises. A smile broke across Hara's face. "You're all my brothers. Now let's eat."

She drew aside the white cloth to reveal a basket full of small, rosy apples. "I went to the east ravine to find them. They're a bit woody and not very sweet, but you can eat them."

The boys weren't fussy. They bit into the tart fruits with gusto and declared them very good.

For a little space there were no sounds but the crunch of teeth attacking resistant fruit, a breeze whispering in the Virginia creeper, and, Hom thought, a faint trickling of water.

"The east ravine is spooky," said Hara. "Nobody seems to go there and the paths are so overgrown you can hardly find them. And you know what I found?"

The boys stopped in mid-chew, interested.

"I found a wooden door almost hidden behind a curtain of vines. You go down a couple of steps and there it is. I almost knocked, but then I got scared and didn't, and then I took a deep breath and I did it. And a voice said, 'Who is it?' and I said 'It's just me out picking apples.' And the oldest woman I ever saw opened the door."

"Waw-aw-aw!"

"Did she say her name?" asked Hom.

"No, but she asked me in and made me some kind of tea. Then she wrapped the tea leaves in a little cloth and held it on my bruise. It taked the pain right out."

"I know her," shouted Hom. "Her name is O and she's Gran's friend. She knows lots of stuff like how to trap rabbits and make medicine out of plants and live on your own in the ravine."

"I wanna see that. The house in the ravine," said Rafu.

"Nobody's sposta go there," said Hom hurriedly. "It's gotta be a secret. O doesn't have any ID." But privately, he planned to ask Hara to take him to O's hideout.

Bim and Jog began throwing their apple cores at the cats sleeping on the higher ledges. But they slept with pricked ears and watch-cats gave the warning yowl.

"Hey, stop that!" said Hom and Hara in unison, Hom because he was on the feline side in this war, Hara because she wanted to save the cores.

"I want the seeds," she explained.

"But they're poison," said Jog, voicing a superstition that lingered from an earlier time. A global agriconglomerate had once successfully promulgated the belief that the only safe seed for domestic use was their patented seed, treated with their proprietary insecticide, Bayosantocidex.

"Nah," said Hara. "Nobody believes that anymore. I want to see if I can grow some apple trees."

"And you can plant them here. In the Roons," said Bim. "We climbed up," he said, pointing to the ledge where he'd scrambled to join Rafu and Hom. "There's an old garden in the middle. You can see it from up there."

Hara jumped to her feet. "Waw-aw-aw. I wanna see that. How do you get up there?"

"I'll show you," said Rafu, heading towards the south-end structure. The others scrambled after, Jog dragging his feet in the rear.

With Rafu leading, they climbed single file up the tumbled walls. Jog watched from below, sighed, and began to follow. The others had reached the fourth-floor ledge before he was halfway up.

"Come on, Jog, his companions cheered. "Go, go, go. Do it, champ."

Bim reached out and drew his brother up the last crumbling step. The five children stood on the ledge, rosy and panting, looking out over their Roons.

"I see it, I see it," cried Hara. "The old garden. It's a jungle of bushes. Red ones and some with no leaves. No wonder we couldn't see it. The rock-pile around it is humongous."

"Our birch tree is just outside the corner."

"We could get in there just beside the tree."

"Let's go down and find the easiest way." Rafu was ready to get on with the task.

But the sun had dropped behind the spruces on the west.

"Another day," said Hara.

They stood sombrely, silent with private hope for the land they'd discovered: Hara for a garden; Bim and Jog for a fortress; Rafu for discovery of its life forms.

But Hom's eyes rose with the flight of the peregrine from the jagged ruin above them. He hoped to leave the safety of the garden. To soar. To see the world. To know. To do brave things.

A soughing wind passed through the naked trees; the birch shook off her leaves in a golden shower: the children felt their hair lift from faces cooled, even caressed. Hom recognized it. His dream wind.

24

Gran is making me watch the RAA's Hour of Power every night. The BO-o-o-RING H of P. She never did before. Now we watch and try to decide if they're telling the truth. It's part of my logic work.

Right now the RAA has decided to change the clock. A day will have ten tems instead of hours. A tem will have ten milims. Kids will be in school 45 tems a week, but workers will work just 42 tems a week. This is so parents have three tems to themselves. The high-hat with the pointer grinned in a funny way when he read that. Gran said he meant that parents would have more time to fuck. All part of the RAA's Grand Plan for the Happiness and Well-being of Loyel Sitizenz.

Gran iz maeking mee woch de RAA's Owr uv Power evry niet. Shee nevr did beefor. Now wee woch and trie too deesied if day ar teling de trood. Its part uv mie lojik cors. . .

As usual, Hom ran out of space before his Uniscrip story was finished.

Though it was still morning, the dim light of late autumn hung in the apartment. Hom brought the solar lantern to the table where he spread his books. He'd absorbed *Anne of Green Gables,* reading it hungrily. He yearned for the freedom Anne and her friends enjoyed in their idyllic setting, envying Anne's "Lake of Shining Waters" and "Dryad's Bubble". "Where are the police?" he'd asked Elve. "They seem to have lots of flowers. Why can't we have flowers?"

Now, at Elve's insistence, he turned to *"Life and Literature".* Lali had read it, cover-to-cover. But Hom leafed through it with little enthusiasm.

Elve sat with her mending. Hom's work in the Roons was hard on his clothes. Besides, he was growing out of them at an amazing rate. Her latest attempt at finding new clothes at the Emp had turned up nothing in Hom's size. The shelves were unaccountably bare. She laboured over rips and split seams.

"AUTHORIZED BY THE MINISTRY OF EDUCATION FOR ONTARIO" stood importantly on the second page of the blue book. But it didn't say when the authorization took place, so the book's stories and poems floated in a kind of timeless cloud. Then Hom found a date in the "Helps to Study" introducing a little poem. In 1924, one Wilfrid William Gibson submitted his poem "The Fowler" to a contest in London.

"How long ago is that, Gran?"

"Well it's 41 of the New Age right now, but in the old CE years it would be 3016. So subtract 1924 from that."

Hom calculated. "1092 years. Is that a long time?"

Elve studied her great-grandson's puzzled face. Out of her formal and self-education, she retained a notion of time and history that was in part nebulous and in other ways quite specific. She hardly knew how to answer him. But she dived in bravely.

"At one time, I learned that the earth is very, very old. There were, at first, no people on the earth. Just rock and air and water. It was like that for maybe millions and millions of years. I forget. And then, life began. At first one-celled life. But the cells changed and grew into more complicated plants and animals, all in the water, I think. And then a sea-creature crawled out of the water and somehow could breathe the air. Or maybe the water disappeared, and some of the sea creatures survived on dry land."

"What survived? Donkeys? Cats?"

"No, no. Not like any animals we have now. They were more likely something like worms."

"Then where did the cats and donkeys come from?"

"Well, it took millions and millions of years. Eons of time."

"If there weren't any people, who was keeping track? Somebody had to count the years and write it down. Worms can't do that."

"When I was a kid at school, the Universal Online Science Curriculum had lots of stories about paleontology. I even wanted to be a paleontologist until I found out that there weren't any working paleontologists anymore. The authorities—maybe government or university people—thought that that body of knowledge was already complete."

"Yabbut who was keeping track?"

"Paleontologists dug down in the earth and rock to find the bones of the animals and birds and sea creatures that lived in the very early time. They had a way to date the rock, so they were able to say which ones were the oldest, and how old they were. I never understood that very well. So they put together the time-line for the development of the creatures on the earth. Every stage was millions of years."

"So maybe after a million years, there were people?"

"Gawdno! People came really late in geological time. The last few years of the Pleo-something Age. And the first people made stone axes and hunted animals to eat. They maybe couldn't talk. For sure even if they could talk, they didn't write or read anything."

Hom suddenly saw his time with his friends in the Roons as something like the life of the inarticulate man. The way they built their rock wall with grunts and gestures. The way they sensed each other without speech. The way they all knew without saying when it was time to eat and time to leave.

Hom looked puzzled. "But the RAA says the earth rose out of chaos just before Yeer Wun, with the holy magic mountain in the very centre. That was the best lesson at school, with the video of the golden mountain and the Hidden Palace floating in the pink cloud above it. And we all clapped and said, 'Waw-waw waw.'"

"What do you think, Hom? Could that be true?"

"I really liked that video. The other lessons didn't have pictures like that."

"You haven't answered my question."

Hom frowned and then sighed. "I guess it's just more RAA garbage. The RAA is only 40. You're almost twice as old as that, so the earth didn't begin in Yeer Wun. And Boat too. Why does the RAA tell us this stuff?"

"Let's just be on the watch. Compare everything we see with what we know from other sources. We might learn what they're up to."

"The RAA doesn't like for us to know things, right?"

"I suspect so."

Hom puzzled about the date "1924". It occurred near the back of the book. Did that mean that all the other stories and poems in *Life and Literature* were written before 1924? He decided that it didn't. And it didn't mean that they were all written later either. It didn't mean anything much. Just that Gibson submitted his poem in 1924, whenever that was.

"Gran," he called. Elve looked up from her work.

"I wanna know when this stuff happened. Or if it really happened. I can't figure it out."

Elve was unwilling to drop her work just then. "You could look for more dates," she said, "likely in the study notes."

On inspecting the notes, page by page, Hom turned up several more dates, the earliest 1314 and the latest 1925.

"I still don't know," Hom said. "Somebody could write the stories a long time after they happened, I guess. But somebody had to remember them in between. For sure, though, nobody that lived before 1470 could have wrote that story about Sir Launcelot, could they?"

"Not if the story is actually history. But a writer could make up a story about Launcelot any time: past, present, or future."

Hom snorted with frustration. "How's anybody gonna know what's true?"

Elve laid aside her mending. There would surely be some new clothes for Hom in the Emp pretty soon.

Together Elve and Hom pieced together a sort of timeline for *Life and Literature*. They could nail down a few historical occurrences. Hom made a list entitled "Blue Book":

1. Robert Bruce told his army "Do or die." in 1314.
2. Sir Thomas Mallory wrote "Morte d'Arthur" in 1470.
3. L'Ile Sainte Croix was a colony in Canada in 1604. The people died of hunger and cold in the winter.
4. Prince Charlie attacked Moy castle in England in 1745.
5. Michael Faraday was an errand boy in 1805.
6. Abraham Lincoln was born in 1809. He was a president of the United States of America.
7. John Keats wrote a funny letter to his sister in 1818.
8. The Crimean War took place in 1854-55. Florence Nightingale nursed wounded soldiers there.
9. The Light Brigade charged in 1854.
10. James de Mille died in 1880.
11. Stephen Leacock lived in the 20th century.
12. Dr. John McCrae wrote "In Flanders Fields" in the first Great War in 1915.
13. Wilfrid Wilson Gibson submitted his poem, "The Fowler" to a contest in London in 1924.
14. In 1925, Albania on the Adriatic Sea gained independence from Turkey and Serbia.

Hom and Elve were able to conclude that the Blue Book must have been compiled no earlier than 1925. The historical material seemed to date from the 13th century, but the book also provided tales and myths from unknown ancient times.

On a later day, Hom looked up from reading "Let us now praise famous men". "Gran," he said, "I guess there were hardly any women in those days."

"What makes you say that?"

"There aren't any in the Blue Book." Hom said. "Well, hardly any. Just Florence Nightingale and Elizabeth Fry."

"There must be more than that. Look more carefully."

Hom was able to dig up two more names: Helen Keller and Margaret Aird.

"Margaret's in a story about a spelling match. She was the best speller in the school. And Helen Keller was a real person. She was blind, it says. Why does it say she was stupid if she was smart enough to write the story about Christmas in the dark?"

Elve shook her head, frustrated. How could she, with her partial, time-bound knowledge, bridge the language and experience gap between the 20th century and the 30th? She understood "blind" in its former meaning 'without sight', but as literal blindness had become very rare, "blind" in ordinary speech had become a synonym for "stupid". Vision impairment was not unknown, but it was unspeakably rude to call it "blindness".

"Hom, Helen Keller wasn't stupid. She had something wrong with her eyes, and she couldn't see. As you would be if your eyes were shut all the time."

Hom experimented with closing his eyes. "But, if I was blind, I wouldn't be able to read or write anything."

Elve dredged her memory and came up with a gem. "Braille! It was called Braille. They had a way to make writing with a system of raised dots. Vision-impaired people could read by touching the dots with their finger-tips."

"How do you know that?"

"It's just something I remember. I used to read a lot when we had everything available on Galaxy and Populopedia. Everything. History and anthropology and biology and medicine and literature. All the stories. All the poetry. Music too." Elve sighed. "Now we have the RAA Hour of Power."

"Waw-waw," said Hom wonderingly. "You could get to know everything."

"Yes, and some people did, in a way. They had a microchip implanted in their brain. By just asking in their mind, they could access Galaxy and get the answer. They didn't remember anything, though. The chip seemed to fuck up memory. They could never find their keys."

"They would always need helpers, I guess. To help find the keys," said Hom.

"I never thought it was a good trade-off. I could have had one. When I was at the Uni, many of the students were getting chipped."

Sighing, Hom picked up the blue book. "Nothing in this but guys having contests and fighting."

"It's not as bad as that." Elve took the book. She turned to the poetry. "This one is about flowers," she said. "A woman called Edna St. Vincent Millay wrote it."

Elve read to the boy a short verse called "The End of Summer".

> When poppies in the garden bleed,
> And coreopsis goes to seed,
> And pansies, blossoming past their prime
> Grow small and smaller all the time. . .

Hom, resting his chin on his hand, picked out the rhythm, tapping soundlessly on the table. He asked for a second reading, and Elve complied.

"There's flowers in the Roons," said Hom. "Hara says the purple ones are asters. She knows the names of lots of plants." It was on the tip of Hom's tongue to tell Elve about Hara showing him O's hideout in the ravine. But he decided not to.

25

Although the day was bitter, with a north wind driving stinging veils of snow, the Day 10 parade to the Emp proceeded as usual, with the school children leading the way with raucous song.

> We are the soldiers of
> The glorious new republic
> The glorious new republic
> Of Asia and America
> A brave new world,
> A brave new world,
> A brave new world
> She inspires our hearts and minds.

Hom spotted the local police pair, Dum and Dee, and walked a short distance behind the crowd. He knew he had nothing to fear from them. Gran always gave them something when they made their inspections—a boiled egg, or a bit of whitefish wrapped in a cabbage leaf. They regularly passed over the fact that no ID was ever presented for him.

Hom crouched behind a scraggly hedge some distance from the stage at the front of the Emp. Through its gaps he could see the risers where the schoolchildren were taking their places to the left of the stage. Hara was there among the students on a low step. Hom smothered an impulse to call out to her.

A high-hat officer stood behind a podium to make the usual speech about the Glorious New World Republic. Hom had heard many speeches like it on the Hour of Power. He shifted to relieve his cramped legs and pulled his head into his hooded jacket.

Then two other policemen half-pushed, half-dragged a woman out of the Emp's great doors. She was wearing a red robe and Hom saw her hair, all red and gold like a fiery crown. The policemen threw her down. Two officers with shears chopped off handfuls of her red-gold hair. The crowd watched in careful silence. Also silent were several civilians with puce armbands posted in front of the crowd.

The officers raised up an X-shaped frame of crossed steel pipes.

They bound the woman to it with wire, hand and foot. And all the time there were workers in prison garb bringing barrowfuls of concrete chunks and dumping them in piles.

When the cross with its victim was raised, a puce-robed woman rose from a front seat and ascended the stage. With ceremony, she broke the seal of a scroll she raised in her left hand. Unfurling it, she read in a loud voice:

Loyel Sitizenz: You see before you the criminal named Meem 2.9.02.42.50. The following charges are laid against her:

1. Against the supreme decree of the GNWRAA, she has refused to use her government-approved name and calls herself [the reader points to the woman and jeers] "Meemee." Led by the designated civilians, the assembly jeers, "Meemee, Meemee."
2. Against the lawful decree of the RAA, this criminal has allowed her hair to grow in disgraceful profusion. [The reader points and jeers, "Hag-head." The people cry, "Hag-head, hag-head," until the reader stops them with uplifted hand.]
3. Against the just and pure decree of the RAA, instituted for the well-being and happiness of all Sitizenz, this evil-doer has been found operating a place of degradation and disgrace, namely a common beer parlour. [The reader shouts "Viltrid shit." The response grows in volume and menace.]

Rolling up her scroll, the reader struck Meemee's cheek with it, declaring, "This malefactor, having flouted three venerated laws of the Glorius Noo Wrld Reepublik uv Az\hu and de Amerikas, deserves to be punished by its Loyel Sitizenz. Who will cast the first stone?"

From the front row, another puce-banded woman stepped forward. Choosing a chunk from the nearest pile, and shrieking, "Asshole," she hurled the missile. Blood spouted from Meemee's face. Others began to select their weapons from the piles. These they flung at their target while the reader still led the chorus of insult from a safe distance.

Children moved down from the risers where they were in some danger from errant throws and began to pile on.

Hom peeked out from the shelter of his hood. He saw Hara run away from the bloody attack, dodging through the mob with her arms shielding her head.

"Hara!" Hom yelled from his hiding place. He darted out from behind the hedge to grasp her hand. "Come on. Here. It's better here."

Together they crouched behind the hedge, trembling and breathing hard. "We hafta get outta here," said Hom, and Hara nodded. "We can't go to my house," Hara said. "My pa's at home." (Officials with the standing of Respected Persons or above were exempt from attending Day 10 assemblies.)

They threaded the streets from the Emporium to Miller's Lane, using back routes that Hom had discovered in the games of the previous summer. As they ran, Hom considered whether they should go home to Gran or take shelter in the Roons. Gran would be pretty mad, he thought. *She thinks I'm just over at the Roons.*

Hom had been venturing much farther afield than the Roons in his daily outings. He had watched Dum and Dee from various lookouts and found that they were remarkably consistent in their rounds. They were easy to evade, and not very dangerous anyway. He had studied the patterns in the next precinct and found that the police there were equally unimaginative in their peregrinations.

The Roons were by no means the only local elements that afforded good cover. Abandoned sheds, piles of rubble, and the occasional well-kept hedge provided concealment enough.

The choice of sanctuary was settled when a branch of thorn snagged Hara's jacket. It was a new jacket. With a sickening rip, the sleeve parted company from the shoulder seam.

Panting, Hara grabbed her shoulder. "What'll I tell my pa? He'll ask all sorts of questions. Why I'm not with my class. Why I'm not at the Emp. How could my new coat get torn like this."

"We hafta go to my place. Gran is real good at fixing things."

Ovid wasn't at his usual post at the back door. Probably at the Emp, Hom thought. He shivered to think that Ovid might be throwing rocks like the others. He led Hara up the stairs to Elve's door. It was locked, but Hom's expert shove dislodged the latch, and they went in.

Elve was mending again, sitting close to the balcony door to make the most of the dull light. When she saw Hara, she recognized her at once as the girl with bright, brown curls as Hom had described her.

Hom didn't bother with an introduction. "Gran, can you fix Hara's sleeve? Like right now?"

"Hi, Hara. Hom told me about you." Elve looked at the children sharply. Their faces were unnaturally red and their breathing still laboured. "What happened to the sleeve?"

"I was running and the thorn bush caught it and it ripped. Just like that."

"Well take it off and let me see." Elve examined the rip. "It was sewn much too close to the edge." She opened her box of precious pins, and after turning the garment inside out, began to pin the edges in place. "What's going on? Why were you in such a hurry?"

"We couldn't watch. . .We had to. . .they were all so ugly and screaming—throwing rocks at her."

"Please—you're not making any sense. Tell me the story, Hom."

But the boy, leaning against his granny's knee, began to sob. He buried his face and dug convulsive fingers into her thigh.

It was Hara who told the hideous story. She took a chair by the table and told it in an even, flat tone. From her place on the risers, she had seen everything. She told the part where the people began to choose their stones, hurling first an insult and then their weapon in a deadly rhythm of shouts and pitches.

Elve let the jacket fall to her lap, listening. She recognized the red-haired woman of the shebeen in Hara's description. Her face went white.

Hara's voice caught in her throat. "The woman with the red hair—she cried out. 'Freedom! Some day, freedom.'" Hara stopped. She laid her head on the table, shoulders shaking.

Hom wiped his eyes on Elve's sleeve. "Why did they do that, Gran?"

Elve paused to think. She shook her body to clear the horror of Hara's account. "It's to warn us all, I think," she said slowly. "A warning that the RAA will be brutal in enforcing the law. We need to be very careful."

A silence followed, broken by the children's trembling breaths.

"I'm sorry, Hara. I have no dark thread to sew the seam. But the red shouldn't show at all."

"Sure. Anything you got is fine."

Elve sewed in silence. Hom joined Hara at the table. She was looking at his chalk wall. "What's that funny writing?"

"That's Trad," Hom said. "It's the kind of spelling Gran learned before the RAA. It's like Inglish only harder. I bet you can read it though."

Hara attempted Hom's Blue Book timeline. With generous prompts from Hom, she did surprisingly well.

"All my books are written in Trad. You oughtta read them."

Hara looked puzzled. "Books? What're books?"

"They're paper sheets with stories and pictures printed on them. All bound in a bunch with a cover."

"Oh, I wanna see those."

Hom was off his chair, ready to run for the book box.

Elve intervened. She stood behind the boy, hands on his shoulders.

"Hara, I've used a few very old books to help with Hom's education. You know he can't go to school—just now. I didn't know where to start, and they were all I had. But the books may get us into terrible trouble. The RAA insists that Inglish is the only language and spelling for the whole world. You will be much safer if you never see them. Please, never tell anyone of their existence."

"I think Bim and Jog and Rafu know about them. I didn't know I had to keep them a secret," said Hom.

Elve sighed. "I was a little careless about that, I guess. But now I see that we must be vigilant about all the rules."

Elve returned to her sewing, finishing off with three tight stitches. She snapped the thread with her teeth. "Your jacket's done, Hara. It wasn't a very big rip."

Hom was rummaging in the bread drawer. "What've we got to eat, Gran?"

Hara took the jacket, thanking Elve with a small bow. The kids took their hunks of bread and peanut butter with them down the stairs. Ovid was home.

"Who's this?" he demanded.

"She's my friend, Hara. What's the rest, Hara?"

Hara supplied the digits to complete her name.

"Does your granny know her?"

"Yeah. She'll be coming back sometimes to do reading with me."

"You owe me some chores. You haven't been around much."

Hom sensed Ovid's displeasure. "OK. I'll come down tomorrow afternoon and do some stuff." Hom nudged Hara out the door before Ovid could ask any more questions. "See you tomorrow at the Roons?"

"No. Pa expects me home right after school. But soon. When he's gone again." Hara hurried away, hoping that Hom's promise of reading was genuine.

That night, Hom took his homemade chalk and tried to write.

> **I have seeed something terrible. So bad I feel sick in my stomach. I went to the Day 10 Parade this morning. I hid behind a hedge. I could see Hara in the school choir beside the high**

> platform, but I couldn't see my other friends.

Hom stopped a moment to draw a deep breath. He continued, although his hand trembled.

> Two policemen dragged a woman out of the Emp. She was wearing a red robe and I saw her hair, all red and gold like a crown. The policemen threw her d. . .

Hom couldn't continue. He curled in the old recliner, rocking and grasping handfuls of his thick, black hair. Elve found him there, and though the RAA would have condemned her for it, drew him into her arms to comfort him.

Hom never wrote the rest of the story.

26

Hom reported to Ovid the next day, washed and dressed in worn but clean clothes. Ovid looked him over. "Yer shootin' up. Soon be tall enough to be some good to me."

Hom ignored the implication that he hadn't been any good before. "What're we gonna do?"

"Sweep down the north stairs. Stuff's been blowin' in."

They put two brooms and a shovel in Ovid's barrow (a clumsy wheeled box) and took the creaking elevator to the nineteenth floor, where they left the barrow on the landing. They walked up to the twentieth floor.

Hom had never been up there. Because of the damage at the north end of the building, the two floors above were blocked off. Hom could see cracks in the improvised roof.

"There's where the stuff blows in. We should fix it."

"With what, I'd like to know? No building materials in the Emp for at least a year."

Ovid began to push the accumulated debris down the steps with his broom. In the sand and gravel that formed its base, dead leaves and twigs were predominant, but there were also birds' nests, wood chips, concrete fragments, and even a dead bird. It was grey with a darker head and rusty breast.

"What kinda bird is that?" Hom asked.

"Dunno."

When a limp, but intact plastic bag turned up, Ovid pounced on it and pocketed it. Plastic was a scarce and valuable commodity. Any kind of twine was also worth scavenging.

Hom on the landing shoveled the debris into the barrow. He collected wood chips in his pockets, thinking he might whittle some little things. It took both Ovid and Hom to push the loaded barrow, its small wheels squealing all the way. They took it to the elevator and then out to add its contents to the rubble at the building's north end.

"Where've you bin? Ovid said as they descended with the first load. "You haven't bin down for a long time."

"Gran gives me lessons in the morning. You know about the decimal system?"

Ovid glowered.

But Hom was undeterred. He had been totally flummoxed by Elve's efforts to teach simple arithmetic until her revelation of the decimal system made everything clear. He was anxious to share the miracle.

"See, everything is grouped in tens. It could have beed in fives or sevens, but somebody chose tens. Gran thinks it's cuz we have ten fingers."

"Yeah, I know that," said Ovid. "Didn't learn it at school. At school we used calculators for everything. Had an old carpenter friend. He showed me how to calculate on paper and in your head. I liked being able to figure things without diggin' out the calculator."

On another descent, Hom chatted. "I'm getting pretty good at calculating too. And we're trying to do history but we haven't got much. . ." Here Hom remembered Elve's injunction against telling about her books. "Gran doesn't remember too much."

"I'll tell you history," said Ovid with sudden anger. "I'll tell you that this RAA is a bunch of crap. Bloody killin' good people for no reason."

"You saw it too? The Day 10 P & C?"

"I was there. I threw some rocks, I tellya. Tried to hit that pucy old hypocrite. Spyin' on us and tellin'. . ." Ovid stopped, knowing he might have said too much. The elevator had come to a jolting stop. They resumed their work, pushing hard on the barrow.

As they progressed down the stairwell, there was less accumulation of debris and the work went quickly. At the back of the building with the last barrowful, Ovid's curiosity prompted him to ask, "What were you doin' at the Emp? Don't you hafta stay home? No ID and all that?"

It was Hom's turn to consider how much he should tell. "I goed out all summer when there were lots of kids out there. The police didn't bother us much. But I'm careful now that school's in. Hara and me, we meet in the Roons with some other guys."

"The Roons?"

"Old Statesfield."

Ovid blanched. "I'd die before I went anywhere near those cats. Statesfield's bad, real bad."

Hom thought it best not to tell Ovid anything different about the cats.

Pale sunshine sifted through thin, grey cloud later that afternoon in the Roons. Hom arrived before any of his friends. He had brought with him a chunk of bread spread with pork fat. He knelt on his favourite flat rock, watching for Roon. The grey tabby, now a glossy, full-grown tom, crouched a little distance from him, while the other cats perched on higher ground.

Hom made his calling sound, a murmur with a questioning tone. He took a tiny bite of the snack. Roon rose from his crouch, tail aloft and waving gently. He picked his way towards Hom and stopped just out of reach. Hom took another bite. Then he extended his hand with the rest of the treat, calling softly.

Roon approached cautiously. The smell of the fat overcame his caution. He stretched to lick the proffered treat and Hom laid it on the ground between them. As Roon devoured it, Hom traced the back of the animal's ear with a gentle finger. The cat purred. He rubbed against Hom's hand, asking for more caresses. He allowed Hom to rub his ears and chin before he trotted off to wash his face with a vigorous paw.

It was the first time the two had touched.

"Halloo!" It was Rafu leaping from stone to stone from their private entrance.

"Shtup! You want everybody to hear us?"

"I forgot," said Rafu, mildly apologetic. Rafu took for granted the safety of their stronghold and Hom had too, but now he was newly watchful.

Jog soon appeared, followed by his brother. They were only a little less noisy as they crouched in their circle with Hom. "Guys," said Hom. "We gotta be careful."

"Sure," they said, but without conviction.

"I mean, really careful. Were you at the Day 10 P & C?"

Their faces went white. They nodded.

"Our school was in the choir. Nearly froze on the west risers," said Rafu. "When they began to throw the rocks, we came down and people with armbands handed us rocks to throw too."

"Puce armbands. They're neighbourhood watchpeople. Ovid told me. They tell the police if they see anybody breaking the law."

"But we didn't throw any. We had to run to the old shed on the other side and be sick," Bim and Jog confessed. Hom told them about Hara's escape with him to Miller's Lane.

"Why did they do that?" said Rafu. "Make all the people kill her with stones?"

"Gran says it's a warning. To tell us all that the RAA is watching. We better keep all the rules."

"But there's no rules about the Roons," said Bim. "Nothing to say we can't be here."

"Yeah," the others chimed in. "We aren't breakin' no rules." Jog even said, "We have a right to be where we like."

Hom looked at them. "Um. I don't think we have any rights. Except to fuck when we're eighteen. They say on H of P."

The muttered responses indicated that they didn't pay a lot of attention to the Hour of Power. But no, they couldn't furnish any evidence that Loyel Sitizenz had rights.

"I got no ID," Hom reminded them. "If the police hear us and come in to investigate, I end up dead like Meemee."

The other boys, reminded of Meemee's awful death, fall silent.

"But she was a bad person. She broke important laws. You're just a kid," said Jog.

"Guys, they kill kids. All the time. 'Imperfect babies'. 'Defectives'. 'Ineducables'. 'Incorrigibles'. The high-hat was on about it a while ago. How this preserves the perfection and the stability of 'Owr Glorius Sesieety'. It's called 'Soeshel Klenzing'.

"He said, 'Mothers, do not weep for your cleansed offspring. Their bones are the true and rightful sacrifice to the RAA. Such weeping is an insult to the Infinit Wizdum uv de RAA's Awsum Dekrees that maintain Law and Order for de Benefit and Wel-beeing of awl Loyel Sitizenz.'"

The other boys chimed in at "Infinit Wisdum . . ." It was a refrain they knew well, being required to recite it daily at school as well as at the Day 10 P & C.

They sighed and for a while said nothing.

Bim was piling little stones to make a tower. "Is our wall against the law?"

Jog began to build too, a construction of rectangular chunks. "Don't see how it hurts anybody's 'Benefit and Wel-beeing'".

Rafu, choosing to be different, ordered pebbles in a line, smallest to largest. "But if a cop saw it. . ."

Hom was choosing jagged pieces. He fitted them to make a rough mosaic. He took his time. Then he said, "Y'know what? The cats would get him. 'Merow-w-w-w'." He jumped up, raking the air with clawed hands.

His friends laughed and jumped up too, yowling and growling.

The sun had succumbed to enfolding cloud. A single snowflake spiraled down into the circle.

"If it snows, our tracks will give us away," said Jog.

"If there's enough to track, we hafta stay away," Hom said. The others nodded.

"We're on custodial detail anyhow," said Bim. "Next week, Day 1 to Day 9. After school, ninety minutes."

"It's supposed to be an honour, isn't it?" said Hom.

"Yeah, we get to wear a star on our sleeve." Jog showed no pleasure in the thought.

Rafu looked from Bim to Jog, surprised that the prospect of Custodial Duty didn't make them happy. In his junior class, TV lessons touted it as a privilege for which they would be eligible in the coming year. He hadn't heard the sarcastic self-designation of the Respected Corps of Toilet Scrubbers.

With renewed care, the boys performed their exit routine, one at a time, scouting the scene for any threat before leaving the sheltering rubble. Jog, hearing the crunch of wheels, dodged back to safety until the sound receded. Following him, last man out, Hom saw Dum and Dee wobbling away in the distance on their cheap bicycles.

A whiteship descended in a leisurely spiral, as if to inspect the boys' constructions: a carefully balanced tower; a miniature fortress, a mathematical progression, a mosaic.

27

The snow began that night. Soft, thick, flakes, falling tranquil and relentless. It snowed for three days. On the second day, the electricity failed.

Late in the afternoon, Elve and Hom lighted candles and studied by their flickering light. Hom wore his outgrown jacket and rabbit fur leggings for warmth. Elve had a long, purple coat older than the RAA. She daren't wear it outside because of the clothing regulations. Purple was worn by ranking civil servants only, people like Respected and Honoured Administrator Garg.

"Gran, what's charity?" Hom was reading "Charity" in the Blue Book. Since their sources were so few, Elve required him to read every selection several times, mining it for information about other times, other societies, world geography, anything to illuminate beyond the narrow time and space presented by the RAA.

"Depends. Read me the sentence."
"Though I speak with the tongues of men and of angels,
And have not charity,
I am become as sounding brass, or a tinkling cymbal."

"Hm. Is there more?"
"Yeah, lots." And the boy read:
Charity suffereth long and is kind;
Charity envieth not;

Charity vaunteth not itself, is not puffed up,
Does not behave itself unseemly,
Seeketh not her own,
Is not easily provoked,
Thinketh no evil;
Rejoiceth not in iniquity, but rejoiceth in the truth.

Hom looked up from the book and saw that his Gran's eyes were wet with tears. "Gran?"

"I knew Meemee. They stoned her to death. They rejoiced in iniquity."

"And charity doesn't do that?"

"Never. Charity is kind. Is kindness and mercy, I think. Who wrote that?"

"It says 'The Bible' at the end. That doesn't sound like anybody's name."

"It's taken from a book collection, I guess." Elve was familiar with the word "bibliography" and the French *"bibliothèque"* meaning library.

"We have *Holy* Bible. It's in the book box." Hom's tone suggested that he was surprised that his granny hadn't noticed the connection. And indeed, she never had.

"It's in such bad condition. I'm afraid to touch it for fear it falls apart even more."

"I wanna see it. See if I can find charity in it."

He ran to unearth the metal box from its hiding place. Scarcely breathing, he lifted out the sheaf of delicate leaves tied between leather covers with a bit of ribbon. He laid it on the table. The singed cover and browned edges showed that the book had been salvaged from a fire. The words, "Holy" and "Bible" could still be deciphered on the spine. As he untied the ribbon, the sheaf fanned into a sloping pile. The pages were completely unmoored from the spine, but some of the binding held. Hom framed the pile with his hands, considering how to proceed.

"I guess I begin at the beginning," he said.

Several loose pages lay on top of the pile. They were a pale yellowish brown, their edges charred and broken. Hom lifted the first.

It bore a colour print, a painting of a white-bearded man carrying a bright lantern. A rock wall rose at his right hand, and a chasm fell away beside his sandaled feet. His clothing was unlike anything Hom had ever seen: a flowing white head covering, a long, white, belted tunic, a dark red robe. Two faint stars shone in the night sky.

Hom felt the threat of the chasm and the salvation provided by the patch of light at the traveller's feet.

The next loose page denoted the presentation of the book. To whom and by whom were rendered in a very difficult handwriting that Hom didn't try to decipher. But the date was clear enough: August 3, 1927.

"How long ago is that, Gran?"

"Don't be so lazy. Figure it out."

Hom figured it out. "More than one thousand years! No wonder this book is falling apart."

A loose page bore the title, **"The Literary Books of the Old Testament."**

Hom, spotting the similarity between "Literary" and "Literature," again taxed Elve with questions. She did her best to explain what she considered the difference between literature and other kinds of writings.

"At school," Elve said, "I read science and history and literature. Science is about what things are really like, especially the tiny things we can't even see like microbes and molecules. Big things too, like the sun and stars and galaxies of heavenly bodies."

"Peregrines and rabbits? Worms? Rafu likes to study worms."

"Yes, worms too."

"And history is about men and war." Hom had gathered this much from his study of *Life and Literature*.

"But there's social history too—about people and how they've lived. What their families were like, the work they did, what they ate. Tremendously interesting." Elve spoke regretfully, unhappy for the loss of historical sources.

"And I read literature too. Stories and novels and poems in Trad and Inglish and some translated from other languages. French, mostly."

"Other languages?"

"In every part of the world, people spoke a traditional language as well as Inglish. They had always had authors who wrote in *their* Trad, and their literature from centuries back was available on Galaxy."

"Wow! Hundreds of books like *Alice in Wonderland* only in other languages!"

"Billions. Trillions. There was no end of books."

The conversation continued to meander, with Elve telling the boy what she remembered, and Hom absorbing like a sponge.

"So the 'literary books' are story books?" said Hom, returning to his original question.

"I guess. Which ones are 'literary'?"

Hom read aloud, "Esther, Job, Psalms, and Proverbs." "Ecclesiastes" challenged Hom's reading ability, but he came up with a good approximation. "And Song of Solomon and Lamentations. It says these ones are poetry, not stories."

At last the light dimmed too much for study. Hom collected the Holy Bible pages and after a long look at the man with the lantern, he tied them up again. He returned them along with the other books to the tin box in its hiding place.

This much he'd gathered from his first study of Holy Bible: the volume was a collection of many separate books. Written by lots of different people. Like the Blue Book.

* * *

On the fourth morning the snow stopped falling. Sunshine and frost crystals turned the fresh mounds into glittering heaps. Hom looked out at the Roons from the balcony, longing to explore its snowy recesses. But he could see no access that wouldn't be extremely noticeable.

Ovid came to Elve's door with two shovels. Hom's services were necessary. He donned leggings and jacket.

Ovid and Hom started to work on the snowy barrier that had laid itself across the back entrance. It was almost as high as Hom. But it tailed off on one side, leaving a place to start. They worked in silence, staggering their digging and pitching so that they didn't get in each other's way. After a few minutes of heavy work, Ovid leaned on his shovel, taking a breather. Hom continued to dig.

"Take it easy there, fella. We've got a fair bit to do yet," Ovid said.

"It makes me feel," Hom grabbed a breath, "strong." Flushed and sweating, he flung off his jacket and kept digging.

The two of them worked until they had cleared a path to the parking lot. The lot itself was navigable on foot, though the snow was deep. There was no need to clear it. No one had a private vehicle anyway, and the garbage truck wouldn't come for another week.

"Good enough for now," said Ovid. "I'll make a path out to the road in a bit."

The two of them returned to Ovid's "office" in the back lobby where Ovid poured himself a mug of tea from a vacuum bottle.

"What's that? Hom asked, eyeing with wonder the steam coming off the tea.

"Says 'Thermos' on it. Guess that's a brand name. Everything used to have a brand. Want some?"

Hom nodded without enthusiasm. Tea was one product that had never been in short supply at the Emp. But the Thermos fascinated him. "Where did you get it?"

Ovid poured Hom's tea into the Thermos lid and his own into a never-washed, stained mug.

"Got it att the midden. We're down twenty metres into an old landfill. Workin' on the back so that it doesn't show from the road. Amazing stuff there."

"But how does it work? Why is the tea hot?" Hom visualized some kind of miniature tea-maker in the bottle.

Drawing from his own observation and a scrap of scientific knowledge from the internet of his youth, Ovid explained the principle of the vacuum bottle.

"So the heat can't get through the empty space?"

"No, because a vacuum is a hundred per cent empty. No air to conduct the heat."

Hom considered this phenomenon. "Why don't we have Thermoses at the Emp?

"Ask the RAA. They decide what we can and can't have."

The two finished their tea.

"Want to come to the midden with me some time? We work at night because there's only one watchman and he's a deep sleeper."

Hom's eyes lit up. "Slooty! When are you going?"

"I'll let yer know."

This time, Ovid sounded like a Brit of many centuries ago.

28

Hom's opportunity to visit the midden didn't come up until weeks later, after rains had devoured the snow. The weather turned dry, but cold.

Ever since her long illness, Elve had kept the habit of retiring early. As soon as the Hour of Power was over and the kitchen tidied up, she would lie down to rest.

Sometimes she asked Hom to read to her. They were trying to work their way through some of Holy Bible's many books. They decided to start with a poetry book, The Book of Psalms, because Elve knew that psalms were songs, and Hom thought he would like to read songs.

There had been singing in the Roons. One afternoon, the boys stopped lugging rocks to their wall, transfixed by a strange, sweet sound. It was Hara, singing as she planted apple seeds in a small area they'd cleared of debris. (Hara reasoned that since apples fall in autumn, and their seeds likely reach the earth then, autumn was the right time to plant the seeds.)

Singing was a familiar activity. Lifting patriotic songs with strained, shouting voices marked the opening of every school day. But the boys had never heard a voice like Hara's. Lilting and fluid, her wordless song was full of a joy unknown in the compulsory songs of the RAA.

Hara stopped singing and blushed when she saw that the boys were listening. But they were anxious to hear more, and know how she made the sweet sounds. There followed a scene with the boys trying to imitate Hara's voice. They squeaked and squawked, grasping their throats and kicking up their legs. Hara lowered the pitch a little for them, and at last, Rafu matched her melody—a simple five-note scale.

Hom failed that day, but on later days he also managed a singing tone. Bim and Jog as well. The children sat by their small birch tree, making new songs, songs deliberately unlike the shouted paeans of the RAA. A bird's chirrup or a cat's meow would inspire a phrase that grew into a sort of plainsong. Rafu discovered harmony, and singing became their delight.

* * *

Reading The Book of Psalms to Elve moved Hom to appropriate phrases he liked for songs that he sang by her bedside. When he sang, "For the Lord is good: his mercy is everlasting; and his truth endureth to all generations", she resurrected a voice she hadn't used for many years to echo his phrases. This voice, though diminished by age, served well enough to give new life to the ancient songs of Israel.

It was after they had sung, and Elve had slipped into a deep sleep, that a soft knock caught Hom's ear. Quickly, he hid the book under Elve's bed. He opened the door cautiously to find Ovid waiting in the shadowy hallway.

Ovid whispered, "Can you get away now? I'm off to the midden."

"Gran's asleep. Let's go."

Hom yanked his jacket from the hook where it hung by the door and scuffed his feet into his shoes. Ovid shoved a spade and a polybag into Hom's hand. "There's a velotruck to take us out there. We meet it at the top of Miller's Lane."

They set out northwards, stumbling into deep frozen boot-marks dimly lit by Ovid's solar lantern. They pulled up their hoods against the stinging wind.

Ovid turned out his lantern. They waited in the loop where at one time velotrams had turned at the end of their route. Just when Hom, shivering, was beginning to regret this adventure, a truck, apparently an old army vehicle, came into view. Electrically powered, noiseless.

Ovid passed a handful of coins to the driver. The two of them scrambled into the covered box, joining several others who looked at them, especially at Hom, with caution bordering on hostility. Ovid greeted one of them, a woman, with a curt "Huah," and she acknowledged him with a nod. The truck lurched away to the north on a road barely better than Miller's Lane.

It seemed a very long drive to Hom. He'd never had a ride before, but the swerving and jolting soon erased any pleasure in the experience. He longed to ask Ovid about the truck. Who was the owner? Where did he get it? How did he get the battery for it? (Rusting velos were a common sight in Tranna. They sat, half-hidden in tall grass, unusable for lack of batteries.)

Hom felt, though, that questions would be a mistake. The silent occupants of the truck huddled in the darkness, faces drawn back into their hoods. "Almost there," Ovid volunteered, after they passed a ruined tower, all that was left of a failed development. A landmark.

The truck stopped. Hom jumped down, glad to stretch his legs. The others followed. A black mound rose high against the night sky, now cleared of clouds by the persistent wind. The moon was rising, almost full, lighting the peak of the man-made mountain. There were stars, more than Hom had ever seen.

A man slumped, snoring, at a desk in a dimly lighted kiosk. He had carelessly left his half-drunk bottle on the desk. Silently, the group filed past, skirting the edge of the heap until, rounding a bend, they came to a place where the face of the mountain was marked with three black holes. Entrances to tunnels, Hom guessed.

He was surprised when the woman Ovid had greeted took charge of the group. "No one uses the old tunnel," she directed. "It is seriously compromised and may cave at any time. In No.2, work towards the left only. I'll go in ahead and check it out. No.3 is OK for now. Everything solid."

With nods and grunts, the workers accepted the woman's directions. The people, both men and women, moved off to the designated entrances. Ovid chose No.2. It was plain, even in the lantern's pale light that the tunnel had been in use for some time. It accommodated two people side-by-side. Hom walked easily under the ceiling and Ovid had to stoop only a little. Timbers shored up the walls here and there.

"Who is she? How does she know about the tunnels?" Hom asked.

"Call her Zeta. Don't know if that's her real name. She was an engineer in the army. Understands things like stress and stability." The tunnel began to slope down steeply. Ovid grasped Hom's wrist, either to steady the boy, or perhaps to steady himself.

"Zeta began to work here after the collapse. Three guys buried in a side-tunnel. Never got them out. No.1 always dubious after that. But a few go in there anyway. Seem to always find something." The tunnel took a sudden turn and led down again in a set of rough steps.

They stepped into a wide, domed space. Three tunnels, or rather, crawl-spaces opened out of it. Zeta motioned them to wait. She gestured to the nearest opening. "Anyone want this one?" There were two takers, so she crawled into the opening, shoving her lantern ahead of her. "Seems OK," she said as she backed out.

Ovid waited for Zeta to declare the third space safe. It was comparatively shallow, and still very narrow. Ovid pushed Hom in ahead of him while he came behind with the lantern and the polybags. Hom could see that because he was smaller, he would be a useful partner.

Hom pushed his spade ahead as he crawled. His own shadow played an eerie dance on the walls and low ceiling. When they could go no farther, Ovid put the lantern down. "Dig," he said.

Ovid began to widen the space to the left, while Hom dug the wall ahead. "Watch for plastic bits," said Ovid. "Old, broken stuff—anything at all."

Hom was hoping to find treasure. Some ancient piece, precious and perfect. Plastic bits hadn't been any part of his plans. But he attacked the wall manfully. The impacted rubbish yielded only a little to his efforts, unlike the snow that he'd shoveled with such verve.

He tried something different. He studied the wall, looking for a spot where he could insert the spade. Finding a slit near his feet, he pushed the spade into it and rotated it as much as he could. Small clods fell from the opening. He knelt and began to scrape away the edges. Bit by bit, the hole widened. He had reached a patch of crumbly material that he could scrape out with his fingers. He could feel something solid. He grasped and tugged.

The object came out with a jolt. When Hom regained his balance, he saw that he held a tiny spoon with an odd curved handle. Tarnished and bent, but intact.

"Hey, look, Ovid. Can I keep it?"

Ovid examined Hom's find in the lantern's light. If it had been larger, he would have claimed it. Metal was a valuable commodity. But it was too small to bother with. "Sure, keep it," he said. Hom put the spoon in his pocket.

"Hua," Ovid yelled as his shovel knocked against a large, solid piece. A little careful digging unearthed a blue plastic helmet. Dark blue with a white sector at the front, decorated with a bird's head and a red maple leaf. Delighted, Ovid shook off the dirt and stuck the thing on his head.

"What's it for?" Hom wanted to know.

"It's to protect a batter's head. There used to be a game. Lots of games. I found them on Galaxy. Way before Franklin's Folly. One guy threw a ball as hard as he could. The other guy tied to hit it with a wooden bat. But he needed the helmet in case the pitcher tried to bean him."

"Did the guy with the bat ever hit it?"

"Oh yeah. Right out of the park sometimes. I used to watch something called 'Baseball Highlights'. But the baseball leagues and teams broke up for some reason. A long time ago. Like centuries. Now the RAA don't like teams of any kind."

"So there won't be any new baseball?"

"No, nor football or hockey either."

Ovid returned to his digging, the helmet firmly in place.

They dug and sifted the diggings for a while, amassing a broken plastic bowl, the cab of a toy truck, some little bricks with short posts on one side and round indentations on the other, and three unidentifiable plastic bits.

They heard a faint whistle. Zeta's signal. It was time to get out. Ovid stuffed their finds, including the helmet, into his bag They bent to retrace their steps.

The moon had set. Scattered stars were fading. The scavengers found the silent truck waiting and scrambled aboard. Hom wanted to show the others his spoon, but heavy silence forbade talk.

When Hom got home, he shined up the little spoon and strung it along with the bear coin and the dove's wing on the thong that he wore around his neck. Then he slept.

29

Hom jumped over a chair on his way to the counter for his morning porridge.

"What's that?" Gran pointed to the little spoon that drew attention to itself by clanking against the bear coin.

"I found it," said Hom, hoping to leave it at that.

"Where?"

Hom hesitated. A complete and total lie would be necessary to hide his night's activity. Gran was fixing him with a penetrating stare. He decided to come clean.

"I went to the midden with Ovid. People are digging in it, trying to find good stuff, mostly plastic or metal. I found this spoon, and he let me keep it."

Elve's face went white. She was aware of the cluster of dangers that surrounded work in the midden. She'd heard of the collapse and the deaths there. At least as dangerous was the possibility of discovery and subsequent punishment, especially for a boy with no ID.

As well, goods found there were the property of some government agency or other, and any trade of the material strictly illegal.

"Hom," she said. "Promise me you won't go there again."

Frightened by her intensity, Hom promised.

"Put it inside your shirt. Don't show it to anyone."

Hom did as he was asked and, sighing, dug into the congealing porridge.

He was reading Holy Bible that afternoon when Boat arrived with a fine catch, the first of the season. He'd been missing most of the winter, as a bout of virulent flu had laid him low for some time.

"What's you real name, Boat?" Hom asked, returning to his reading. "Boatman isn't a real name, is it?"

"Why do you wanna know?"

"I'm doing Holy Bible names. They have great names like 'Methuselah' and "Nebuchadnezzar'."

"Yeah?"

"And some Holy Bible names are real people's names too. The Blue Book has lots of them, and the Anne book too." Hom opened the blue reader to the contents page, where he'd underlined the names of several authors: David Grayson, James De Mille, John Keats. "There's Adam, and a story about Abraham too. Abraham Lincoln. He was like me. He liked to read and had hardly any books."

"Yeah," said Boat. "Lincoln was a real guy. An American. President or something. Quite a while before the dictatorship. Got a lot of respect, I think."

"Abraham in Holy Bible did too. You can tell by the story. The Lord God talked to him."

"Funny thing. That's what my mother called me. 'Abraham.' Dad called me 'Abe'. But no god is talkin' to me."

"I'd like to have a real name that goes back a long way. Not three letters picked out of the RAA's approved baby-name list." Hom was turning pages randomly. "Waw-waw! Here's 'Matthew'! There's Matthew in the Anne book too."

"Yup, that's a real name too. I knew a Matthew at school. Named for some great-great—I don't know how many greats—grandfather. Always had to be a Matthew in the family."

Hom was quiet. He felt suddenly alone with his little name that had no connection to anything. Not to parents or grandfathers or the people in his books. Did my mom and dad choose 'Hom'? he thought. If they did, why?

His wanderings in Holy Bible had led him to read with wonder the first chapter of Numbers:

And these are the names of the men that shall stand with you:
of the tribe of Reuben; Elizar, the son of Shedeur.
Of Simeon; Shelumiel, the son of Zurishaddai.
Of Judah; Nahshon, the son of Amminadab.

And on for eight more verses. Sons known by their fathers and great-great-numberless-great grandfathers: Reuben, Simeon, Judah, Issachar, Zebulun, Joseph, Benjamin, Dan, Asher, Gad, Naphtali. Hom wondered if he himself had an ancestry too. Just as many greatgreatgreatgreats. But if he did, their names were lost to him. He had just Gran and Grandma Jema.

After the simple meal of trout and rice, Elve and Boat retired to her room and this time, shut the door. Hom heard their voices, lowered, he thought, to be sure he couldn't make out the words. Then all was quiet except for the familiar accompaniments of fucking.

Hom decided to organize his study of Holy Bible. He made a narrow column on the left side of the black wall. Under his title 'HB", he listed in abbreviated form the titles and page numbers of the books: Gen 5, Ex 83, Lev 113, Num 150. It was tedious work, but he persisted, and had reached The Book of Job before Boat reappeared.

"Your granny's gonna rest now. We'll clean this up," Boat said, gesturing towards the remains of the meal. As they worked, Boat said, without looking at Hom, "How would you like to come down and stay with me on the boat?"

"Slooty glor! Can I really?" Then Hom realized that staying with Boat would mean not going to the Roons. "But not all the time, right?"

"That's what I was thinking. Live on the boat and learn how to fish. I could use a hand with the work."

Hom pretended to concentrate on cleaning the wok. Then he said. "I can't go just now. We're doing something in the Roons. Me and my friends. We had to stop when the snow came, but we're back working now. It's a wall, and it's almost done."

"Me and Elve think you should get away from here. Be safer down on the lakeshore."

"I'm OK here. Dum and Dee never bother us. They know I got no ID."

"Yabbut diggin' in the midden is askin' for trouble. No end of probs. How did you get there anyway?"

So Hom recounted the story of his night with Ovid: the velotruck; Zeta, the engineer; the other hooded passengers.

"See, I found this little spoon." Hom fished in his shirt to show off his new treasure. His efforts at cleaning had revealed two kittens etched in its bowl. The curved handle was split in a heart shape and rejoined in a decorative cluster of tiny spirals. "It's got two cats. Tabbies like Roon."

Boat examined Hom's find. "Looks like silver. Tarnished, but the real thing. Surprised Ovid would let you keep it. Worth something, maybe."

"We were looking for plastic. Ovid says there's guys that melt it and make new stuff. Plastic is better than silver. Gold isn't even worth bothering about. Can't make anything useful with gold. But steel and aluminum, they're the best. Good prices for them."

Boat's eyebrows rose at Hom's knowledge of the market for trash. The blackest of black markets. Apparently lucrative, given the risks people were taking. "Ovid shouldna done this," he muttered.

Hom remembered the cold, bone-shaking ride with surly companions, the airless, dirty work, and Ovid's gruffness. "I told Gran I wouldn't go there again," he said.

"For sure. No matter what Ovid wants." Boat reached to hang the wok on its hook. "I gotta be going now. Fishing is best in the early morning. Take care of your gran. Don't give her a hard time. And think about my offer."

Hom completed his table of contents for Holy Bible the next morning, as much as the condition of the volume allowed. A bundle of pages was missing near the middle of it, so that his list had a substantial gap. At the end, scattered loose pages were all that remained of the books following The Epistle of the Apostle Paul to the Galatians. Among them were a couple of maps, one titled "The

Ancient Eastern World up to the time of the Exodus" and the second, "St. Paul's Missionary Journeys."

The name, "Peter" turned up among the pages. Hom laughed to find his friends the Pumpkin Eater and Peter Piper in the solemn text. For he had already sensed that the books in Holy Bible were solemn texts, even the most joyous of the psalms.

"Gran, what are these?" Hom asked, showing her the maps. So Elve did her best to draw for him a map of the world and to place the biblical maps within it. She had no means of correcting her errors. He conception of Africa was innocent of detail except for Egypt's Nile and the pyramids. China and the Americas were huge, while Europe had dwindled to a mere afterthought. Some areas were left out altogether—Indonesia, New Zealand, Greenland. Korea was marked, however. Its brief but dramatic period of domination was surrounded by a mythic aura, and the story was part of common lore.

In the first chapter of The Gospel According to Saint Matthew, Hom found another set of wonderful names: the familiar Abraham, David, and Joseph, but also Salathiel, Zorobabel, Aminadab. Hom marveled at the seventeenth verse:

> So all the generations from Abraham to David are fourteen generations; and from David until the carrying away into Babylon are fourteen generations; and from the carrying away into Babylon unto Christ are fourteen generations.

The detail of the genealogy, with all these men and their sons remembered by name, seemed to Hom a rare and wonderful thing. How could this be done? Did someone write it all down? Did people just remember all the names? Were there special people whose job it was to remember all the names?

Elve wasn't much help with his questions. Her knowledge was so scattered. Again, the loss of her sources stymied her. Her mind was never keyed to remember details, but only to note the best sources of information and save her favourites.

"I wish I had a name like Zorobabel and I knew who was my father and grandfather and way, way back to Abraham," said Hom, with his finger on the mellifluent name.

"You have an ancestry too, and not a bad one," said Elve. "I can show you quite a bit of it." She went to the black wall, took up the chalk, and wrote "Amma." She constructed, as well as she could, a family tree for Hom.

30

"Amma Newberry. She is the ancestor farthest back that I know anything about."

"How far back?" Hom turned a chair around to sit with his arms laid across the back.

"Don't really know. I had a photo of her in my ComD. She was tall and black, and magnificent. She lived in Canada in the Maritimes."

"Huh?"

"Maritimes. By the sea. The Atlantic Ocean. She went to Parliament. Leader of the Opposition. Shamed the government out of selling the roads and schools to private business."

"So she was your grandma?"

"No, no. Way farther back than that. But we used to be able to look stuff up. We knew that her family escaped slavery long before her time. But that's all I remember.

"My great-grandmother, Jamila, came along many generations later. I remember her a little, because she was like Amma. She died when I was six or seven. Her daughter was Atlanta, my grandmother. Grandma Atlanta lived in Mimico on the lakeshore here in Tranna. Her son was Aaric, my father." Elve listed the names down the board.

Hom rested his chin on his arms. "The Israelites remembered all their generations. Why did your family forget?"

Elve thought for a moment. "The Israelites remembered important men. But they forgot almost all the women. And there were scads of ordinary men whose names they forgot too. My family was mostly ordinary."

"And you lost your pictures and stuff. When the RAA taked the ComD's."

Elve nodded. "Over here," she said, moving to the right side of the board, "we have my Grandma Kumi. She never talked much about her family. Just the story of the old blue jug. Grandpa Joe and her had my mother. Her name was Emily."

Elve drew two lines from Aaric and Emily, joining them in the middle of the board. "They were partners and they had a baby—me." "Elve" appeared at the conjunction of the lines.

"But they both died when I was just three. They ate canned meat from Patagonia. It was bad, and they died."

"Lucky you didn't eat it too."

"Yes, I guess I was." Elve looked surprised. "Anyhow, then I went to live with Grandma Kumi on her little farm in Muskoka. When I was old enough to go to school, I came down to Tranna and lived with Grandma Atlanta."

"Did they make you sit on your hands?"

"Never. And I went back to the farm in the summers."

"And Luky Sadano was your joog and you had Max and Mungo." Hom had always been fascinated by stories of Max and Mungo."

"And I had a little girl that died when she was three days old. I named her 'Kumi Atlanta Amma Sadano. And then we had Grandma Jema. 'Jema', because the RAA didn't allow 'Jamila'. "

Hom was tired of genealogy. But he hung in there. He was waiting for the big reveal.

"Grandma Jema's first baby was Reba. When Reba was just eighteen, a military unit from the west coast was posted to Camp 46."

Elve seemed to have forgotten her audience. She laid the chalk down and sat by the table. "It was a special unit—you could tell by their greenish uniforms and light gear. Not like the others with armaces and boots and high hats. They never marched. They ran in twos and threes, and not on the streets. Ran among the trees and disappeared like shadows.

"Reba met one of them in the ravine. She told me. They kept on meeting there. Then he was posted away. At least, we think so. One day he was there. The next we saw nothing of any of them."

Hom raised his chin. "So what about me?"

"You were born nine months later."

Hom processed this information. "They fucked. Reba and the soldier."

"Yes." Elve touched the boy's cheek.

"Who was he?"

"His name was Lev."

"He begat me."

"He did."

"He might still be alive somewhere."

"Yes."

The word dropped into a pool of silence, woman and child lost in its implications.

BOOK III
Elve

31

At sun-up, Elve went out to stand at her balcony rail. Spring rains had been constant and the temperatures warm. She looked down on the overgrown copse of lilac, a remnant of landscaping that had once graced the property. Not that Elve had ever seen it in its former manicured state.

The light west wind carried lilac scent. Elve straightened her body. She felt well. Truly well.

She went in to make the morning porridge. Hom was off to the Roons as soon as he'd had breakfast and made himself a peanut butter snack. Elve didn't object. There would be rainy days when he could stay home to read and study.

Someday when Lali comes, we will go to see O, Elve thought. It would be better to go together.

O hadn't ventured to visit again after Elve's injury had healed safely. But throughout the winter, Lali had been faithful in coming to cook and talk. Lali was a fine source of news because her basket business brought a variety of customers to her door. Through her, Elve knew that the RAA had become vigilant in enforcing the reg against unlawful gatherings. No more than two unrelated people could congregate anywhere, even on a street corner. Groups of three were regularly broken up, though not prosecuted.

Lali arrived before noon. She brought a ham bone and wild leeks. Elve was able to supply two small beets and a blackened carrot from her winter store. Cheerfully, Lali peeled the carrot's powdery coating and sliced the remainder into the soup. As it simmered, the women leaned elbows on the table drinking cups of black tea and exchanging what tidbits of information they had.

"I only know what the RAA has been saying on H of P," said Elve. "They're gonna abandon the metric system. New measurements will be based on the sacred body of Owr Preshus Leeder."

"Yup. The basic unit will be the raes. The distance His Precious and Perfect Highness can run in four minutes. He'll be doing the run tonight, live on H of P."

"Another op to show off how fit he is. I'm getting bored with seeing his pecs like bricks and bulging biceps."

"OPPL considers himself the prime example of human excellence. A model for us all."

The women chuckled bleakly.

Lali moved to check the soup. "Lem at the bridge came in yesterday," she said, throwing a little salt into the pot. "He keeps the cops happy with handy things he makes. They can sell them easy among their fellow enforcers."

"Dum and Dee always seem to be hungry when they come to check us out. I've bought them off with food. No trouble with them even though they've figured out that Hom has no ID."

"Looks like the police force is seriously underpaid."

Elve nodded. She finished her tea. "I've a notion to go and see O one of these days. Would you come with me?"

"Slootly. When do you wanna go?"

Elve glanced at Hom's board. Day 9. Not tomorrow then. So far, she had never been missed at the Day 10 P & C. She wouldn't press her luck by appearing out of doors.

Lali agreed to go early on Day 2. They would meet where Old Rathburn Road met the ravine and continue together from there. If each left home at first light, they estimated that they would arrive at the spot at about the same time.

Mist still lay in the grassy hollows when Elve arrived at the meeting-place. She watched for Lali from a spot behind a sturdy oak that leaned into the ravine.

A rising sun rosied the stratus cloud above the flat-topped buildings on Old Rathburn. Elve figured that it must be April of the pre-RAA calendar. There was just enough chill in the air for that.

A lone man labored up the sloping street, pushing a barrow. Then Lali appeared, a dark-clothed figure with a broad-brimmed hat. She toted a blue polybag in her hand and a brown one on her shoulder. Lali bearing food, Elve thought, and wished she herself had more to offer.

"Yo, Lali," Elve said, stepping out from behind the tree.

"Yo." A single syllable, rich with trust and friendship.

The two women made their way into the ravine following a tenuous path that disappeared at intervals. The dense tangle of leafy shrubs served to conceal their progress, although the larger trees weren't in full foliage yet. They proceeded as silently as they could, startling flights of little brown birds from the bushes. O's hideout was well concealed by grape vines and a creeping plant that Elve couldn't name. Elve knocked at the sunken door.

The door opened a crack and then fully. O greeted her friends with extended hands and a joyful smile. She didn't speak until she'd drawn them inside and closed the door. Lali pushed her bags into the old woman's hands. "Fiddle heads," she said, "and a tunic that's too small for me."

Three rustic stools provided seating for them all. Elve was grateful for a chance to rest.

She looked at O carefully to see how she'd come through the rigours of winter. She found her friend thin but still wiry, her crinkly hair springing from her forehead as thickly as before. The black eyes hadn't lost their brilliance.

"You're looking well," she said.

"And you?" O asked. "How are you?"

"It's been a long time, but I think I'm OK. Really OK again."

As O busied herself with tea, Elve turned to Lali. "Did you watch H of P last night?"

"Slootly. Couldn't miss OPPL's historic run. A lackey helped take off his whopping hat and uniform. But he looked just like anybody else, climbing out of his pants." Lali snorted.

"Had to show us his muscle and sinew." Elve lifted a clenched fist in parody. "They claim he broke an ancient record—the four-minute mile. But there's something wrong with that. It didn't look like much more than one kilometre and a mile is quite a bit longer than that, I think. Besides the fact that they try to tell us that history began with the RAA. How can there be ancient anythings?"

"Anyhow, we have a new way to measure. The raes. We don't really know what it is because they didn't convert it. I'm totally discombobulated."

"First they take away time and now they've taken away space too. We float in immeasurability."

"I still have a watch," said Lali. "A wristwatch. Been in our family from time immemorial."

"They didn't get it in the sweep?"

"They didn't know it was a timer. You wind it up, so it doesn't use batteries. Not very useful, because nobody else has one. But I set it by the noon sun to help measure the day."

"That will be next," said O, setting out small cakes. "After ten months a one hundred day year. No relation to the sun or seasons or anything. History fails."

O went to a high shelf lined with blue canisters. She pulled *Mother Goose* from between the containers. "I've had this a long time," she said. I've memorized all the verses—the ones I didn't already know."

Elve received the book with trembling hands, moved again by this memento of a lost time. "I hafta give up on my writing project," she confessed. "There's just too much. A page or two of *Alice in Wonderland* used up most of the paper you made, Lali. And it's barely readable, the ink splattered so much."

"It scares me silly to think what the RAA would do if we *did* produce a bunch of written stuff," Lali said. "Even if I could somehow make the quantities of paper."

The three were silent, contemplating the RAA's probable attitude.

"So if there's no law forbidding writing, there soon would be if our work was circulated."

"Contradicts their declaration that the world began with the RAA."

"Slootly."

They nodded. They shrugged, lifting their hands in a gesture of resignation.

O recovered first. "But we mustn't give up. It's criminal, the RAA telling kids that there was no time before."

"Adults believe it too. My own Jema . . ."

"Before we die," said Lali. "We're gonna fix this. It's ridiculous. The RAA has control of everything—makes up its own 'truth'."

"I got just five—four and a bit years," said Elve.

"I got ten."

O laughed. "I lost count. It's that long since I should have died at the hand of the RAA."

"We're illegal right now, you know. Three unrelated people meeting under one roof."

"Plotting sedition and treason."

"Don't laugh. That's exactly what we're doing." Elve rose and collected the cups. She cleaned them in the dishpan with the bit of hot water that remained in the water boiler.

"Remember how you could read anything you liked?" Elve waxed nostalgic. "There was an empire—the Roman Empire. Lasted hundreds of years. And then it didn't. I read all that."

Lali likewise. "Travel was my thing. Couldn't go anywhere much, but I read about people who did. I wanted to climb Mount Everest."

"Lali, can you draw a map of the world? I tried to do it for Hom, and did a terrible job."

"Oh I think so."

"Do it. Make some more paper, a big sheet. Draw us a map."

"Slootly treasonous. The RAA has its own map. But I'll do it."

"I'll see if I can improve the ink," said O. "Oak gall and vinegar, perhaps."

"Somehow we hafta get in touch. There must be many more like us. People who remember the time before the RAA."

Together, the women named everyone they knew who lived before the RAA. They suggested, they discarded, (too loyal to the RAA, too wimpy, too ill). The contacts had to be made one person at a time. No meetings. No protests. No riots.

"We need a sign. A secret handshake or something."

O brought a basket from behind the curtain that hid her bed. "I can't stop collecting these things. They're so small and so perfect." She held up a tiny, roselike brown cone, the fruit of the hemlock tree. "If anyone will join us, give them a hemlock cone. It will be our sign of loyalty to truth."

Lali and Elve accepted a handful each. They tucked them away in their pockets. In turn they locked right forearms with O and left wordlessly.

32

A few days before school closing, Hom went down with Boat to spend the summer with the sun-bitten fisherman. The two left Elve's place just before dawn. The thug-gangs had gone to ground after their nightly rampages, and the police were in their headquarters writing up reports.

Elve had misgivings about the plan. How safe would Hom be with Boat? Out on the lake would be OK perhaps, but at the docks, nosy people would ask questions.

"It's OK," said Boat. "I know who my friends are, and the others we can steer clear of."

Certainly, Hom couldn't spend the summer in the streets as he had last year. Bim and Jog were slated for "Glorius Shiening Woterz Expeereeuns". Hom, though legally young enough to escape, was tall and sinewy for his age. If seen outside by police (other than Dum and Dee), he would be questioned, and when found without ID, dispatched to a hard-labour camp or worse.

Rafu had been chosen for a special government program called RAAGERS. When Hom told her of this, Elve feared greatly for the youngster. It sounded to her like some sort of special indoctrination—brainwashing?—program. Rafu seemed to have an unusually intelligent and inquiring mind. The RAA would try to bend it to their own purposes. She was thankful that his escape from school protected Hom from similar notice.

Hara, as the daughter of a ranking official, was excused from camp.

So Elve was alone late on a summer evening when she heard a faint knock at her door. She set aside her mending and went to listen. Silence.

Then she heard a soft thud. Something or someone had fallen.

She peered through the peep-hole. Nothing.

She opened the door a tiny crack. A burden shifted against it. She opened farther to see a slumped figure with short, brown curls. Hara.

"Hara, can you hear me?"

Hara lifted her face. Bruises were swelling on cheek and forehead; blood seeped from her eye. She tried to stand.

Elve linked her arm under Hara's armpit, half-lifting, half-dragging the girl inside. She engaged the ineffectual lock and stood panting, back against the door. Ice, she thought. Ice would help.

But first she needed to make a bed on the floor. She brought blankets, pillows, and a sheet to make a pallet. Hara was able to roll onto it and stretch out. Elve saw no other signs of injury.

The trays in her old fridge were laden with frost. Shrunken ice-cubes lined the little compartments. Enough for a cold compress. Elve wrapped all the bits and the frost too in a soft old towel. She held it to Hara's face. "There, there, lassie," she crooned.

When the girl seemed a little more comfortable, Elve asked.

"What happened? Who did this?"

"My brother. My step-brother. Urgo. He's in charge when Father is travelling."

"And he beat you up?"

"He. . ." Hara struggled to speak. "He put a pillow over her face. I couldn't stop him."

"Your mother?"

Hara could only nod. Dry sobs shook her body.

Elve looked for a way to keep the cold towel on Hara's face and yet offer the comfort of an embrace. The best she could do was to lie on her side, the length of her body providing a warming touch. Hara's sobs ebbed. After a time, she slept, but lightly.

Elva lifted her improvised ice bag. Hara's left eye, swollen shut, still bleeding. Bruises darkening on her brow and cheekbones. The nose caked with blood and knocked askew. He must have hit her with something. A blunt instrument. The eye appeared to be pierced. A knife. Or an armace, Elve thought. An armace with a bayonet.

She needed more ice. She would see if Sor was at home. She went next door and knocked. She waited and knocked again. Still no answer. She would have to ask Ovid.

Elve made her way down the stairs to Ovid's workshop. He wasn't there.

She went down the first floor corridor. She had never seen Ovid's partner, and knew only that she existed, hermit-like, in the superintendent's suite. She knocked tentatively.

When the door opened a mere crack, Elve was knocked back by the odour of the place. Pot smoke, food smell, the miasma of illness and neglect. A face, yellowish and haggard, peered with blood-shot eyes. "Whaddya want?"

I shouldn't have come here, Elve thought. Ovid was trustworthy in his way, but this woman was an unknown quantity. She blurted, "Have you got any ice? I need some for a bad bruise."

"Sure."

The woman stepped back, allowing Elve inside. "What happened?"

Elve couldn't fathom the situation. She suspected that caring for Hara was against regulations. This woman wore no purple armband, but informing on neighbours was a way to stay on the good side of authorities. If she was a pot smoker, which seemed evident, she likely needed protection.

Since she didn't know what kind of lie would be useful, Elve decided to be truthful. "I'm Elve from upstairs. My friend got beat up. A family row. She's come to me for help. I thought Ovid. . . He's been a good friend in the past."

"Ovid's gone," the woman said flatly. "They took him away a while back. Not long. Couple of days."

"Oh. Sorry. Are there charges or something?"

"Haven't heard a word. But they likely caught him with stuff from the midden. He was doin' a pretty good business." The woman steered her huge bulk towards the fridge. She extracted an ice tray from the freezer. "Not much here, but yer welcome to it."

Elve bowed her thanks. "Decent of you."

The woman shrugged. "Not much I can do for anybody anymore. It's OK."

"Your name?"

"Used to be Penelope, like the woman in the old Greek story. But the RAA made me change it to Pen."

Elve was startled by Pen's reference to ancient Greek literature. She wasn't well-read in it, but had come across some of the stories. She remembered Penelope.

"Pen. Could be worse."

With a grunt, Pen let down her bulk into the large upholstered chair that appeared to be her usual station.

Elve asked, "Are you OK, now that he's gone?"

Pen answered with a shrug and wave of her hand. Obviously a signal for Elve to leave.

Elve climbed the stairs with Pen's gift wrapped in the front of her tunic. She pondered the woman's misery and helplessness. She wondered why she felt somehow responsible. And then she knew. It was Grandma Kumi's voice in her head. "Love your neighbour. . ." It was Grandma Kumi who was neighbour to all, herding strayed cows back to their pasture, giving away Elve's outgrown clothes, sitting long hours with the sick and bereaved.

Elve found Hara asleep but feverish and restless. She applied her new supply of ice, securing it with a strip of polybag. Hara muttered and fought off these ministrations, but Elve prevailed. She watched uneasily as the bandage reddened. Too much blood.

The fever rose as the night wore on. Elve considered hospital treatment. As the daughter of a ranking official, Hara should get the best. But she had no means of summoning help, and felt that she shouldn't leave her patient alone. Elve clenched her fists in frustration.

She would have to wait until Dum and Dee made their morning rounds. About the time the young spruce outside her balcony drew its shadow back from the road. Ten o'clock by the old system. New clocks were promised by the Respected Ministry of Measurements and Weights. None had yet appeared at the Emp.

The police could use their Apsams to call a veloamb. But Elve feared the upshot of the questioning that would precede admission to hospital. Would Hara's ID be sufficient to ensure a routine admit, or would they ask about Elve and their relationship? If the registrar thought it irregular, Hara might be denied treatment, or Elve might herself be charged, with what she couldn't guess.

While Elve tried to order her fears, Hara stirred. She scratched at the bandage which covered both eyes, pulling it askew. Elve knelt beside her to remove the sodden rag. It seemed that the bleeding had stopped. Livid swellings closed the child's left eye and distorted that side of her face from chin to brow. The ice treatment had largely failed. The fever persisted.

Elve decided. In the morning, she watched the spruce tree's shadow and went down to wait at the roadside well before she expected Dum and Dee. She pulled a handful of radishes from her garden and shook off the dirt against her thigh. These guys were always hungry.

Children too young for the camps played in the roadway and on the tumbled masonry outside the Roons. Elve's heart ached for Hom; she missed him acutely. She stood in the shade of the spruce, and continued to wait.

But Dum and Dee didn't round the corner on their wobbly bikes. The shadow shrank to a patch beneath the tree and they didn't come.

Then Elve heard the crunch of boots. A pair of tall men in uniform marched down the middle of the road. Their caps were noticeably higher than those of run-of-the-mill soldiers who were a familiar sight in town. Their tunics of dark greenish black fitted precisely, unlike the loose puce garments of ordinary service persons. Most noticeable were their gleaming weapons, one on each hip, and resting on their shoulders. Elve froze in her spot, though she longed to take cover. The children scrambled out of the way, then watched, google-eyed. The men looked neither left nor right as they goose-stepped in unison, high boots gleaming. They marched over a low rise in the road and were gone.

Cowed by this show of authority, and knowing that that was the intention of the show, Elve gave up her hope of getting Hara to the hospital. She would have to consult her most trusted friend. O.

33

It was now high noon. Not a good time. A walk to O's place would be unmercifully hot, as well as dangerously conspicuous. People, including the purple-banded snoopers, were out and about.

These were Elve's thoughts as she climbed the stairs to her rooms. She heard Hara's sobs even before she opened her door.

Hara was on the floor among the rumpled sheets, knees drawn up, arms protecting her bowed head. Her body shook. Her voice rose in a crescendo of pain. "Momma . . . Momma."

In her concern for Hara's injuries, Elve had barely thought of the girl's bereavement. She felt a swift stab of resentment. She barely had her own health back in order, and now this.

She'd become used to the codified mourning allowed at RAA-ratified deaths and funerals. But for this Elve went to the well of memory. Grandma Kumi. Nanna Atlanta. Both dead within one year. Luky, taken away from her side for execution. Her sense of being utterly abandoned. Rage at the unfairness.

RAA-approved terms of sympathy (there was a list) would not do. Elve knelt at Hara's side, enfolding her in comforting arms.

"Darling, darling." She whispered the forbidden word. "There, there, there."

They rocked together, encompassed by pain. Hara's sobs were harsh and dry, but Elve's tears flowed without sound, a gentle, inexorable rain. Tears for Hara and for her own losses.

Their paroxysms subsided. Elve adjusted her cramped knees. Gently, she lifted Hara's face to assess her injuries. The swelling was tight and hard. Painful as hell. There was no fresh blood, but the fever hadn't abated. How to get a message to O?

As the afternoon wore on, Hara's fever mounted. She writhed with pain and called out in delirium. She shouldn't be left alone. Elve cursed her isolation, her inability to call anyone for help. The calculated malice of the RAA in confiscating all means of communication.

Jema would be coming someday soon. Elve had lost track of the days without Hom's blackboard notice. Jema, so good to bring food and do up the laundry. Jema who'd planted the vegetable garden when Elve didn't feel able.

But Jema now wore a puce armband. She was a trusted spy for the local authorities, minions of the RAA. Trusted because of her unquestioned loyalty to the RAA and valuable for her detailed knowledge of all the regs.

What would Jema think of Elve's harbouring a fugitive? Elve dared not guess.

Still, there was one possibility. Her communication with Boat, coded in small stones, a black for yes, please come, and white for better not. They had fallen out of the habit of using their code, with Boat coming up from the lake whenever he thought it safe enough. The harmlessness of Dum and Dee had soothed their fears. They'd become careless.

Boat and Hom hadn't visited since their departure together. Though H of P had been consistently bland, adorned with obviously posed photos of youngsters enjoying their camp experience at Shining Waters and Green Hills Vistas, Elve had sensed a new watchfulness in her fellow shoppers at the Emp. The skies too seemed threatening, with the frequent passage of silent whiteships in pairs and threes. The jack-booted soldiers on Miller's Lane. Ovid's disappearance.

Boat must have a reason. Maybe Hom is the reason. They probably shouldn't be seen walking together.

Nevertheless, Elve found the black stone in her kitchen drawer and went out late in the summer evening. She went to their old spot, the shadowy niche at the base of a skull cairn where Boat used to leave fish for her. She laid the stone inside and hurried home. She could only hope that Boat would think of checking the niche. But why would he do so? It must be a year since they'd used it.

She found Hara still rocking and moaning with pain.

"Hara, I want to get you up off the floor. You'll be more comfortable in bed."

Hara shook her head. "I can't."

"We can do it together. Your legs must be OK. You ran all the way from your house. Let me help you."

So Elve linked her arm under Hara's shoulder. With a heaving effort she helped the girl to her feet. Together they took a few steps to the big chair, its bulk providing temporary support. From there to Elve's bed was, they felt, an impossible journey, but with a rest at the doorframe they were able to make it. They collapsed on the edge of the bed, breathless.

After tucking Hara in, Elve contrived another ice pack that she hoped might ease the pain. Then it came to her that a story might provide a distraction. She pulled out the book box. What should the story be?

Hara had come only once after Hom invited her to read with him. It was hard to get away from Urgo's surveillance. At the time, Hom had been reading Holy Bible with puzzled interest. Elve turned the fragile pages, looking for a story. She found one near the front of the book. She sat on the low stool and read aloud:

> And God said unto Noah, the end of all flesh is come before me; for the earth is filled with violence through them; and behold, I will destroy them with the earth.
>
> Make thee an ark of gopher wood; rooms shalt thou make in the ark, and shall pitch it within and without with pitch.
>
> And this is the fashion that thou shalt make it of; the length of the ark shall be three hundred cubits,

the breadth of it fifty cubits, and the height of it thirty cubits.

The story proceeded in a leisurely way, detailed and repetitive, telling how Noah, following God's instructions to the letter, was saved, along with his family and a pair of every living species; saved from a mighty flood, when the windows of heaven were opened and rain fell for forty days and forty nights.

As Elve read, Hara quieted and was asleep when God's rainbow appeared in the cloud.

34

Elve startled and woke. Holy Bible slid from her lap to fall in a disordered heap. What was it?

A thud at the door echoed the thud of her heart. She turned out the lantern and waited. For what? Who?

The door creaked. Thumped. Footsteps, light and quick.

"Gran? Where are you?"

At Hom's voice, Elve broke into tears. She held out her arms and he leapt into them. "Hom, Hom, oh my little Hom."

First order of business: food and drink. Elbows on the table, Hom chomped on cold sausage wrapped in a tortilla. Soy milk in a blue mug. Small dill pickles. He talked with his mouth full, and Elve didn't correct him.

"I snuck away after dark. I came home. I just wanted to come home."

"Boat doesn't know?"

Hom shook his head. "He wouldn't have let me come. We're lyin' low just now. The pucers are everywhere. I hafta stay below deck all the time. It's dark down there and it stinks. Bilge-water stink."

"You took a terrible chance. And what will Boat think? He'll be frantic."

"I left him a sign. I hope he gets it."

"A sign?"

"I left my spoon where he would see it. The one with the tabbies on it. He knows I miss Roon something awful."

Elve had supposed that she herself was the irresistible draw. She smiled wryly. Then, "Hara is here."

"Hey! How come?"

So Elve told the story. Hom listened, sometimes with clenched fists, sometimes with a tear.

"Urgo is a shit," he said. "He always was mean to Hara and her mom when her father was away. And sweet as syrup when he came home. Hara told us."

"The police will be looking for Hara now. They've likely been called to the house. Urgo will have some kind of covering lie, and Hara will be the suspect."

Hom held out his mug for more milk. "Do you think they'll bother much? Sometimes they don't."

"Hara's father is a ranking official. They'll have to make a good show of investigating. Arrest somebody. ASAP."

Quite suddenly, Hom's eyelids began to droop. Elve saw that he was exhausted. He must have run most of the way from the lakeshore. She scooped him off his chair and half-carried him to the cot in his tiny room. He was asleep before she'd pulled off his shoes.

Elve didn't sleep. Her beds were full of children, children in mortal danger. Her mind roved in the past, a past long before the RAA, when she slept on white sheets in Gramma Kumi's farmhouse, her window open to soft winds scented with sweet clover.

She drew strength from the peace and safety of that time. She would not give in to the RAA—to its uncertain justice and profligate power. The children must survive.

Hara woke in the night, fevered and delirious. Elve did what she could, which was very little. Hom woke and stood by the bed, fearful and anxious. He knelt and touched his friend's cheek.

"Hara," he whispered. "It's Hom." But Hara didn't seem to hear.

"Hara," he said more urgently. "Hara, remember the Roons. The wall and the birch tree. Singing. Singing with Rafu and Bim and Jog."

Hom began to sing one of their wordless songs. A song echoing the call of the small, brown bird that made her nest in the young birch.

The song brought Hara out of her hellish mental state. She quieted. She offered a faint note here and there. Like a bird's song, it had no real ending. Hom let it die away as Hara slept.

"Hara needs medicine," said Elve. "But I can't leave her to go to for help. O might know what to do."

"She had good medicine for your head. I'll go get some."

"But you don't know the way."

Hom looked a little uncomfortable. "Yes I do. Hara showed me last summer. She found O's place when she was picking apples in the ravine. She even went in for a while."

Shocked, Elve realized that Hom had had adventures that she knew nothing about. She'd been lulled into complacency by the assumption of Hom's safety in the Roons, guarded by the myth of the feral cats.

"You're sure?"

"Yup. I don't forget stuff like that."

Elve was satisfied. Hom had demonstrated that he seldom forgot things.

Although his sleep had been brief, Hom seemed invigorated and ready for the task. He set off at first light, threading the creekside path, dodging across the intersection of the two deserted streets, and diving into the leafy dimness of the ravine track.

A thicket of brambles guarded O's door. Hom crept behind it and knocked softly. The door opened the merest crack.

"Hom! My dear boy! What's wrong? Why are you here?" O ushered Hom inside.

"It's Hara. She's sick. She's at Gran's and she's hurt."

"Hara? What's wrong with Hara?"

"Her brother—her step-brother—beat her up. He smothered their mom and beat her up. She ran to Gran's, and she has a fever. Her face is all purple on one side and her eye is swelled shut." Hom opened the drawstring bag Elve had sent. O brought a plate for the bread and marge. They shared the bread and washed it down with spring water.

As they ate, O asked about Elve's health, and how Hom was spending the summer.

"Gran let me go down to the lake to stay with Boat. I help him fish in the mornings. He takes his catch to Camp 46, and I hafta stay on the boat. They're watching the docks all the time now, so I hafta stay below. I hate it there. That's why I ran home."

O asked for more details about Hara's injuries. "I can give you something for the fever. Maybe an ointment will help with the pain and swelling. But I worry about you going home in daylight. I can't let you do that."

Hom looked at her. There was no use resisting that look. "Hara is too sick. I gotta go back." He grinned his gap-toothed grin. "I'll be OK. I know lots of ways to hide."

O went to her shelf of herbs. She selected two items. "You make a tea with this one," she said, and tucked it in Hom's bag. "She should drink a cupful every hour or so. This is the ointment." She held up a small round jar.

Hom hung the bag round his neck and let it fall underneath his tunic. He remembered his manners then. "I haven't asked about you. Howya doin'? Gran will ask me."

"Tell her I'm doing OK. Tell her," and here O hesitated, "tell her I wish her well."

"I'll say you send love."

O looked at the boy, surprised. He had used the ancient word, a word that had fallen out of the language. "Love," forbidden in the early days of the RAA and almost forgotten.

"Yes," she said. "Love." She pulled the boy's head into her gaunt side.

Hom went out and made his way into the thicket.

35

Elve heard a knock at her door.

"Boat! Come in!" Elve drew him in and deposited him in the easy chair. Boat slumped, heaving breathlessly.

"Damned sun. Hell out there," he wheezed. "Where's the kid? Is he here?"

"He turned up here late last night. He's off on an errand. I had to send him to O for medicine."

"You idjit—he shouldn't be raisin' his head above ground. They're out to git anybody for any infraction whatsoever. No ID—he's dead quicker than spit."

Elve called over the kitchen counter where she was making tea. "I know, but I had no choice. Hara's so sick."

"Hara? Hom's friend from the Roons?"

"That's the one. Fell against my door two nights ago all bruised and bleeding."

"The one that sings. The kid sings too, while we fish."

As she brought the tea and soy cakes to the table, Elve told the story. "I suspect she's in the police crosshairs this very moment. Somebody to pin the murder on. Her brother—if he hasn't already absconded—has likely made up a story to protect himself."

A weak voice came from the bedroom. Hara, calling for help. Elve hurried to the bedside. Hara was sitting up, wild-eyed with terror. "I heard somebody. I heard a man. Is it Urgo? Police?" She covered her face. "Oh, they've comed... Comed to get me."

"It's all right, Hara." Elve took the girl's hands. "You do hear a man. It's Boat. My friend, and Hom's friend too."

Boat came in. "It's OK, lass. I don't hurt people. Hom told me you play in the Roons. Along with Rafu and Bim and Jog."

"I wanna go back there. To the Roons." Hara slumped back on the pillow.

"You're way too sick for that," said Elve. "But Hom is bringing medicine. Something from O. He tells me you know her."

"Yeah. She took me into her house under the vines. She's gonna show me things. The good things. . ." Hara's voice trailed and she seemed to sleep. Like a kitten, Elve thought. Awake and active and then donk! Asleep.

Elve drew the bamboo curtain to cut the afternoon sun. She pulled up a kitchen chair near Boat in the recliner. They talked in the shadowy room. Elve hid her anxiety for Hom's return as well as she could. But Boat knew, because he shared it.

"If anyone can do it, he can," said Boat. "The kid has an uncanny knack for hiding. Just backs up into the shadows and hides in plain sight. People walk right by and don't notice."

"I wish he didn't need to depend on camouflage for his safety."

In the silence that followed, Elve laid a hand on Boat's. It could be said that they prayed, if prayer had been a procedure known to them.

"It's murder out there all of a sudden. Must be Tranna's turn for a clean-up. Inspectors and the military everywhere, all entitled to stop a guy for any reason or no reason. Pucers too, of course."

"Jema is a Neighbourhood Watcher now." Elve couldn't bring herself to call her daughter a pucer.

"Can you trust her?" Trust her to keep her mouth shut?"

"She won't betray Hom, if that's what you mean. She has already taken considerable risk for him."

"The pucers are under pressure though. They hafta report every day, and they're in trouble if they haven't contributed any dirt."

"How do you find out this stuff?"

"I have my sources. We're getting a bit of a system set up. An information pipeline. There are resisters here and there. Just gotta know who. Have you seen one of these?"

Boat fished in his pocket and drew out a tiny brown rosebud—a hemlock cone. He held it out in the palm of his hand.

Without a word, Elve drew something from her own pocket. "How did you get that?" they both said together.

So each described their acquisition of the sign. O must be the common source, they thought.

"O has friends that I know very little about," said Elve. "Like Lem, the wood-carver. There are several others. She credits them with providing for her modest needs beyond what she can harvest in the ravine. O's friends are resisters for sure. Else they would have betrayed her long ago."

"Lotsa stirrings. Can't quite call it a movement yet. But we'll bide our time. Stay underground. Figure out ways to get out from under the RAA." Boat paused. "Hey! You know there was a big jailbreak?"

Elve sat back. "No! In Tranna?"

"Yup. Maybe a couple hundred got out. Not enough police to stop them. Did it with sheer muscle. That and surprise. The RAA don't figure that anybody has any git-up-and-go any more. Kids all cowed and dutiful. That's what's so great about our boy. He wouldn't sit on his hands."

After a pause, Boat said, "You got any more of that black paint? I got me an idea."

"I have about a litre if you want."

"There was a couple small paint brushes. You put them in the tool bag. Remember?"

Elve nodded. "I do."

"With a bit of paint, I could put out messages. There's still driftwood and other flotsam I could write on. Even Porgel, and there's lots of that around."

"What kind of messages?"

"Names. The old countries. The cities. People. Remember that woman? The one that ran Blue Planet Council at the time of the mass migrations? All the countries in temperate zones were building walls, and she got people to stop that. She was 'Min—min—something."

"Minerva."

"Yeah. That's her. And there have been others. Malala. Moses. Obama—the girl, not her father. That queen—Elizabeth. Mandela. Confucius. People gotta remember."

Elve stood up. "I'll get those paint brushes."

At that moment, the door opened, and Hom burst in, flushed and sweaty. "I got it," he said, waving the bag of medicines. "I had to crawl through a culvert, but that was OK. What's to eat, Gran? How's Hara? Hi, Boat. What're you doin' here?"

Elve intercepted the waving bag. "She's asleep. There's soy cakes and tortillas. Peanut butter."

"Lookin' fer you. Whadja think?"

"Didn't you see my sign?"

"The spoon? You betcha I saw it, and knowed you'd took off to see that darn cat."

Hom looked up at Boat from under a lowered brow. "I was lonesome," he said. "It was lonesome below deck. And stinky too."

"Nearly gave me a heart attack."

"Sorry." But Hom knew, and so did Elve, that Boat was more pleased than angry at Hom's sin.

36

Elve made the medicinal tea. Besides medicine, Hara badly needed to be given a bath and clean clothes. So the two of them were occupied for some time. Boat took a much-needed nap in the recliner.

After he stuffed himself with peanut-buttered bread and soy milk, Hom turned eagerly to his books. Almost as much as he'd missed Roon, Hom had been missing his books. He still had many of the books in Holy Bible to digest. Because The Book of Daniel appeared to have no missing pages, he chose it for his continued reading. The archaic language bothered him very little. He learned it with a child's inborn facility for learning any language.

Life and Literature had provided a story called "My Dog, Simba" in which a little dog bests a ferocious, man-eating lion when eleven spear-carrying Masai are unable to do so. When Hom read that Daniel was thrown into the den of lions, he understood that Daniel was condemned to a terrible death. But there was no illustration, and Hom was left to imagine for himself what a lion might be like.

He went to his chalkboard, and drew a tiny Daniel, dressed like the Holy Bible man with the lantern, falling headlong from the hands of a crowd of baleful men into a cave. At the bottom of the cave he began to draw a large ferociously-toothed beast.

Boat roused and watched the unfolding drawing. Interested, he came over to stand beside the young artist.

"Who's that?" Boat indicated the diminutive human figure.

"It's Daniel. He's in Holy Bible. He got casted into the lions' den because King Darius signed a law that said everyone had to pray just to him, and if they prayed to somebody else, they'd be casted into the lions' den. But Daniel kept on standing at his window praying to his god three times a day like he always did. And the king was sorry because he liked Daniel, but he had signed the law, and it was a law of the Medes and the Persians that couldn't be changed. So the presidents and the governors and the princes and the counsellors and the captains casted Daniel into the den of lions."

"And this is the lion?"

"The first one. I think there was a whole bunch."

"Um. I think you've just drawn a cat. A big cat."

"Yeah, well the only dangerous animals I know are the cats in the Roons. Like everybody thinks they're dangerous. Everybody but me and my friends."

Boat's grunt suggested that he still harboured doubts about the cats.

"So I'm just making him the same but bigger, with his claws out and spitting. They do that."

"You got it spot on. Lions really are extra big cats. But he needs something more." Boat took the chalk and with a few deft strokes, added an impressive mane to Hom's big cat.

"Waw! Is that what a lion is really like?"

"Pretty much. What happened then?"

"King Darius stayed up all night, he was so worried about Daniel. And in the morning he goed to see if Daniel's god had saved him like he hoped.

"And did he?"

"Yup. He sended an angel to shut the lions' mouths and they didn't hurt him. If Daniel hada had some fish guts, he could've tamed the lions himself. The way I've tamed Roon."

"Well if you haven't got the guts, an angel will do."

Hom looked at Boat, trying to fathom his wry tone.

Hom returned to his drawing, adding more vicious beasts and the bones of a previous victim. Boat sat down at the table with Holy Bible.

It was difficult. He'd learned Trad just as it was being phased out and hadn't seen any for forty years. But he was interested in the Daniel story, especially the role of the presidents and the princes and the other officials who trapped the king into honouring a very bad law. He wondered if officials were pulling strings in the Magic Mountain, influencing Owr Preshus Leeder into proclaiming some of the more egregious regulations that bound ordinary people. Where are the angels, he wondered.

Hara and Elve came into the room, Hara looking immensely better in spite of the ugly swelling of her face. She leaned only a little on Elve's arm. Elve helped her to sit in the recliner and began to make preparations for the evening meal.

Hom deposited his chalk in its bag and reported for kitchen duty. Without much instruction, he did the things that required reaching and bending. He collected utensils and ingredients and put them away when Elve was finished with them. They had perfected a routine that kept Hom active and spared Elve's energy. It suited them both. Elve felt that soon she would be able to retire to a supervisory role. Hom would be able to make their simple meals himself.

The atmosphere at Elve's table was subdued. The adults were aware of the illegality of their little gathering. More than two. Unrelated. One with no ID. One in compromised relationship with police. The children sensed their concern and were silent.

Impulsively, Elve grasped Boat's hand and reached for Hom's. He in turn took Hara's and she completed the circle. There was no faked recognition of the RAA's beneficence. Only a sense of whatever it was that held them together. Elve recognized it. It was love.

Before they had finished eating, they judged that it was time for H of P. It was hard to tell without a clock.

Hom turned on the TV. A silent progression of beautiful landscapes moved across the screen. No captions or voice identified where or when such pictures had originated. Not in Tranna, for sure, or any other locale that had suffered the indiscriminate warfare of the previous century.

The pictures stopped, and the screen was filled with a familiar view. Ranks of puce-uniformed soldiers stood at exaggerated attention. The voice-over extolled this unit of the MagnificentPeople's Republican Military Force who had shown exemplary courage, and unfailing loyalty to Owr Preshus Leeder. The commentator didn't give any hint of the operation that required this courage and loyalty. It would be most incorrect to imply that there might be pockets of rebellion or dissension anywhere in the GNWRAA.

Owr Preshus Leeder himself was reviewing the troops. His white uniform glittered with a double row of medals. At his side hung a ceremonial rapier. A golden medallion of noble size adorned his officer's cap with its enormous wheel. The cap kept him at a distance from the soldiers as he passed down the front rank, unsmiling.

But it was the officer accompanying Owr Preshus Leeder whose face made Elve blanch. He marched beside, but a little behind the Commander-in-Chief, his trim figure matching OPPL's vaunted fitness. He also was uniformed in white with medals and a hat of impressive height, though significantly smaller in circumference than his superior's. Like the Leeder's, his expression was impassive.

"It's Max," Elve said. "I'm sure it's Max,"

37

Abruptly, the screen faded to black. H of P continued with the customary poster printed with the new regs and a puce-uniformed official reading them while pointing word by word with a white baton.

Elve sat, stunned, pale, speechless. "Turn it off," she said wildly. "Turn the viltrid thing off."

Hom jumped to obey.

"He's alive. I could only hope. All these years I've hoped." Elve twisted her hands in painful knots.

A terrible clarity came to her mind. She straightened and her voice was strong. "I would have wished him dead if I had known. If I had known that he would rise in this vile regime.

"But oh my son. My lovely little son." And now violent sobs rose in her throat. Elve was overcome with her memory of a sturdy, brown boy with mischievous dark eyes and endearing grin. How had he become this flint-faced purveyor of the RAA's propaganda?

Boat came to Elve's side. What comfort could he give? He knew only to offer his body, where Elve buried her stricken head. He cradled it with his gnarled fisherman's hand, and they rocked in awkward unison, Elve's cries smothered in Boat's grubby tunic.

Hom and Hara turned to each other. "Will she be OK?" Hara asked. The possibility that her helper would fail struck her with a new terror.

"Gran is tough," Hom said. "I think she'll come through all right."

"Who is Max?"

The children had moved off to the big chair, which held both of them well enough.

"Max is Gran's son. He's my Grandma Jema's older brother. I guess he's my uncle. When Max and Mungo turned eighteen, soldiers came for them and they marched away. Gran hasn't heard from them since."

Hara wasn't surprised by this. In her short life, she'd known only the limited communication allowed by the RAA. Even her father, a Respected Health Inspector, had no means of sending messages home. His Apsam accessed only the government network.

"Max was very smart," Hom said. "He could make stuff. We still have a barbecue that he made out of scrap metal and wire. Gran says he made a solar lantern before they got them in at the Emp. He could read Trad too. He read Gran's books."

Boat had shepherded Elve to the bedroom where they closed the door. The youngsters respected this sign that they should stay out.

"Let's read something," said Hara. "Something in one of your books."

Hom had rather carelessly moved Holy Bible to one of the barstools when he went to help with supper. They brought it back to the table and pulled up chairs side-by-side.

"Your gran read to me out of this book. A story about Noah and the animals. I liked it but I fell asleep before the end."

Hom turned again to The Book of Daniel. "Here's a good story." He turned to a page headed "Belshazzar's impious feast."

"You read," said Hara. "I have only one good eye."

So Hom began to read aloud the chapter about Belshazzar's lavish party, a feast for thousands: Belshazzar and his lords and his wives and concubines. He read:

> In the same hour came forth the fingers of a man's hand, and wrote over against the candlestick upon the plaister of the wall of the king's palace.

Here Hom kept his place with his finger and continued with a rather loose interpretation. "Belshazzar was so scared his knees knocked and he shat himself. He didn't understand the writing and neither did all his smart guys, the astrologers and soothsayers. So he called for Daniel to come and explain it.

"First Daniel told Belshazzar what he'd done wrong—drinking wine from the gold and silver vessels his father Nebuchadnezzar had stealed from God's temple—him and his lords and his wives and his concubines."

Hom returned to the text.

> And thou hast praised the gods of silver and gold, of brass, iron, wood, and stone, which see not, nor hear, nor know, and the God in whose hand thy breath is, and whose are all thy ways, hast thou not glorified.
> And this was the writing that was written, MENE, MENE, TEKEL, UPHARSIN.

"So what does that mean?" said Hara, just as puzzled if not fearful, as Belshazzar himself.

Hom read.

> God hath numbered thy kingdom and finished it. Thou art weighed in the balances and art found wanting. Thy kingdom is divided and given to the Medes and Persians.
> "In that night was Belshazzar, the king of the Chaldeans slain", Hom finished in solemn tone.

"Was it because they drank out of the gold and silver vessels?" asked Hara.

"That was part of it. The children of Israel believed in just one god that they couldn't see. And they had a temple to honour him. That's where the vessels were stealed from. So this big god was real mad when Belshazzar and his gang drank and then worshipped all their stupid little gods—the statues they made of iron and wood and stone."

"So who do you think wrote on Belshazzar's wall?"

"Had to be Daniel's god. Or maybe the hand of Abraham. God really liked Abe."

"Anyhow, that was the end of Belshazzar. Gone for good."

"Yup."

And the children wondered. They wondered about the demise of a powerful person. They wondered if some god could make it happen. They felt the weight of the RAA, but didn't understand why the bible story brought their oppression to mind.

38

The summer sun still poured through the western window outlining the tumbled rock of the old ruin with an eerie yet enticing glow.

"Hey, we've lots of time. Won't be dark for hours. Let's go over to the Roons." Hom was out of his chair already. But Hara's face, its livid bruise, reminded him. "Can you make it, dya think?"

Hara squared her shoulders. "I'll go if it kills me." But when she stood, she swayed uncertainly.

"Sit down. I'll get your shoes." Hom selected Hara's worn runners from the heap at the door. He knelt at her feet to put them on. "Should we tell them we're going?"

They heard the adults' intense dialogue from the closed bedroom. "Leave them a note on your wall," said Hara.

So Hom wrote beside his HB book list: Gon too de Roons. Bak at sundown.

"Gotta have something for Roon." Hom looked in the fridge, which was basically a somewhat cool cupboard, the hours of electrical power being still unpredictable except for the RAA's H of P every evening. He found half a tin of Sprem. He daren't take much, because meat of any kind was precious.

"I'll just shave off a bit. Maybe Gran won't notice."

"Mom would notice. . ." Hara's voice faded. Mom. Momma. Oh Momma. She hid her face in her hands.

Hom mixed bits of meat with torn-up bread. All went into the pot that had made many trips to the Roons.

"Let's go."

Hara clung to the rail at first, but found her feet and made her way down the stairs steadily. They passed through Ovid's empty station and rounded the building choosing a route well hidden in the dense shrubbery.

Miller's Lane was nearly empty at this early evening hour. RAA regs insured that most workers were home for *Nue Wrld Gloree*. The parents had joined the grandmothers and children in the squat dried-brick residences to the north. These were one-storey duplexes mixed in with occasional two-storey structures. A condominium or two in bad repair like the building where Elve lived. A single three-storey grey stone house of ancient build, once the palatial home of a lawyer, his wife and son, now occupied by four or five little clans—grandmothers mostly, each with an assortment of related hangers-on.

Hom saw no threat in the passing stragglers, and slipped across the road without incident. Hara, more cautious, waited until the road was deserted. She had no wish to explain to anyone why she wasn't away at camp.

Their entrance to the Roons was now hidden in new growth. They pushed their way into their old playground, alive now with verdant abundance. A persistent south wind caressed their sunlit faces. They stood hand in hand in the unearthly light, awed and immensely happy.

39

Elve's windowless bedroom reeked with old blood and new fear. She curled on the thin mattress while Boat sat on the edge, a hand on her shaking shoulder. Paroxysms shook her body and with each spasm she called her son's name. Boat pulled up the sheet to warm her cold sweat, but it was no use.

She quieted under the warmth of his hand, the sound of his gravelly voice, "Easy, easy, old girl. Take it easy."

Elve cried out her pain. "Mungo is gone. Jema is lost. And now Max is lost too. The RAA has taken all my children. God damn them. God damn them to hell."

Neither Elve nor Boat knew from what tribal well she drew that oath, not heard among the people for many generations.

Their silent tears beaded and fell to the clammy sheet.

Elve thought she would weep forever. That she would never rise from that bed of sorrow. That she would die.

But her rage outbid her sorrow, and she sat up. "I will go there. To that hellish Magic Mountain. I will see my son and take him back."

Boat pulled on his earlobe, as he was wont to do when thinking. He was silent in the expectation that Elve would soon see the folly of her impossible plan.

A retraction was not forthcoming. Elve was muttering. Something about backpacks and food—Hom, Hom and Hara.

He sighed and said gently, "Elve. We've no idea where to go. Nobody knows the location of the Magic Mountain. It's the RAA's most closely guarded secret."

"But Max got there. There has to be a way. You have a boat. We can go anywhere in the world."

"But the Magic Mountain might not be in the world. You've forgotten the moon bubbles and Mars settlements. We ain't got rocket ships."

"Those settlements are dead. Their communications stopped long before Franklin's Folly."

"Yeah, maybe so. But there was always Brankoch and Buffcom. Even old Gatamazoogle. The possibility of mounting new expeditions. Could have had something up there again before Franklin."

Elve shook her head. "The Magic Mountain is right here on the Blue Planet. I'm sure of it. Those guys on H of P are breathing air just like you and me. No space suits, no moonwalking, just ordinary clothes and flowers and vehicles on the ground. No ear-buds. Not even chip-scars on their foreheads." The argument cleared Elve's mind. She stopped raving.

"Maybe so. But what about the bubbles? They've got the artificial gravity/atmosphere bubbles just like they had on the moon."

"Could all be a sham too. To fool us. The RAA is one big systematic lie. You know that."

Boat sighed. "I'm tired, Elve. Tired of trying to strain the truth outta the fiction. So let's not shoot before we aim. Gotta do the intelligence thing before we try anything so crazy as a trek to the Magic Mountain."

"Got any sources?"

"No. Guys I trust, but not sources."

Burdened with the cloud of uncertainty, they lay close for a while, dozed a little.

They roused to the sound of the children's return.

Elve laid a finger to her lips and Boat nodded.

40

The garden, planted and still tended by Jema, was now yielding leaf lettuce, green onions, and radishes in abundance. In early evening, Elve selected a generous batch to take to Pen. She'd been down to see her regularly since Hara's injury. On impulse, she tucked the sign of resistance in her pocket. The little cone reminded her of her pact with O and Lali, Boat, and others unknown but involved in resistance.

She left Hara absorbed in reading *Anne of Green Gables*. Better than Holy Bible, Anne was enabling Hara's growing facility with Trad.

Pen's place still reeked, but not of pot. Elve judged that Pen's source must have been cut off. There was still the miasma of old food and illness. Of sealed, airless space.

"Can I open a window for you? The sun has passed over the building, so your side shouldn't be too hot. There might be a breeze."

Pen nodded listlessly from her post in the big chair. She had no objection to fresh air. She was just unable to summon the energy to do anything about getting some.

Elve pushed open the balcony door, ignoring its squealing protest. Because of the thicket encroaching on the old patio, only the faintest current of air entered the room, but it was tinged with the scent of unseen flowers. Elve breathed it gratefully.

Elve took a chair by a table covered with a soup-stained cloth. The women exchanged enquiries for health. Pen's face was creased with the pain that pot had eased before.

"Perhaps my friend, O, can give you something for the pain. She lives on the land and knows many useful plants."

"O?" Pen's face was a curious mixture of wariness and interest.

Elve realized that she'd stupidly unveiled O's existence to a relative stranger. She paused in confusion.

"I believe I know the person, in a way," said Pen carefully.

"How so?"

"You know you take serious risk by visiting me? As Ovid's joog, I'm under suspicion, and special police have been here. They searched the place, but not thoroughly. They seemed to be looking for something in particular, which they did not find." Here a suggestion of sardonic pleasure twitched Pen's mouth. "I know someone named O by a means that I cannot reveal to you. I know nothing of the person but the code name Oyyz."

At this, Elve dug into her pocket to finger the hemlock cone. Wordlessly, she held it out in her palm.

At this, Pen lifted her tunic to reveal a thick pad covering her torso. She pulled it aside to reveal a black box strapped to her rather scrawny torso. The appearance of huge obesity had been a sham. What was she hiding? Elve wasn't sure.

"A ComD?"

"Nope. Two-way radio. The RAA seems to know nothing about them. A long- forgotten technology. Fairly simple to make. Ovid made this one."

"So you know O by radio? Do you know her location?" This at least, Eve could keep to herself for now. Well, maybe she'd spilled that too.

"Tranna, judging by the yyz. That was originally an airport designation. Long before the RAA. Even before the annexation of Canada."

"'Cone' is a code word we use in the system," said Pen. "It means the source can be trusted. So I took a chance when you showed your sign."

"A huge chance, seems to me,"

"I'm old and sick. Can't do much for the resistance. If they get me, what will it matter? But we need to consolidate our resources in whatever way we can. Build the network. Multiply radios. If they get this one, it doesn't matter. Radios aren't like a ComD, storing every transaction it ever did. Radios keep their own secrets."

Elve went into the kitchen area to clean the vegetables she'd brought. The women commented on the recent rains and new shortages at the Emp. After storing the food in the "cool box", Elve took her leave, first linking elbows with Pen, who had resumed her disguise as a mound of obesity. She left the hemlock cone in Pen's lap. "Use it when you don't want to reveal the radio," she said.

Pen quickly stored it in her pocket.

Instead of going home, Elve went past Ovid's old post to the neglected gardens east of her building. Strangely, there were narrow paths under the trees and bushes, paths untrodden by human feet. A scuttling rabbit startled her, followed by another. They were clearly the path-makers.

She stopped to listen. An unfamiliar sound, a clear "Tee-prettee-prettee". A flash of red. A bird—it was a bird. Except for the peregrines and sparrows, Elve had seen few birds in the area. In O's ravine, but not here.

Borne on the scented wind, an unreasonable hope coursed through her, body and mind. Gladness unearned. A gift.

41

Hara's recovery took its deliberate course. The swelling receded until one morning when she awoke, she sensed that her right eye had opened.

Elve heard the cry from Hara's (formerly Hom's) room. She hurried in. "What's wrong, lass?"

"My eye is open, but I can't see. Can't see anything at all."

"Sit up. Sit up and let me see." Elve turned Hara's face toward the window where the morning light was already strong.

The iris of Hara's right eye, which should have been walnut brown, was shattered to form a milky starburst, white against a bloodshot eyeball. Elve couldn't suppress a shudder.

"Cover your left eye. Can you see the window?"

"No. I can't see. I can't see." A wail of despair tore Hara's throat.

Elve sat on the bed and took Hara's hands. "Open your eyes. Both eyes. You can see, Hara. Your left eye is fine."

"Yabbut I just thought it would be OK. I thought I would get better just like before."

"I hoped so too. But I saw the bleeding. I knew it would take a miracle to save that eye. I'm so. . ." Elve was about to offer sympathy, but changed her mind. No point in engendering self-pity. Better to be matter-of-fact. Positive. Encouraging. She squared her shoulders and took a deep breath. ". . .glad you still have one good eye. Urgo gave you a terrible going-over."

At Urgo's name, Hara's spine straightened. "May heaven rain pig-shit on him. Hey—he's turned eighteen! Last week or so. The army has him. Good-bye, Urgo. Square-bash your brains out."

Elve was startled at this outburst from one so normally mild. Heartened too. Hara would not be defeated.

The weeks of recovery had accustomed Hara to navigating with only one eye. The blinded one was mercifully pain-free. The yellowing bruise was no impediment to her becoming an indispensable help around the condo. She even ventured to the vegetable garden with Jema, learning the names and growing conditions of the plants. She picked the first ripe tomatoes, presenting them to Elve as a precious gift.

There was time for reading. The Anne book proved sufficient for Hara's mastery of Trad. She sampled Holy Bible, using Hom's list as a guide to books that might be interesting. The Book of Esther was present and complete in the loosened pages, as was The Book of Ruth. Elve guided her to favourites among The Book of Psalms, and Hara, sensing that they were songs, sang them to tunes of her own making.

But she was sad, and one day looked up from her book to announce, "I'm going home. I hafta go home."

Elve had been pondering the wisdom of Hara returning to her home. She was certainly well enough to go. What she would find there was an open question. Urgo wouldn't be there, almost certainly. Her father? Had he come home to an empty house? If so, what then? A police search for Hara?

Hara's sadness grew daily until she was barely functioning. Elve decided they had to risk a return to her home. They both had ID, which was good, but Hara's might reveal her relationship to her father if they were accosted. Who knows what data police Apsams could access? If she and Hara were discovered to be unrelated, what then? Besides, Hara's blind eye might mark her for immediate liquidation. The RAA hated disability, congenital or acquired.

"I think we should go someday soon. How far is it? Do you feel able for the walk?" Elve asked as dusk reddened the western sky. To make use of the evening light, they were patching pants beside Elve's houseplants at the balcony door.

"Oh it's not far. Maybe twenty minutes." Hara had forgotten that minutes were obsolete. But she didn't know how to convert to minims anyway. "I can do it easy."

"We'll go early in the morning. Always the best time. Tomorrow." Elve spoke with a confidence she did not feel.

They put on clean tunics. They wound their heads with their brightest polycloth scarves.

On impulse, Elve chose two fat tomatoes from the bowl on the kitchen table. She dropped them into a bag. Hara, who'd come with nothing, travelled light. They were ready.

They walked south on Miller's Lane for a short time and turned onto a curving road into what was once a prosperous residential area. Stumps of large old trees remained here and there, trees long since used for fuel. Slender, young alders were taking hold, and a few homes of a long bygone era stood among stands of healthy trees. Ugly blocks of recent construction stood cheek-by-jowl with the old homes. All appeared to house several families.

A few children too young for the RAA summer camps played tag in the street, watched by thumb-sucking toddlers. A mother called from her front step and two youngsters detached themselves from the group to obey her call.

Hara soon indicated a side street, where they veered off again. This road was better kept than the others, and newish, single-family homes lined its snaking course. Alders grew here in abundance and there were attempts at landscaping, though without flowering plants. These were government houses, and Hara's was the last before the road ended in a clump of alder and a path down to a trickling creek. Hara took the path on the run. She wanted to see her wild garden behind the house.

"Ugh! What a mess! I can't see anything." A disappointed Hara stood among the tall weeds that had overtaken her planting.

"What did you have?"

"Mallow and daisies and chicory. Queen Anne's lace—oh, there it is!" Hara squeezed through the vegetation to lift a small, lacy parasol to her nose. "It smells so sweet and strong at the same time."

"And here are the daisies," said Elve, coming round a huge burdock. "Dandelions too."

"They just came up by themselves. I didn't hafta plant them."

"Huah, there. What're y'doin?" A short woman with a baby on her hip accosted them from the back stoop.

"I'm Hara 05.06.33.43.79. This is my garden. I live here."

"Not now, you don't. I moved in here three months ago. Me and my joog and our kids." A boy of about six appeared at her side. He adopted a belligerent stance.

Hara seemed unable to speak. Elve spoke up. "We're looking for Hara's father. Dag is his name. He is an Honoured Health Team Inspector."

"Respected," Hara whispered.

"Respected Health Team Inspector. An RHTI."

"Respected or honoured, don't make no difference. They took him away in handcuffs. The very day we was movin' in. We had to wait in the street while they doed it." The woman's face softened. "You'll hafta ask the police. Though it probly won't do you any good." She shrugged.

Elve recognised the beaten attitude of so many Loyel Sitizenz. Consciously, she straightened, resisting. "Are you sure he was Dag? The previous occupant?"

"Yeah, pretty sure. He was crying. 'My daughter. My pretty lass. My joog and my son and my girl gone too."

Hara cried out and buried her face in her hands. Elve moved to comfort her.

"Come in a while. Come and sit down."

They went into a dim, sparsely furnished room. The woman gestured them to sit on the orange sofa. Still carrying the baby, she cleared breakfast bowls from the table and turned on a water boiler. The boy remained suspicious. He watched from the corner of the room where he kept his playthings.

Hara recognised the sofa. He mother had lain on it for hours in her times of distress. Hara couldn't sit there. She moved instead to a straight chair.

The woman made tea and brought the pot and cups to the table. When the baby began to fuss, she invited Hara and Elve to help themselves. She took another chair and pulled up her tunic to offer her breast to the infant.

The clink of cups, the baby's vigorous latch, the tumbling of the boy's blocks: these homely sounds comforted and calmed. They talked softly, exchanging names. The woman introduced herself as Fel, her son Var, and the baby, Resa. Elve introduced herself as Hara's grandmother. It seemed better than complicated explanations.

"Do you know anything else? Can you tell us any more about Dag?" asked Elve.

"Not much. But the house wasn't properly cleared out when we moved in. Bits and pieces everywhere."

The baby had fallen asleep. Fel rose to lay her in a crib near Var's corner. "I didn't throw everything out. Like we needed the sofa." Her glance at Hara was apologetic. "And I guess these should have been disposed of."

Fel knelt and opened a cylindrical stand with twin brass door handles. She rooted among the odds and ends stored in its hollow interior and pulled out a handful of small, dog-eared pages.

Pictures! Elva hadn't seen privately owned pictures since childhood. In her time, photos were rarely printed. They were stored in ComDs or the Galaxy and viewed on ComDs. They could be streamed to wall screens for group viewing too.

"Are these yours?" Fel laid the pictures on the table. Hara moved to examine them.

"They're ours. Dad never wanted us to handle them, but Mom got them out when he was away. He was always away."

Fel nodded with a sigh. "My joog is always away too. It's like that for the RHTI."

"This one is Mom and Dad at the Shining Waters. That's Urgo when he was promoted to Super Scholar. And me on my first day of school. And Dad in his RHTI uniform." Hara paused. The photo of her mother brought a tear, but she controlled her emotion. She turned the pictures over sadly.

"Would you like to have them? You don't want the police to catch you with them. Likely your dad used hospital equipment to print them. Strictly Ultra."

Hara understood "Ultra." Civil Service jargon for Ultra Regulations or unlawful at her dad's level of authority.

"Likely. Yes, I'll take them off your hands."

Elve was curious. "Why did you risk keeping them?"

Fel looked ashamed. "I thought there might be a market for them. Like, under the table."

With this, Elve remembered the tomatoes in her bag. "How about two ripe tomatoes? An Ultra deal as well, since the Emp claims all produce as their own." She laid the fruit on the table.

Var jumped up. "Momma, can I have one?" He eyed the round, red globes hungrily.

Fel laughed. "It's a deal, I guess. Might as well be shot for one as hanged for the other."

Hara dropped the precious photos in Elve's bag. It was time to go.

Making their way through streets alive now with moms and babies and playing children, Elve reflected on the trust she felt in this new acquaintance. How it grew in spite of an inauspicious beginning. Fel was solid. A potential ally in what Elve saw as a growing, though as yet inchoate threat. She fingered the tiny cones in her pocket. Next time, if I'm sure.

Hara was quiet. Counting her losses. She saw that she was alone. Alone and homeless.

42

Again, Hara fell into a state of immense sadness. She would not eat. She wandered about Elve's rooms like a wraith, unable to settle at anything. Jema couldn't coax her to go out to the garden. She mourned her losses and could not be consoled.

The Respected Ministry of Measurements and Weights continued its assault on everyday measures of time, space, temperature, and now, even the terms to describe the weather, outlawing clouds and sun, preferring measures of barometric pressure.

Elve too suffered a sense of disembodiment, of floating in a confused space, of pervasive disorientation. The sun became the guardian of her sanity.

The H of P announced the requirement that each Loyel Sitizen reorganize their name to reflect the change from the twelve-month to the ten-month system and report same to the Noble Office of Citizenship and Documentation. H of P provided a conversion formula. But the Loyel Sitizenz found the formula difficult and confusion reigned.

Strife arose between the Respected Ministry of Citizenship and Documentation and the Respected Ministry of Measurements and Weights. The latter demanded that the conversion be complete and immediate; the former, aware that its local offices accommodated conjoogaeshuns and pleasant interactions with new babies, but not much else, insisted that they needed much more time and resources for the conversion. Their pleas aroused the Respected Ministry of Tax and Resource Allocation which resisted mightily any designation of increased funds to the local Noble Offices of Citizenship and Documentation

Loyel Sitizenz like Elve and Hara knew nothing of these ructions on the Magic Mountain. They feared being caught by local police with obsolete IDs. They calculated as best they could what their new names should be and prepared to visit the Noble Office.

The office was located in a corner of the building housing the local division of the Awesome Force for the Administration of Law and Order. That the Noble Office was governed by the Respected Ministry of Citizenship and Documentation, while the Awesome Force was administered by the Respected Ministry for the Establishment and Maintenance of Law and Order did not make for harmonious residence under one roof. Sit & Doc, being chronically underfunded, envied the wealth of their co-tenants: their Apsams, their velos, even their bicycles. Also their control of the heating/AC.

Elve and Hara found the Noble Office staffed by one harried Respected Clerk in his official hat and a bunch of befuddled assistants wearing green bibs marked S & D over their grey civvies. They sat in pairs behind scarred metal tables. (L & O cast-offs). Hara and Elve lined up at the table with the most likely looking assistants, where they thought the procedure might be efficient.

But Elve watched the other tables, and observed that the assistants two tables over were quite flummoxed by Loyel Sitizenz who hadn't done their own calculation. They seemed unable to apply the chart provided. The room was already hot, but these two dripped with anxious sweat. The line in front of them was long. Elve nudged her companion.

"Let's switch," she said, pointing to the suffering assistants. She didn't explain.

The wait was indeed long, but rewarding. The S & D assistants printed up their new cards using the numbers Elve and Hara presented. They asked nary a question and appeared grateful for this little reprieve. Elve felt emboldened to ask:

"Would you please make the card for my great-grandson who lives with me? He's away at camp right now. His new name is Hom 35.04.43.79." Elve was surprised at how effortlessly she lied.

Assistant No. 1 began to make up the card immediately. Assistant No. 2 made a half-hearted noise about the need for an original. "They're sposta be turned in." But she shrugged too when No. 1 shrugged and finished the job.

Elve's triumph was short-lived.

As they were leaving the Noble Office of S & D, Elve and Hara were accosted by two uniformed individuals whose high hats designated their superiority to Dum and Dee and others of the common rank.

"Sitizen Elve?"

"Yezroe."

"Sitizen Hara?"

"Yezroe," Hara whispered.

"Your attendance within is required." The officers herded their quarry into single file and marched them into the Awesome Office.

Don't think, Elve instructed herself. Don't try to figure it out.

At one time, well before Franklin's Folly, Elve and her fellow citizens knew that the government in Canada, as in most countries, had complete dossiers on all citizens. Eye and fingerprint ID were established in a child's first year. After that, every change in address, every school registration and leaving, every employment stint, hospital admission and diagnosis, and, of course, every interaction with law enforcement. It was so easy. Officials and their helpers entered the information on voice-activated devices which transferred it immediately to the central files in remote storage.

But now, with digital efficiency so fragmented and the central files lost in the ether, Elve had no idea what the officers knew about her or what might be the reason for this arrest. For she had no doubt that this was an arrest, even though no handcuffs or billy clubs appeared.

Hara's safety and her own needed Elve's utmost in clear-headedness and ability to lie. If only she knew what to lie about.

The little retinue passed by rows of metal desks where assistants retrieved data from Apsams and recorded it by hand with stick-pens on yellow legal pads of a kind that hadn't been seen for generations. Elve noted the generous supply of paper with envy and wonder.

These assistants worked under a stark white light that radiated from rectangular screens high above exposed steel beams. Footsteps and voices echoed in the cavernous space. Voices were few but harsh. A high-hat woman appeared to preside over the workers.

The leading officer turned abruptly into a small room, similarly lit and furnished with a battered metal table with four chairs, two plain and two with armrests. The officers took the armchairs behind the table, but kept Elve and Hara standing.

The female officer, the superior (judging by the rows of insignia on her sleeve), spoke peremptorily to the other officer. "Read the charges."

He fumbled with his Apsam, scrolling with increasing desperation through its pages. As he failed and started over for a second time, Hara began to sway. She grasped at the edge of the table.

Elve took her arm. "Couldn't she sit down? She has just recovered from serious illness."

The top officer nodded coldly. "Both of you." She treated Officer No. 2 with a gaze of utter scorn.

At last the Apsam yielded up the appropriate file. No. 2 cleared his throat and began.

"In the name of Hiz Moest Esteemed Prezens, Owr Glorius Leeder and Proetektor uv de Peepl, I charge you Hara 33.06.05.43.79 with murder in the death of your mother, one Kiela 10.01.01.43.79 and attempted murder in the dastardly injury of your brother, Urgo 24.07.01.43.79."

No. 2 scrolled again, this time with better luck.

"Similarly, in the name of Hiz Moest Esteemed Prezens, Owr Glorius Leeder and Proetekter uv de Peepl, I charge you, Elve 25.29.07.43.79 with unlawfully harbouring said miscreant in your home and offering succour and sustenance to an accused criminal."

"You are both, therefore, sentenced to five years hard labour."

Elve had a vision. The Red Queen yelling "Sentence first. Verdict afterward." Alice vanquishing the pack of cards.

Emboldened, she questioned: "No trial? No defence? What kind of justice is this?"

High-hat smiled. "Our business is Law and Order. Justice is not in our job description."

Elve prayed desperately for time. This charade would surely fall apart if she could just gain a little time.

Hara provided the reprieve. She stood and stepped forward menacingly. "My father is Respected Health Team Inspector Dag. What have you done with him?"

It wasn't her father's name. It wasn't even her adamant stance. It was Hara's blazing white eye that threw the officers into confusion. They feared bewitchment, instant death, they knew not what. Their faces turned grey.

Hara still fixed the officers with her stunning gaze. "What. Have. You. Done. With. My. Father?"

At a nod from High-hat, No. 2 scrolled hastily through his Apsam. "RHTI Dag Charged with irregularities, stripped of office, sentence ten years, incarcerated 10.05.42 MNA."

"Where?"

"Awesome Facility No. 5." The man's voice was a trembling whisper.

"Come, Hara."

Elve scooped her arm around the girl's back. Together they left the room leaving the shell-shocked officers gaping.

43

Elve and Hara made their way home using side streets where there was more shade and fewer people to be greeted with the designated salutation. They were in no mood to be grateful for this glorius dae uv de RAA.

Far above, ghosts against the blazing blue, three whiteships flew in close formation. Their silent hovering raised the hairs on Elve's nape.

"Do you think they're watching us?"

"Oh no. They're much too high." But Elve could only guess at the surveillance capabilities of the ships.

A sizable gravel hill blocked their way at old Dundas. This was where the Tory Transit Station had stood before the system foundered altogether and all the stations were filled in.

"They say that there is a humongous system of tunnels under the city," Elve panted. "Fast-moving trains carried millions of people every day to all parts of the Urb." She wiped sweat from her brow with her head-scarf.

"What happened to the trains?"

"The city had no money for maintenance. After three terrible accidents where hundreds of people died, the whole system was abandoned."

"So then they filled all the stations with dirt and gravel?"

"Uh-huh. To keep people out. Probably the tunnels are dangerous. Likely to collapse at any moment."

"I'd go in anyway," said Hara tossing her head. "Anything to get out of this sun."

They were following the cut where tracks had formerly run. It would take them close to a creek where they could take a path through the trees.

Where the track resumed an underground route, the entrance to the tunnel was roughly blocked with concrete. They sighed and began to clamber up the grassy side of the cut.

In a flash of purple, something flew past their faces.

"What was that?" Hara tried to follow the object's flight.

"A bird," said Elve. "A starling, I think."

"Where'd it go?"

The bird had vanished. Elve and Hara turned to search the spot where it seemed to disappear. They came face-to-face with the concrete wall blocking the Octotrans tunnel. As they stood, puzzled, the bird reappeared through an aperture in the upper corner where the concrete had crumbled away.

"She has a nest in there," said Elve. "I hear the babies squawking."

"Yeah. They must be hungry."

Very soon, the bird returned with a cicada in its beak. As Elve and Hara watched, it flew through the aperture, and the squawking subsided instantly.

Before they resumed their trek, Hara took a closer look at the barrier. She picked up a rock and used it to score the surface. Bits of it broke away and rolled clattering down its slanted face. "You could break this down," she said. "You could get in there."

44

When Elve returned from an early morning errand at the Emp, she found a shred of Porgel stuck under her door. Dropping her bags inside, she stooped to pick it up. Strategically, because quick action of that kind could bring on a swirl of vertigo.

The torn missive had only one word, "Pen."

Who delivered this? What does it mean? Elve pondered as she stored her groceries away. The fridge was barely cool, as the prolonged hot weather and shortened periods of electricity were having their effect.

She decided to visit Pen. The message might have had some other source. It could be some kind of threat, given Pen's compromised status with police. But it seemed more likely that Pen had somehow had it brought up to her door. That Pen herself had climbed the stairs didn't seem possible.

Hara was in the garden picking new green peas. Elve left the door unlocked for her and went down to knock on Pen's door.

"Who's that?"

"It's me, Elve. Did you send me a message?"

There was a long pause, a clicking of bolts, then Pen in the doorway. "Come in," she said, turning heavily to her chair.

The fug in the room was overpowering, as before,

"Can I open the balcony door? The air today is pleasant—not too hot yet."

"Whatever you like."

Elve slid the protesting door to one side. A welcome breeze, sweet with summer blossom, wafted into Pen's virtual cave. Five of the six pot lights in the ceiling were non-functional. The room had no other light.

"Did you send me this?" Elve held out the Porgel scrap.

Pen nodded. "Sent it up with your neighbour's boy. Kal. He's around quite a bit. I see him smoking in the bushes."

"Kal must be eighteen by now."

"Yeah, and avoiding the draft. Something irregular for sure."

"Haven't seen him recently. Guess he's laying low." Elve sat down at the table. "But Hara and I have our new IDs. So we're relatively safe for a while."

"Not gonna bother. I never go out anyway."

Elve felt a stab of guilt. Hadn't been down to see Pen for quite a while, she realized. Should've brought some tomatoes today. "So what can I do for you?"

"Better go see your friend, O. I had a bit of a garbled message from her. Our radios are nearly useless, the reception is so bad. But I thought she said your name."

Another stab. A visit with O was long overdue. Still, her concerns with Hara and Hom had been all-consuming. The next time Lali turned up, they must plan to see O.

Elve sighed. "We've returned to the Dark Ages." Literally, she thought, looking at Pen's pitiful light. "We have no transportation but our own two feet. No way to get in touch but face-to-face and the RAA hardly even allows that. If three people chat on the street corner, they all hafta give account of themselves."

"Oh but the RAA is generous. A parent with a minor child may say hello to one other adult." Pen snorted.

"Hello? Never hello. 'Giv gratitued and danks for dis glorius dae uv de RAA'." Elve vented her resentment of this RAAtic imposition. "But that's neither here nor there." And she told Pen of her experience with Hara at the Awesome Administration of Law and Order.

"Hmph. Don't see how your fancy new IDs make any difference now that you're in the cops' sights. You need to lay low too."

Elve was shocked to realize that she hadn't considered this. Their triumph in the office of L&O was probably a one-off. Those officers would recover and redouble their efforts. Unless they were mortally scared. Or humiliated. "They might prefer to forget the whole thing," she said.

"You can always hope. The cops can be counted on to be unpredictable."

They contemplated this truth for a moment.

Elve stood up. "Thanks for the message. I'll visit O as soon as I can. Want the door closed?"

"Leave it be. Come again."

"I'll send Hara down with some peas right away. Stay well, Pen." Elve let herself out and went round to the garden to find Hara.

Lali came that evening.

Lali had said little months ago when Elve confessed her disillusionment with their writing project. "It was a long shot anyway," she'd conceded. Now she was hard at work making baskets and hats. In summer the Emp wanted all she could make. She had little time for paper-making.

"I got me a helper," Lali announced as they sipped cold tea. "An illegal kid, well, a boy of eighteen. He harvests the reeds and lays them out to dry."

"How illegal?"

"Don't know. He didn't tell and I don't ask. But he should be in the army."

"Not Kal?"

"Yeah. Do you know him?"

"Lives next door, unless we have two illegal teens around."

"Kal's in. He has the cone. Left it where I would see it on my worktable. So I nodded and fished mine out of my pocket."

"Something is growing. Resistance. I see it in faces at the Emp. There's a brightness, an alertness. Just here and there. Most are so very dull."

"What can you expect with every spark of good sense whacked out of them at school? Most of the younger people are stupid beyond belief. Only fit to follow orders."

Hara came out of the bathroom freshly washed and combed. Her curls clustered softly, quite a little below the RAA's regulation length. So pretty, Elve, thought, and a distraction from her injured eye. The girl poured herself a cup and sat with the women at the table.

"How did you keep from going stupid at school?" Lali asked.

"I played all sorts of games in my head," said Hara. "We watch the same lessons over and over because so many kids fail the tests. So I made up stories. Songs, but that's harder. Sometimes I did arithmetic. Counting and multiplying. Ears. Fingers. Fingers and toes. Boring, but better than the same old lessons."

"Still sitting on your hands?"

"Yeah, but I found a way to do it without hurting. And a way to fake it when the teacher isn't too near."

Chuckles all round. The RAA couldn't outlaw laughter.

"Y'know what?" said Elve. "I think I had a birthday a day or so ago. Number 80. Should have been Death-Day. I guess the RAA lost count when they went to the ten-month year. I almost did too."

"They've over-reached in lots of ways," said Lali. "Trying to govern as if they still had Galaxy."

Elve nodded. "I doubt that they have the digital capacity to keep track of all the details as most governments used to do."

"And not enough smart people to do it anyway," said Hara with a sardonic grin.

When the tea was finished, they exchanged gifts: from Lali, a new basket; from Elve, fresh vegetables. The women planned their expedition to O's place for dawn of the next day.

The path beyond the oak tree was nearly impenetrable. Lali went ahead, parting the bushes for Elve, who used her walking stick as defence against lashing branches. O's door seemed to have not been opened for some time, so thick was the concealing vegetation.

Lali knocked and called, "It's us—Elve and Lali." A faint voice came from within.

They pushed open the door, sensing that all was not well with their friend. They found her on her cot almost in the dark. Vines had overgrown the skylight, cutting off both light and ventilation.

Elve propped the door open with one of the stools to clear the heavy air. Lali followed her nose to the chamber pail. She took it outside to dispose of the contents. She found the pit with a trowel stuck beside it in the dirt. She dumped the pail and ladled in a cover of earth.

Elve was busying herself, making broth with the onions and tomato sauce she'd brought. She longed for a bit of beef, but the best she could do was to add a couple of "mystery cubes," the meat-flavoured substitute offered at the Emp. Fortunately, both plentiful and cheap.

O lay with closed eyes, making no attempt to direct her friends' work or initiate conversation. Her face was cadaverous, her hands on the knitted coverlet blue-veined and inert. Her crinkly hair had grown into a wild silver bush springing in all directions from her scalp.

"Did you send a message to Pen?" Elve had propped up her friend with a rolled-up blanket. She was spooning broth into O's obedient mouth.

"I tried. Radio's almost done. Haven't got any more batteries and the reception's bad anyway."

Elve was grateful for O's answer. Coherent and relevant. She had feared both delirium and dementia. How old was this woman anyway?

"Pen got me down to see her. She sent a messenger with a scrap of Porgel. Just her name on it. She got your signal OK."

"I'm OK too. Just need some assistance. Can't get up to clear my window. I hate living in the dark."

"We'll get your lantern out to charge up. Don't know if Lali's able for the window job. 'Fraid I can't do it. Not steady enough on my feet."

"Two invalids would be a very bad outcome. I had a friend who did heavier work, but he has not turned up in a long time. Months. I fear that disaster has overtaken him."

There was no need to elaborate.

O rested again while the other two did a few necessary chores. The skylight would have to wait, Lali decided. She didn't have tools for the job.

O sat up. "What about our writing? We aren't quitting, are we?"

Elve sat down on the edge of O's cot. Lali pulled up a stool. "You up for trying again?" Lali asked.

O's voice was weak but determined. "I am. It's what I want to do with the last of my strength."

"Whole books out of the question." "Haven't the resources." "Books are too bulky." "Impossible to hide." "Single sheets." "Pamphlets." Voices overlapped as their ideas tumbled out.

"How can we choose what to write?" Elve felt overwhelmed at the prospect.

"I would write 'Humpty Dumpty'," said O. "It suggests the fall of an elevated person. Makes it seem possible."

"Sing a song of sixpence," suggested Elve. "The poor maid in the garden gets her nose pecked off."

"While the king counts his money and the queen eats bread and honey," said O.

"Maybe we shouldn't be too pointed about preaching," said Lali.

Elve agreed. "Some nonsense to muddy our trail. 'Jabberwocky'"

"What's Jabberwocky?" Lali asked.

"'Twas brillig and the slithy toves did gyre and gimble in the wabe,'" quoted Elve.

"Nonsense all right. Could be useful."

They agreed that Lali would bring Kal to clear O's skylight and dig a new, deeper pit. She would also bring a few sheets of paper for O to use. O still had ink and two of Lem's feather pens. Lali undertook to examine the blue reader for suitable short passages.

Elve thought that with a little more instruction, Hara would become good at handwriting. Together they would find nuggets in the other books. Holy Bible should be a good source, Elve thought, and Hara knew the Anne book from cover to cover.

"Do you need *Mother Goose* again?" Elve asked O.

O laughed. "Not at all. It's firmly entrenched in my memory."

Elve and Lali left with promises to return soon.

BOOK IV
Hom

45

Hom continued to spend his summers with Boat and the winters with Elve. By the time he was eleven (by the old reckoning) he was tall for his age, his brown skin enriched to a ruddy sheen by hours spent outdoors. He let his springing, black hair grow longer than the RAA law allowed. He kept it in a thick braid down his back.

He kept the official ID in his RAA issue pants pocket. The leather thong continued to swing on his bare chest, flashing the bear coin, the dove's wing, and the little silver spoon. He put on a tunic under protest in the summer, and donned a winter jacket unwillingly.

The Roons continued to be a place of refuge for Hom and his little group of friends. Their meetings were occasional, since Bim, Jog, and Rafu still attended school and couldn't get exemptions from the summer work camps. Hara divided her time between Elve's place and O's cabin, where she helped the old woman survive while learning all the lore of plants and animals that O could impart.

The group (they called themselves "the guys") worked out a system of signals—rocks arranged at the base of the tallest alder at Fel's house to tell when each might be able to meet in their hideout. They were runners, all of them, stealing at speed through streets pocked with rusted machines and dilapidated buildings, all increasingly hidden and broken down by rampant vegetation. Hiding places abounded.

After a summer of no meetings, they were able to get together one afternoon some weeks after school opened. Hom was still bare-chested in summer mode, but the others had donned a second layer over their regulation blue tunics. The Emp provided drab hooded sweaters made of a rough cotton knit and closed with a loop and toggle arrangement. (The metal toggles conducted the cold.) But they each had a bright polybag to carry snacks and water.

"Hey, guys," said Hara as they crouched in their usual circle by the birch tree. "Elve helped me make an eggless raisin cake this morning. Have a piece."

This brought cheers all round. They savoured the treat with smacks of delight and unspoken appreciation of this symbol of their old life together.

"When I was six," said Hom, "Gran made a cake like this for my birthday. But we had to give it to the police to keep them from reporting us for having too many people together. I was hiding under the table at the time."

"Why?"

"I didn't have any ID. They would have taked me away pronto."

The others nodded. Hom continued with the details.

"Gran did make me another cake like she said. I still remember how good it tasted," Hom concluded in a wistful tone.

Of the oldest cats, only a couple of gaunt females remained. The kittens of the past summer were now half-grown and vigorously batted away by their mothers if they tried to nurse. They lounged with the adult cats on their favourite perches in groups of two or three, cosied up for warmth.

Roon, clearly the dominant tom, approached Hom diffidently. He took the sphinx position just close enough to receive a treat or friendly pet, but safe from any indignity like being picked up. A lap cat he was not.

Hom reached into his bag for the chunk of Sprem he'd saved out of his lunch. Roon accepted it from his fingers and permitted himself to enjoy Hom's stroking him behind the ears.

The cake had disappeared. Bim jumped up. "Let's climb up there again," he said, pointing to the ledge whence they had seen the outline of a walled garden. "It still looks solid enough."

The others agreed, though day-by-day, debris was crumbling away from the standing ruin. Their protective wall on the east side was still functional, though somewhat diminished.

They began to climb, Rafu in the lead. Jog came up in the rear, taking advantage of secure footholds discovered by those ahead of him. After quite a bit of sliding and scrambling, they all achieved the goal and stood as before, silently surveying the scene below.

The summer's growth had obscured a good deal of the garden's outlines. Alders had found their way here, and several young trees were well established within the borders. Their leaves had begun to take on their autumn gold. Virginia creeper was rife, its leaves red against the green of high grass.

In spite of the presence of the cats, bird life seemed abundant. Sparrows, the children thought, but they were wrong. The small brown birds were warblers and wrens. Their twitters mingled with a barely audible purling of water.

Jog shifted and broke the silence. "You could hide in there easy."

"Just needs a good place to get inside. Must have had a gate or something once," said Bim.

Rafu saw the multiplication of living things—plants, mostly, but a pile of rock near the centre of the garden seemed to frame a low entrance. "Something lives in there," he said, pointing.

Hara saw that her dream of cultivating the space—neat rows of vegetables and an orchard—was unrealistic, given her lack of heavy tools. She would have to scratch out little patches at a time.

A transient wind passed through empty windows. It rose and whistled in cracks grown large with weathering. The children shivered, all but Hom. He felt it as a blessing, clearing his mind for what was to come.

They met again in a few days. The boys chose a likely spot to begin creating an entrance on the south side of the garden not far from the wall they'd built years ago. After they moved the slabs most amenable to their efforts, they found the rotted remains of a wooden gate. Bim claimed the rusted hinges and hasp immediately.

"I can use these," he said. "I'll make a spear."

"Oh please," said Hara. "Make something to dig with. I need something strong and sharp. Elve's little trowel is too round on the end."

Bim was noncommittal.

A huge, immovable slab guarded the opening. They levered another sizable piece to form a triangle with it. Bending low, the youngsters could pass through the opening.

"We'll get the vines to grow over it. Make a sort of curtain," said Bim.

"It'll take some time," said Hom, "but it'll be a great hideout."

At their next meeting, Bim presented Hara with a tool much like the mattocks of a long-ago time. The handle he had liberated from a worn-out mop, discarded in the janitor's room at school. The triangular hinge he had separated into two parts with a hacksaw, also available in the janitor's room. He and Hom had joined forces to file it sharp with a rasp in Ovid's tool supply. (Kal now presided as Ovid had done at the back door of Elve's building.) The whole was bound together with twine, a stout sisal which was at present available at the Emp.

Hara seized the mattock with joy. Within the hour, she had cleared a little space inside the garden where short grass resisted the encroachment of thistles. "Hey, look at this," she called. "It's big enough for something. O will know what I should plant here. Something that will live over the winter."

The boys scrambled over the rocks to see her work. "It smells nice," said Jog. "The dirt smells almost like you could eat it." "Yeah," in notes of surprise.

"Eeow-w-w." Rafu came screaming from the rock-pile. "It sprayed me. With its tail." He waved his arms trying to disseminate the miasma that enveloped him.

"Pee-ew!" ""Yecch!" "Get away from me." The others waved Rafu off and dispersed in order to get away from the stench.

From a safe distance, Hara asked, "Who did it?"

Behind Rafu, four small, furry, black-and-white-striped animals progressed, led unhurriedly by their dignified parent. She led her offspring into the cavity in the rock-pile that Rafu had noted earlier. Unwittingly, he had blocked her access.

"That one did it. The big one," said Rafu, still trying to shake off the smell. "Funny-looking cats."

"Those aren't cats," said Hom. "I don't know what they are, but they're not cats."

"O will know," said Hara. "She knows that kind of thing."

Rafu took off his hoodie. He hung it on a shrub to air out. Fortunately, the animal hadn't scored a direct hit. The guys said he didn't smell too bad, and thought he might get home without attracting unwanted attention. He raced home, shivering, the offending garment stuffed into his polybag.

The others soon made their way out, satisfied with their day's work. A whiteship circled high above them, unnoticed.

When they met again, Hara produced two garlic bulbs from her polybag. "O gave me these to plant. She says they will start to grow now and be OK over the winter. Then they'll come up early in the spring."

The boys were a little disappointed. They'd hoped for early tomatoes or maybe green peas. But they knelt with Hara as she peeled away the dry, white skins and separated the cloves.

She said, "See, this is how you plant them." With the trowel, she dug down a little more than the width of her hand into the soil she had loosened with the mattock. She nestled a clove in the hole and covered it with earth, pressing down firmly.

"I want to try that." "Let me do it." "Me too." One by one, the children took turns in the planting ceremony until all the cloves were safe in their winter bed.

There was another day of digging and planting—beet and turnip seeds, this time. Nobody's favourite vegetables, but they'd learned long ago not to be fussy. Good food was too hard to come by for that.

After the planting, Hara continued to dig with the mattock, planning to create a good spot for wildflower seeds she'd collected on the roadside. Hom, Jog, and Bim worked on pulling Virginia creeper vines to cover their entrance to the garden. Rafu explored.

In a short time, he came leaping rock to rock. "I found it. I found it. The water. The fountain's broken, but the water's still running."

Rafu led the way over a barrier of rubble to his find. Remnants of the form that had once graced the fountain lay half-hidden in long grass. Hara parted the grass with her foot to find a woman's face, black with lichen, a travesty of its original beauty. A broken stone jug lay close by.

Hom knelt where the water bubbled from a pipe between two rocks into the remains of the fountain's basin. He caught a handful and tasted it. "It's good."

Hara began to sing. A new song, wordless. The others sang too, their own, different tune, but in the same key. Jog grabbed a couple of bones and picked up the beat. Mischief lighting his eyes, he upped the beat striking hard on the offbeat. The song wavered, then took on energy. An elemental song. A spiritual.

46

Hom went back to the lakeshore in the early morning. He was buoyed by Boat's decision to allow him to come on his daily trip to Camp 46. What Boat had once considered impossibly dangerous seemed now to be the lesser peril, considering the acute surveillance of the docks.

"Boat," said Hom, as they hauled in their fishing gear, "why don't we find another way?"

"Another way for--?"

"To get to Camp 46."

"How?"

"Well, the camp is pretty close to the lake, right?"

"Yeah."

"So instead of going back to Long Branch, sail west along the shore and find a spot to dock close to the camp. It'll be a shorter route to push the cart."

"I dunno. Might be worth looking into." Boat looked chagrined that he'd never thought of this himself.

"And then maybe I wouldn't need to stay below deck so much. If there's a cove or something. Some place where nobody goes."

Boat merely grunted.

But he steered off shore instead of returning to Long Branch. He turned "Old Girl" (that was the only name he'd ever given his boat) into the wind, moving westward at some distance from shore. Sufficient distance to at least prevent easy identification by the naked eye. Hom kept watch for a likely haven along the shore.

Little by little, the forest had been returning to the area for decades. Now young trees crowded the shore with exuberant growth. Boat brought her in close, estimating that they'd come fairly near to their destination.

Hom yelped. "In there, Boat. In there." He'd spied a derelict dock dipping precariously into the water, barely visible behind a curtain of drooping willow branches, still covered in golden leaves. He danced, pointing. Boat cut the motor and steered her in behind the sheltering branches. Hom leaped to secure the line to a remaining upright post.

They needed to reconnoitre the area before Boat would set out for the camp. A gravelly bank stood in their way, but a little exploration yielded the ancient stairway built of logs sunk at intervals into the soil. Steep at first, it soon levelled into a barely visible path. Breaking through the choking brush, they came upon the remains of a stone house of considerable size. The chimney still stood, overshadowed by stand of spruce. The tile roof, sagging dangerously at best, had utterly fallen into the extension on the right. Slender, young trees mixed with spruce rose inside the tumbled walls, and shrubs sprang from the detritus between the stones.

Hom was scrambling inside before Boat could stop him. Feeling his old bones, Boat followed, cautiously making his way over the debris. He found Hom standing motionless, awed by what he saw.

Hom waved a "stay back" signal. He pointed to a fawn-coloured animal barely visible among the trees. Its antlered head was lifted, nostrils flared in wary alertness.

The boy whispered, "What is it?"

"A stag! They've been gone for centuries."

"It's beautiful, said Hom. Neither he nor Boat understood why tears came to their eyes.

The animal gazed steadily at their frozen forms. Then it turned and bounded out of the ruin, its raised white tail signalling its distrust of the intruders.

Hom was eager to explore the rest of the house, but Boat vetoed the idea. "We're trying to find Camp 46, remember? There should be a road, or what's left of one, in front of this place. So keep a sharp eye. It's gettin' on for noon, by the looks."

Hom soon discovered a trail running in front of the property. Bits of asphalt suggested that it had once been a major paved road. "Old Lakeshore Road, I bet," said Boat, kicking aside a knob of pavement.

They followed it towards the west until it merged with a gravel road obviously in present use. "Youpee! It's the camp road. She's just over that rise." Boat was elated at their good luck. He'd taken a guess in choosing their westward course.

By unspoken agreement, as men do, they took a leak in the bushes at the side before altering their route. Back to the boat to load the cart, and manoevre it up to the road, no easy job.

As they pulled and pushed the cart up the bank, Hom recalled his work with Ovid's clumsy barrow. He pushed mightily, and they got it done.

The trail was relatively easy. When they reached the road, Boat motioned Hom to go back. "Don't want to hafta explain you at the camp. Wait for me at the boat. Below deck if anything crops up." Even as he spoke, Boat knew that his instructions were in vain.

Hom hoped to sight the deer again. In that he was disappointed. But his exploration of the ruined house was of almost equal satisfaction.

* * *

When Boat returned with his clattering barrow, he found the boy splashing his feet over the side of the dock and eating a peanut butter sandwich. "I saved two for you," Hom called.

"Shtup, boy, Maybe we got more company than we think. There was a patrol on the gravel road." Boat pulled back the cover on his barrow and brought out a packet wrapped in polycloth. "A present from the cook."

"Sticky buns?" Hom craned to see the treat.

"Apple dumplings. Apples are good this year, he says." Boat handed over the packet. "Now get on board. We should be getting back."

Hom left the food in the cabin and went to help wrestle the barrow on to the deck.

Once away from the dock with its overhanging trees, Boat cut the motor. They sailed east to Long Branch under a high sun and spanking breeze.

"I wanna go back there," said Hom, licking his fingers. "There's lotsa good stuff in that house."

Boat's curiosity outran any resentment at being disobeyed. "What kinda stuff?"

"Nothin' in the back where we saw the stag. But somebody used the main part for a workshop, I think. Wire and small metal things. Pliers and tape. Drawings on the walls, mostly numbers for names, but I saw 'radio'. And there's been a fire under the chimney. Maybe quite a while ago."

"You shouldna been in there. The roof's ready to cave."

Hom just looked at him. "We ought to go back there tomorrow. There's lots more stuff."

Boat's grunt was negative. But his nod was definitely assentive.

47

Bim and Jog quit school. It wasn't too hard.

The Reespected Ministree of Sitizenship and Docuementaeshun, while respecting the ten-month year as legislated by the Reespected Ministree of Mezhurment and Tiem, were highly annoyed to find that the abrupt change in the digital names of Loyel Sitizenz rendered the school attendance files obsolete. Teachers accustomed to taking attendance via devices somewhat like the police Apsams, found that their files no longer matched the students' IDs. The practice of taking attendance by calling out the numbers didn't work.

For reasons unexplained, but probably related to economy, the classes had become very large with upwards of sixty students per class. With teaching by TV, it seemed not to matter, as long as there were spots for all the bodies on the benches.

Policing the ranks for violations of the hands-under-bums rule kept teachers busy. They knew only a few of their students by name and reputation as troublemakers. Jog and Bim had been careful to maintain a low profile and slipped under the radar as the attendance recording failed. Somebody was missing, but the teacher didn't know who. He shrugged and was grateful for this slight reduction of his workload.

Rafu stayed in his class. Like Hara, he'd developed ways to avoid going stupid. He also respected his teacher, RI Lam.

While careful to seem to adhere to the Ministry line, Lam stole a few minutes from the RAA's presentations every day to tell a story. Her stories were about kids who were honest, or brave, or learned from a wise parent. Animals too. And a story she remembered from childhood called "The Giving Tree".

Besides that, Lam made use of the Digital Manipulation Recovery Exercises. These had been recently provided by the Respected Ministry of Health and Well-Being to offset digital weakness and deformity caused by the students' sitting on their hands. She added words to the finger exercises: funny, factual, and fantastic. Sometimes she sang.

"Guess what RI Lam sang today," Rafu said to his companions in the Roons. He sang to an invented tune:

> The time has come, the Walrus said,
> To talk of many things:
> Of shoes and ships and sealing wax
> And cabbages and kings—
> And why the sea is boiling hot
> And whether pigs have wings.

"Hey, I know those words," said Hara. "They're in *Through the Looking Glass*. Tweedledee recites the whole seventeen verses to Alice. Wonder where Lam heard them."

By this time the guys had become well acquainted with Elve's books. They were free to come and read them whenever they could do so without attracting attention.

"Lam is the best," said Rafu. "She puts me on the front bench by the door. If I hear Garg's clunky boots, I quick give the high sign and she stops singing. She turns up the sound on the TV and we all put our hands under our bums."

"She'll get caught." There were nods all round. Rafu looked dismayed.

"Us too. We might all get caught. For not being in school."

"For singing bad songs."

"Not even RAA songs."

"For planting flowers."

"Not *flowers*! Oh-h-h-h."

They capered in laughter. But they stopped abruptly. The sky above was a sharp autumn blue marked by one hovering whiteship. It spiralled downwards.

"Can they see us?" Rafu whispered.

"Don't know. Keep still."

They turned their faces to the ground, crouching to emulate the rocks that still dotted the area. A soft hissing became audible as the ship seemed just above their heads.

It hovered, then shot straight up, its trajectory marked by a white trail. It was gone.

When the hissing receded, the children unwound.

"Waw-waw," said Jog. "I thought we were cooked."

"Don't know what those things can do," said Bim. "H of P showed them shooting poison gas. But that might be a lie."

"Yeah. But anyhow, we need better cover. That was way too close," said Hom.

"Time to go," said Hara, ever the timekeeper. After they had sung a song of parting, they went out.

48

The Guys got together infrequently after that. Hara's attendance to O's needs took her to the ravine almost daily. Rafu continued at school.

Bim and Jog laboured in the Roons, digging under the garden wall to make a shelter safe from aerial surveillance.

Since Hara occupied his old room, Hom stayed with Boat at the lakeshore.

Boat kept Hom busy with repairs to Old Girl in addition to their usual routine. Hom welcomed their daily trek to deliver their catch to Camp 46. Exploring the lakeshore house and its surroundings while Boat completed the delivery was almost as good as time in the Roons. Though he missed the Guys and his feline friend too. He considered how he might lure Roon to join him by the lake.

"Boat, can I borrow the radio?" They had hauled in their catch and were heading on their usual course some distance from the shore.

"Maybe. What for?"

"I want to see how it's put together. That workroom in the house has lots of stuff—tools and little things I don't know what they are. And diagrams on the wall."

"So what you got in mind?"

"The first one is labelled radioempfänger. I think it shows how to make a radio. And if I had yours to go by, I might be able to make one."

"Hmm. Well, for a day or so."

In what had once been a spacious living room, the rough worktable stood in front of a wide mullioned window. No vegetation blocked the light, so Hom went out to find out why that was. He found the bushes and young trees had been cut away from that side of the house. Three solar chips were mounted on the windowsill, well exposed to the sunlight.

The clearing must have been done just last spring, Hom reasoned, or it would have mostly grown up again by now. The cuts were pretty fresh—not weathered much at all. The chips meant that the outlets in the workroom were live. Good.

A couple of days were all Hom needed. The radioempfänger diagram and the working radio enabled him to construct a simple radio from the materials at hand. True, it only made crackling noise, but Hom wasn't discouraged.

When Boat came back from the camp, he knocked on the window. Hom yelled out, "Come and see my radioempfänger."

Boat shook his head when he heard the radio's feeble signal. But he put his finger on the problem. "You need to fix your aerial. Get it up higher."

Hom hopped up on the worktable. He drew the aerial wire up tautly and anchored it to a handy nail in the beam above. A sprig of tinsel on the nail suggested its original purpose—to support decorations for a Holiday celebration.

He crouched on the table as Boat fiddled with the tuner. Static like hail on the roof. A tortured whistle. Then, loud and clear, a signal.

"Four-three-seven-nine. Brillig. Adit six-eight. Shovel ready. Over."

Boat and Hom exchanged puzzled looks.

"Forty-three seventy-nine. That's the Urb. Old Tranna," said Boat.

"Brillig is a time, three o'clock I think. In the afternoon. It's in Gran's Alice book."

"Shovel ready sounds like a job for a work crew."

"Somebody is reading Gran's secret book. Who?"

"And somebody's organizing a work party somewhere in the Urb. Dunno who or where. The sender should use some kind of ID," Boat grumbled.

The radio crackled to life again. "Adit six-eight. Twenty mans west past Tory Station."

Hom and Boat recognized the unit of measurement that men on the docks had developed since the official units were so counter-intuitive that few understood them. A "man" was a distance from head to foot of a tall man. Laid horizontally, a "man" was the distance travelled in two strides. "Mans" could be measured by pacing off the distance. One stride, or half a "man" was a "kid".

"That'll be a tunnel entrance on the old Octotrans," said Boat. "I think I might just know the place." Boat had long ago explored all the routes to Miller's Lane, looking for shortcuts.

"Can we go there? At three o'clock?"

"First we hafta get back to our berth. Not sure about the three o'clock thing. This doesn't sound like a daytime job, dya think? And nobody has a clock. Three o'clock is anybody's guess."

It was true. The RAA had diligently collected all the twelve-and twenty-four hour clocks soon after the establishment of the ten-tem day. Timepieces geared to the new system were promised, but never appeared. The Ministry erected a few public clocks throughout the Urb and furnished each government office with one.

They left Hom's radio in the workshop for further improvement and experimentation. Hom chattered about his hope to make one that could send as well as receive.

Old Girl made good headway toward Long Branch with Hom at the wheel and Boat beside him, supervising.

A rhythmic, screaming pip-pip-pip assaulted their ears. They looked up.

A dark arrowhead shape was sailing towards Old Girl. The sun gave it a purplish glint as it whirled just above the shoreline trees. It was gone as quickly as it had come.

"What was that?" Hom yelled, peeking up from under his hands.

"Dunno. But the RAA is up to something. The whiteships were bad enough, but this is a different animal."

"Slootly."

"Yeah. But that's all it might be. Remember the month we had the jack-boot crew on the premises? Marched around like dragoons. But they never did anything. And then they went away. Just here to scare us."

"We better watch H of P. It might tell us something."

Boat had little hope of that. He snorted and turned the boat into the dock.

48

Boat snored in his bunk most of the afternoon. Hom read for a while. Elve was allowing him to dismember Holy Bible and bring a book or two to read in his downtime on the boat. He was working his way through The Book of the Prophet Isaiah and The Gospel According to Luke.

As the sun approached the horizon, Hom prepared a meal of flatbread and seasoned lentil mush. As they ate in silence, they watched the sun fall blazing into the lake leaving the sky streaked from west to east with rosy cloud. Hom felt the touch of a wandering wind. He heard for a moment the humming voice of his old dream. "Hom-m-m-m."

The wind carried the smell of the oily water around the boats, but also the pure scent of the waters rolling gently in the distance. There was a whiff of food being prepared by sailors on the dock, cooking on makeshift barbecues. Also something metallic that caused Hom's nostrils to flare.

Pip-pip-pip. The dark arrowhead screamed and whirled above, tracing a swooping course out of the northern sky towards the Urb. It hovered briefly over the city before disappearing utterly.

"We're being singled out for attention," said Boat. "Something's going on."

At dusk, when Boat and Hom collected their tools and began to take a cautious route to the disabled Octotrans, their way was untrammeled by police.

"Come to think of it," said Boat, "there haven't been many officers around. Nobody at the docks for a couple of weeks, maybe."

"I didn't see any on our way to Gran's last time either."

Two others, a woman and an older man joined them at Tory station. A third man was ahead of them on the track allowance. He turned to meet them. He tossed and caught a small object, then displayed it on the back of his hand like a coin. A tiny cone. He looked questioningly at the approaching workers.

Boat fished in his pocket. He produced a similar cone, squashed and disintegrating, but recognizable. "He's OK," he said, indicating Hom with his elbow.

"I know," said the questioner.

"Is this brillig? Nightfall?" Hom asked. The man gave a quick nod, turning to the other two.

They also showed the sign of the cone. Hurrying up, another young man quickly offered his sign. Hom recognized Kal, the caretaker of Gran's building and gave him a thumbs up.

Pocketing their cones, the group moved down the track allowance, led by the man who first showed the cone. "Call me Nik," he told them.

When they reached the adit, it was much as Hara and Elve had seen it, though the opening where the starling had flown in and out was somewhat enlarged. On the concrete barrier, barely discernible in the falling night, were roughly painted numerals 6 and 8. Adit 68.

Nik and the old man had pickaxes. They attacked the concrete with a will and soon had a pile of gravel and concrete at their feet. Hom and Boat moved in with their shovels to shift the debris to one side.

From time to time the wind drove cloud across a gibbous moon. The workers pushed on in the fitful light. Silence but for the hack and scrape of tools.

Kal took over the old man's pickaxe. Nik handed off to Hom. They struck alternate blows at a likely spot. Under this onslaught, the concrete crumbled. A piece almost the size of a fridge was loosened.

Assisted by shovellers, they levered it out of the entrance. Triumphant shouts mingled with the crash of its fall.

"Shtup!" hissed the woman, who'd been keeping watch. "Somebody's up there." She pointed to the north rim of the cut.

In the darkness, Hom detected a moving shadow. A man? It didn't seem so. A man walking low to escape detection? Maybe. Or a woman. Or a girl. An animal? Then, nothing. Nothing to see. Not a sound. "It's gone," he said.

Subdued, the workers surveyed their handiwork. The opening would admit a man easily. Nik went in, feeling his way to determine whether they had actually opened up the tunnel. "Hallo-o-o," he shouted, and the echo assured him that they were in.

Before they dispersed, the group exchanged names. Nik. Boat. Hom. Kal. Lem. Fel.

"Stay tuned," said Nik. The others nodded and moved off to wherever they laid their heads for rest.

50

There was no sleeping in the morning after. The fish must be caught, the trek to Camp 46 accomplished, the delivery made.

Hom sat with Boat on the deck on their return voyage. A good breeze sent Hom to the storage box for warm jackets. They munched on Cook's treat, a pretty good berry tart.

"Have we opened up the whole Octotrans, dya think?" Hom asked.

"Nope. Just the west arm. The biggest part is the other side of Tory station under old Tranna. Six more branches to the north and east and a short one to the lake."

"Should we dig out Tory station next?"

"Dunno. Don't know what Nik has in mind. Don't know who else he has contact with. I think we should go west. The line used to go all the way to Niagara. Branch lines off it too."

"Did you ever go there? To Niagara?"

Boat laughed. "How old dya think I am? Octotrans was abandoned in my grandfather's time. I just know about it from what he told me when I was a kid. Even then it was sort of a myth. How huge it once was, how fast the trains were, how it operated without human hand. One central station with a crew of three to watch the blinking lights."

"Waw-waw! Three guys. And now it takes five of us to dig out one tunnel. Will it ever get fixed up again?"

"Not unless digital power is restored. Don't see much sign that the RAA is getting it done. They'll keep it to themselves if they do. Use it for military purposes. And to keep us all in line."

"What about H of P?"

"H of P is very old technology. Doesn't need Galaxy to work. Galaxy was something else. A huge network. Everybody could use it. Could find out anything you wanted to know. Too bad I've forgotten most of what I looked up. But I know the world is a whole lot older and bigger than the RAA wants us to think."

"A-w-w. I wish we still had that." Hom rubbed the last flake of tart from his chin.

Hom hadn't heard any more radio signals in his workshop that day. But how could he know if any had come in during his absence? Perhaps Nik had tried repeatedly to reach them.

In the days that followed he worked hard to produce the device labelled "funksender" in his guiding diagram.

The diagrams were recent. They were drawn in pencil on paper only slightly buckled and yellowed. They were detailed and expertly drafted. Hom wondered about his absent instructor. Who was he? What was the language of the labels? Could he be reached?

"I nearly have it," said Hom when Boat came into the workshop. "It took me five days. I need this thing." He pointed to "microfon" on the diagram. "I can't find anything like that in here. There's boxes and drawers with lots of bits and pieces, but nothing like this."

"To send, you need a microphone. To talk into. We had them before the RAA. Even after. You could talk on a ComD."

"I never seed a ComD."

"No. The RAA took them away early on. Before you were born."

"There's a place I couldn't open." Hom seemed reluctant to mention this.

"Yeah?"

"It's upstairs." As Hom expected, Boat growled his disapproval.

"So you went up there even though the roof's ready to cave?"

Hom reddened and nodded. "There's old furniture up there. Falling apart, except for one big wooden thing. It has drawers, but I couldn't get them open."

"Well, let's go look." Boat's curiosity overcame his caution. The stairway curved upward from the wide front entrance.

The steps were firm. They didn't even creak. Boat surveyed the ceiling. It was supported by sturdy black beams.

"It's in here." They had reached a small room at the head of the stairs.

Boat recognized a long outmoded kneehole desk. He'd seen one in a movie eons ago. Solid oak, by the looks. The finish scratched and marked with two round stains, the edges nicked as well, but it stood secure on a moulded base.

Hom was pulling ineffectually at the drawer handles, two on each side of the kneehole. Boat stood by, rubbing his cheek. Trying to recall.

Then Boat moved forward to pull open the centre, shallow drawer over the kneehole. Just a little until he heard a soft click. The bottom left drawer rode out, tossing Hom back on his behind, and ending up on his stomach. "Yerks! It's a secret trick. Hey, get this thing off me."

Boat lifted the drawer and slid it back into place. Hom began to rummage in it. It contained a Medusa of cables. Thick black ones. Thinner black ones. Slim ones, black and red and yellow. Some with black boxes attached. Entwined in what seemed a hopeless mess.

But Hom was not discouraged. He began to untangle the mess, taking note of the varied plugs and prongs on the ends of the cables. He laid them out, sorting as he went.

"These look perfect. Not rotten or anything."

"Not all that old," said Boat. They used to be needed for some of the digital stuff. Everybody had wi-fi mostly, but not everywhere. Like here in this place maybe the wireless was never installed. The guy that liked this old desk maybe stuck to outdated tech too."

Boat was opening the top drawers. In one, a tray held three pencils and a box of stick pens. A pad of yellow paper lay beneath. "These are for your gran," he said. "The writers are desperate for paper." In the others, he found yellow pages covered with fine, neat writing in a pre-RAA language. "We'll take this too. They can bleach and recycle."

Hom left a few cables still tangled in his eagerness to get into the last drawer. "What're these?"

On his knees, Hom handed up the items to Boat, who ranged them on the desktop. Nine of them.

The colorful collection represented most of the portable digital devices of the late 30th century. The oldest were thin, rectangular tablets, the newest were designed to fit in the hand and be operated by just the index finger. The two ComDs were homely black slabs, cheap, simple, yet once immensely useful.

"Waw-waw," marvelled Hom, scrambling to his feet. "I've never seed anything like this stuff. What are they?"

"Phones. You used them to send and receive messages—like to talk to a friend or order in your dinner. Or call for help—the police or fire department. Lots of other uses too," said Boat.

Hom didn't understand fire department. There hadn't been any in the Urb in his lifetime. But he was much more interested in turning over the devices, examining their buttons and holes. They all had round holes, obviously portals for plugging something in.

"I like this one best," said Hom, holding up a satiny red ovoid.

"Yeah, that's an Oprah. Best of the best. The rich guys' phone. It had direct access to Galaxy. You asked Oprah anything you wanted to know and she would tell you. She would read to you too. Books, jokes, poems. Anything."

Hom was already poking about in the pile of slim cables. The ones with small round plugs. "If you can talk to it, it has some kind of microphone, doesn't it?" He chose a likely looking cable, a red one.

"Guess so. I never understood how the mike worked."

"Got it!" The red cable snapped into the Oprah. A perfect fit.

"I want to see if the mike will work with my funksender. Let's come back for this stuff after." Hom raced for the stairs. But Boat stayed behind to replace the cables and phones in their drawers. He was careful to properly position the centre one.

By the time Boat entered the workshop, Hom had the red cable attached to his contraption with electrical tape. He called into the tiny aperture in the Oprah's surface. "Nik, Nik. This is Hom. If you can hear me, please talk."

The radioempfänger crackled. It whistled. Then, "Nik here. You're loud and clear. Glor, boy!"

"Slooty glor!" When do we dig again?"

"Wait one sundown. Brillig at 68."

"OK. Bye."

"Bye."

Hom's happiness encompassed Boat's old body. They leaped together slapping raised palms like rejoicing ballplayers of old.

51

At brillig, under a glowering sky, a file of dark figures armed with tools moved through the aperture at Adit 68. Boat and Hom were last in line. Last, except for a straggler who came sliding down the grassy bank, calling softly, "Wait, Wait."

Hom recognized the outline of a mattock on a sturdy shoulder. "Hara, for grood's sake. What are you doing here?"

"Kal told me. He got to know Lem at O's place. So I want to dig too."

Dumping their jackets in a heap just inside the tunnel, the workers activated their lanterns. The lights played faintly on the dome high above them as they stood in the bottom of the metal tube. Nik led the way, testing the soundness of the walls with a crowbar. Boots crunched and tools clanked with every stride. Echoes and re-echoes bounced from the curved surfaces like the voices of ghosts. Hom shivered, recalling Boat's tale of accidents with hundreds of deaths in the Octotrans.

The group encountered no obstacle until they reached a platform. "Alderwood" was the name inlaid in the tiled station wall. Here a substantial pile of stone and coarse gravel blocked the way. The workers attacked it with vigour.

Hom and Hara jumped up on the platform where passengers had once waited for the train. Here the pile sloped away to a lesser depth. With mattock and shovel, they broke up and moved the mass aside. Their work opened a narrow passage along the wall.

Hara giggled. "We're the toves. Gyring and gimbling. Gimbling, anyway."

Hom shrugged. "Digging holes? Well, OK."

"And slithy too." Hara sidled along the oozy wall. Hom followed.

They went to work on a second impeding heap. It was tough. Their breakthrough to the other side left them panting and leaning on their tools. Hom swung his lantern, inspecting the newly discovered space.

"There's a dark opening in the wall ahead."

It was the opening to a broad stairway. A black streamlet oozed down the cracked and crumbling steps. Hara and Hom were halfway up before Boat was done yelling at them, "Don't you guys go up there."

The stair led to an area where the passengers had passed through turnstiles to access the platform. Water stood in sunken patches of the floor. Everywhere rust, mould, mildew.

Hara could decipher "S" on the wall of a passage angling off to the right. She scraped the mould with her mattock with little effect. The edge of Hom's shovel proved even less efficient.

Boat, trudging up the stairs behind them, managed to catch up when Hara bent to shake a stone out of her shoe.

The three followed the passage in single file, lanterns bobbing bright circles on the tile walls. Short flights of steps raised the floor level at regular intervals. Though no wider than a man's arm span, the passage was well-constructed in the same manner as the main station.

The light from Hara's lantern dwindled. Its last flicker fell on a door. The kind of half-glassed door common to public buildings for centuries. People in a hurry could straight-arm its wide metal bar to barge through. Hom tried it and it worked.

They entered a small, square lobby decorated with Grecian pillars and plaster cornice surrounding the entrance opposite. A once luxurious carpet, mildewed and malodorous, squished under their feet.

On the far side, the door hung askew on one hinge. Boat leaned in, swinging his lantern. They saw a hallway blocked with chunks of masonry.

"Major digging here," said Hom, disappointed.

"Another night," said Boat. 'This lantern's going out in ten."

When they made their way back to Alderwood Station, the rest of the crew were returning, also with failing lanterns.

"Got through to Rattray Station," said Kal without enthusiasm. His pants were wet to the knees. "Most of the tunnel has a kid or so of water in the bottom."

"This much?" said Boat, indicating the depth with his hand. Kal nodded.

But Hom and Hara were jubilant. As they'd turned to leave, they had spotted the framed sign above the door: OCTOTRANS and beneath, **Statesfield**.

52

Bim and Jog had laboured daily to develop a shelter under the garden wall. Their digging was halted by a flat concrete barrier. A good floor, if only it had allowed more head room.

The boys crouched on the concrete patch to consider their strategy.

Bim said "Maybe we should try another place in the garden. The skunk den?"

"Are you crazy?" The skunks still live there." They hadn't seen any recently, but occasional pungent whiffs announced the skunks' continued residence.

Bim reconsidered. "Well, maybe we can go sideways and find the edge of this cement."

They poked the cave's edges with their shovels to find the easiest digging. They were rewarded with the exposure of a massive crack in the concrete, a crack accomplished by a vigorous network of tree roots. "It's our birch tree," they yelled.

Leaving shovels and caution behind, the boys wriggled down among the roots and dropped from a thick strand into unknown territory.

"Yerks! It's dark!"

"We should've had a lantern."

"How will we get out?"

Their eyes adjusted to the murk. In the light from the crack, they distinguished large rounded shapes. Silent. Unmoving. The hair rose on their necks.

And then. Wheels. Definitely, wheels with rims resting in deflated tires. Velos, each tethered to a post with a thick cable.

"These are real old. Older than shit."

"Waw-waw."

Jog, a reluctant climber, proved brave in the exploration of depths. He felt his way from velo to velo towards a glimmer at the far end of the gloomy space. Bim followed.

The light was sifting in through broken masonry surrounding a dark, rectangular frame. Jog stepped into the black recess. On a hunch, he explored the wall by the opening. His fingers found two ranks of push buttons.

"It's an elevator."

"You sure?"

"Think so."

Bim stepped in to check it out.

A heavy thump over their heads. The boys screeched.

Breathing hard, they clutched each other and listened. Voices? Ghosts. The calls of the Roons' dead.

Thumps, but softer, rhythmic, patterned. A message?

The thumps paused. The pattern repeated.

Another pause. Then the rhythm sped up and Jog picked it up, slapping his knee since he had no other instrument. "It's the song. The water song." He began to sing, and Bim as well. Two muffled voices joined in.

"How'd you get down there?" It was Hom for sure.

"How'd you get up there?" Bim countered.

"Are you coming up?"

"We hafta. We can't get out the way we got in."

Hara's mattock served well. After a few sharp blows, the ceiling of the cage rained glass, tiles, and dangling light fixtures. Bim and Jog jumped back out to safety.

When the ceiling was reduced to a framework of steel bars, Hom and Hara stared down at their friends.

By dint of strong arms and much shouting, a supporting chunk of masonry and a cable liberated from a velo, Jog and Bim climbed up to join their friends in the mouldy Statesfield lobby. They crouched together, panting, laughing, and wiping tears from their chins with the backs of dirty hands.

53

Rafu skipped school to join his friends in the Roons. It was one of those rare, warm days in what was once November and once called Indian summer. Rl Lam had handed him a Porgel chit with the message, "Roons—Noon."

Boat was over at Elve's. Hom had barely said hello before heading across the road with a treat for Roon. Hara came with him. Bim and Jog would be there as a matter of course. They hunkered down where the sun was warm in the lee of their old wall.

Roon adopted his customary sphynx position beside Hom, just out of arm's reach. Other cats, sleek from a summer rich in prey, basked on sun-warmed ledges. With perked ears and half-closed eyes, a tawny watch-cat stretched on the highest vantage point beside the twisted pine.

"How's school?"

"Bout the same," said Rafu. "Lam's still good. Mutes the TV and teaches real stuff. Garg patrols the halls. You guys ever going back?"

"You kidding!"

"Does your mom think you're still at school?"

"She doesn't say nothing," Jog said. "She takes the little ones early to the care centre and goes to work. Yells at us to get up on her way out the door."

"Your dad ever come home?"

"Not since last summer. Mom thinks he might be in jail."

"Or dead," said his brother. "She cries in the night sometimes." Bim and Jog scraped sand into little heaps as they spoke.

Hara fiddled with the frayed edge of her tunic. "Elve and I tried to see my dad. He's in Awesome Facility No. 5 They wouldn't let us in. We were only allowed to send a word-of-mouth message. There was no answer."

A silence. The boys swept their little sand-piles away.

A starling's note dropped like a pearl. Running water sang soft beyond the garden wall. High above, a whiteship circled, then climbed and disappeared. No one noticed.

"Do you think this will work?" Jog held up the rope he'd fashioned with two strands of vine, tied at the ends with tendrils.

"What's it for?"

"To climb up out of the velo garage."

"Not strong enough," said Hara. She chose a thick vine from the pile at Jog's side. With strong, brown fingers, she wove it into Jog's work. She took a knife from her pocket to strip the bark from another vine, revealing strong but pliant fibres inside. She used them to bind the ends of the rope securely.

"How'd you do that?" said Rafu.

"O showed me. It's a great way to tie things tight."

More stripped branches secured the rope to the trunk of the birch tree.

One by one the guys swarmed down their rope to play hide-and-seek among the dusty velos, until breathless and filthy, they agreed that they were all hungry.

Hom was quite sure Gran could pull together a meal for seven people.

Maintaining their cautious routine, they arrived one-by-one at the back door. Rafu was last because he had taken a moment to check the skunk den, hoping for a glimpse of the animals. He was surprised to find his teacher, RI Lam, at the doorway talking to Kal.

In answer to his dropped jaw, she explained. "It's OK. Sor—she's Kal's mom—is my friend. I'm staying here now."

"Are you going back to school?"

Lam shook her head.

"Me neither," said Rafu.

Up in Elve's suite, the shower was already running. Hara first, and then the boys shrieking and splashing together. Rafu came late to the party and was greeted with a few snaps with wet towels which he eluded without much trouble, dropping clothes as he leaped.

Though not exactly a meal, Elve's provision of heaped flatbread with chowder and the inevitable peanut butter satisfied her famished guests.

They were a motley group. The boys wore whatever Hom had been able to find—worn, mended, faded, outgrown. Hara's alone was new, an unusual indigo. Their complexions represented a selection of the world's human hues, no one more beautiful than another.

The muted TV showed a succession of unnamed landscapes: glaciers, mountain crags, badlands, deserts. No trees or other vegetation. No animals, birds, amphibians, reptiles, or even a lowly worm. All was dead, yet beautiful in an awesome way. Nobody watched. They had seen them all before and given up guessing whether the scenes were real or manufactured.

A parade of troops and armoured vehicles heralded the beginning of H of P. Hom punched up the volume for the raucous and out-of-tune military band. Hara flinched.

The band music continued in the background as a high-hatted officer began to read from a teleprompter. Behind and to the right, a lesser female officer pointed word-by-word to a poster where this message appeared in large Arial print.

"Wrong speaking is Treason. Loyel Sitizenz of the MNWRAA are hereby reminded and warned that ANY use of ANY language other than Inglish is both offensive to Owr Preshus and Perfect Leeder and deleterious to the good order and governance of the Magnifisent and Glorius Noo Wrld Reepublik uv Azhu and de Amerikas. Wrong speaking is Treason."

Boat had settled in the recliner, Elve sat with Hom and Hara around the table. The other boys swiveled the barstools to face the TV.

The poster and reader disappeared. High-hat continued, "You have before you a person of many crimes, not the least of which is the removal of materials from his laboratory in the Reespected Ministree uv Sie-ens and Teknolojee."

The prisoner, a tall man of unusually pale skin and blond hair, was marched in leg-irons by two guards to a centre-screen position.

"This theft pales, however, in the blazing glow of his most treasonous action: he was found to perpetrate handwriting in German, the language of the RAA's most persistent enemy. He not only wrote in German, he had the gall to sign with an illegitimate name: Wolfgang von Funksender."

"Huh?" Hom was bug-eyed.

"You are now to witness the fate of a traitor to the RAA. This execution will be executed in person by Owr Preshus Leeder."

The band music swelled as OPPL took his place on an improvised throne to the left of a post sunk into a concrete platform. The sound faded and died.

The action took place on a green hill topped by a magnificent tree, tall, with an umbrella-shaped canopy.

"What's that tree?" Rafu had never seen such a tree.

"An elm," said Boat. "So rare that they were protected by government decree. Way before the RAA."

The guards bound the prisoner to the post with practised hands.

The rest of the drama unfolded with natural sound unnaturally amplified. The stomp of army boots. The prisoner's quick breathing. A sound that might have been his fluttering heart. OPPL unsheathing a short sword with metallic flourish. Grunts as guards and prisoner struggled.

The intent seemed to be to force open the prisoner's mouth and draw out his tongue. The guards hadn't counted on his vigorous resistance. The prisoner succeeded in chomping down on one guard's thumb. The guard's amplified howl raised laughter in Elve's kitchen.

OPPL moved in to slice out the offending tongue. His short stature forced him to reach in order to do the deed. In so doing, he knocked his huge hat askew, lurched off balance, and was saved from falling by alert bodyguards.

Wolfgang, spared the dismemberment, uttered his last word, "Bastards."

The guards fell upon him with truncheons. An obvious splice in the photography brought the beating to a quick close, with a last close shot of Wolfgang's bloodied carcass. The camera receded until the body appeared distantly as a cluster of red flowers on a serene hillside. The screen went black.

After the shocked silence, Boat spoke. "The whole thing is a lie. That wasn't live TV. The elm tree was still green. The leaves are all down now."

"The RAA thinks we're all stupid," said Jog.

"Stupid like a pile of rocks," said Bim.

Hom is thinking about Wolfgang von Funksender. "Gran, do you still have the pages we found in the old desk at the lakeshore house?"

"I keep forgetting to take them to O to see if she can read them. Pretty sure the language is German. O knows Dutch and might know a little German too." Elve opened a kitchen drawer. The neat sheaf of yellow pages lay inside.

Hom turned the pages looking for a signature. What he found was the initials, "WvF" on the lower right corner of each page. "Wolfgang von Funksender. That was our guy. Our radio man. He stole all that stuff from his lab. And then he got caught."

"That's what we're sposta learn," said Boat. "Don't mess with the RAA. You'll get caught."

Hara began to clear the dishes. "Why do they care so much about Inglish?"

"Maybe they don't really. But they sure wouldn't be pleased with all the little messages you're putting out there," Boat said pointedly to Elve.

"They're all in impeccable Inglish," Elve replied with elevated nose and eyebrows. "And Arial too."

Rafu was thinking of something else. "How long will it take the RAA to make everybody stupid?"

"They're working on the third generation and doing pretty well, judging by the clerks at the Emp," said Elve.

"We got out of stupid school just in time," said Bim with a grin.

Elbows on the counter, Jog was resting his chin on his fist. "Somebody making H of P hates the RAA. The cameraman made OPPL look silly. Like he could've took that part out. Where he almost lost his hat. And the part where the guard got bit."

Hara nodded. "Hope that cameraman's running away from the Holy Magic Mountain as fast as he can run."

"Maybe we can get a message to him to come and hide in the Octotrans," said Hom.

In spite of the horror of the execution, an air of confidence settled on the little group. Traitors, all of them.

54

Winter set in. Grainy snow, sparse but biting. Numbing cold. The boats were frozen into the harbour well before Aech. After the holiday, many of the fishermen tried their hand at ice fishing, an unusual pursuit for them. Hom and Boat had the knack.

Hom enjoyed fishing with Boat, but hauling their catch to Camp 46 was a killer. The entire distance had to be navigated by pushing and pulling the barrow on rutted roads. Boat still left Hom at the lakeshore house while he completed the route.

Though he built a fire under the chimney, the house was cold. He dragged the workbench near the fireplace, collected his materials, and worked there on making another radio. All the while, he kept the first one tuned for messages from Nik. Nik came in just before Aech.

"Operator N calling all Toves."

"H here," said Hom into the shiny red Oprah. "Come in, N."

"RAA threat. Mimsy."

"Gotcha."

By "Mimsy" Hom understood that Nik was nervous about his personal safety. Or maybe about the wisdom of further digging in the Octotrans. It was clear at any rate that Nik was recommending caution.

Two more "Mimsy" messages came through early in the new year. Then silence.

In spite of the cold, Hom completed a second radio fixed with a ComD sender. It was good enough to communicate with Kal. They exchanged cryptic messages. Enough to know that the Toves were quiet. Nik seemed to be out of the picture. No one was ready to take his place.

Hom kept warm by trekking outdoors to explore the surroundings. He hoped to see the white-tailed stag again. His hope was disappointed. What he did see was a plethora of cottontails. The rabbits popped up ahead of him whatever path he took. Recalling his rabbit skin leggings, he undertook to hunt them. He fashioned a slingshot from a stretchy polybag and a forked stick. He became expert in felling the creatures.

Boat knew how to skin and dress them. The meat was a welcome replacement for Sprem in Elve's household and those of her friends. Hom took the entrails to the Statesfield cats as often as he could. Roon became tame enough to come to him for pets even before he dealt out the food.

Skunk scat around the feeding area proved that others were enjoying Hom's generosity. He never saw them, but supposed that when they came out to feed, the cats wisely gave way.

The condo on Miller's Lane became a *de facto* school. Elve did her best to extend what could be known from "The Books" into a reasonable curriculum for her students. History, natural science, stories, and writing. In the unit next door, Lam undertook to teach the guys all she knew of mathematics and geography, which her students took in hungrily. She undertook sex-ed as well. She saw the boys' puzzled awareness of Hara's puberty and ignorance of their own.

Hara made sure there was singing every day, usually after lunch. Jog improvised percussion devices to provide the beat for it all. An old plastic pail made a pretty good drum. Bones, so easily found, served well as clappers. Finger snaps, knee-slaps, table thumps, there was no end of percussive alternatives.

When Hom and Boat visited bearing meat and news, Elve and her students greeted them joyously. They abandoned book-learning for science in the kitchen. The arts of butchering, of peeling and slicing, of simmering and seasoning found ready pupils.

Elve was challenged to find enough plates and bowls for the rabbit stew, but somehow it was done. Aech offered no feasting like these occasions.

Hom continued to take sections of Holy Bible with him to study in the chill of the boat's cabin. A tiny solar lantern provided light. Its glow was enclosed on three sides and could be hidden altogether by a sliding panel.

Sometimes footfalls on the dock made hiding the light advisable. But the policing was sporadic. A frozen rabbit carcass kept on hand just in case proved a more than adequate bribe.

After Aech, the snows fell in earnest. Depths unheard of in living memory clogged the streets. The summer failures of the ancient sewage system were matched by complete ineptitude in winter snow removal. A city without local government failed on all scores of civic services. But that was the way of the RAA. The people sighed and shovelled.

Hom and Boat were stuck at the docks. Before pedestrians had made good paths through the mounds of soft snow, a quick thaw followed by a freeze turned the mounds into icy mountains. Ice fishing had become difficult and the transport of the catch to Camp 46 impossible.

Boat chose to stay put. A knee injured in his youth was now reminding him that it had never quite recovered. Hom made the necessary runs to the Emp and a few treks to Miller's Lane. He upgraded Boat's radio with materials he'd brought in his pockets from the lakeshore house.

Hom took the second radio home to Elve. Elve was pleased, but it was Bim who took to it, calling Hom every morning for an update. He figured out how to tune it and mark the frequencies for Kal, O, and Lem as well as Hom. The Toves had a functional, if primitive, network. Nik remained silent.

And then, the great thaw. Nights and days of heavy rain wore down the ice, but slowly. Rivers raced through the city skirting the icy heights, flowing where water had never coursed before. The torrents swept debris from many sources: garbage dumps, jerrybuilt sheds, even the skull cairns.

Citizens corralled floating debris to construct rafts but few of these vessels were sea-worthy. Brave ones drowned trying to navigate the waters.

As fiercely as had the snow and the rain, the sun began a merciless attack. The melting ice contributed to the new waterways, breaking in chunks and forming dams that crunched and clattered.

In a few weeks, all subsided. The dams broke up; the rivers seeped away; the debris heaped itself in new configurations. Creeks returned to their beds, gurgling as if nothing had happened. The mud left by the erstwhile rivers dried and hardened. People made their way along these new roads, finding useful shortcuts.

Hom and Boat took Old Girl out into the placid lake. Catching a breeze under a tender blue sky, they set their nets.

"Time to haul," Boat yelled at his first mate, who was reading a fragment of *Micah*. Hom secured the prophet's pages with a rock before jumping to his post. They pulled in nets bulging with silvery catch.

"Waw-waw," yelled Hom. "We've never caught so many."

As they neared the lakeshore house, the sagging dock dipped perhaps a little more, but appeared to have survived the winter's ravages well enough. The bare willow branches provided less cover than they would wish as they brought Old Girl alongside. Better than nothing, and the willows would be the first to leaf out as spring came on.

Bound again for the Long Branch docks, Old Girl sailed easily while her crew munched Cook's fresh buttered biscuits. A faultless day marred only by the presence of whiteships, a menacing trio high in the sky.

55

Except for H of P, which continued to laud the RAA and announce niggling new regs, the authorities seemed extraordinarily quiet that spring. There were no reappearances of the arrowhead ships. Whiteships were rare in the sky. The necessary police personnel to enforce the new regs seemed to be lacking. For instance, although there was to be no more cooking on the dock (an arbitrary interference in the sailors' way of life), after the first inspection no one came to monitor the situation. Dockside barbecuing soon resumed as if the reg had never been issued.

Two moons after Equinox, evenings had warmed and lengthened. Hom loaded two fresh rabbit carcasses into a tough polybag fitted as a backpack with braided sisal straps. A Porgel sac held the cats' meal of fish and rabbit guts. He set out for Miller's Lane.

A new path now cut around Tory Station. Hom took a side track to look at the track bed and Adit 68. There were no signs that anyone was working there. Rich vegetation was taking over the track bed and hiding the Troves' entrance. Hom wondered about Nik's fate. Imprisoned or disappeared. Silenced.

On the path again, he met others in ones and twos. He exchanged the required greeting, universally truncated to a mumbled "Glordyraw". The mumble matched dull eyes and discouraged posture. All seemed burdened: bundles and baskets on head or in hand, toddlers tethered by sisal harnesses. A few young mothers with infants tied to their backs. Middle-aged and older adults, because younger people were all in the Magnificent People's Republican Military Force.

Hom traveled quickly, skirting mud holes and scattered debris. A steady south wind pushed at his back. In spite of its chill, he shed his tunic, freeing the swing of coin, wing, and spoon. The moon rose in silvery fullness to light his way.

Just outside Elve's building a lithe figure darted out of the Roons and began to run northwards on Miller's Lane.

Hom recognized the silhouette. "Rafu," he called. "What're you doing here?"

Rafu stopped and turned. "Watching the skunks and other night life. Lots of stuff happens in the Roons at night. I gotta get home. Ma doesn't know I went out."

"You think. Bet she knows and doesn't know how to stop you."

"Maybe. She kinda lets me do what I like."

The two boys walked on together.

"She knows you come to Gran's every day?"

"Yup. She knows Lam. Knows Lam teaches better than school. Ma trusts me more than my brothers. They're almost ready to join the RAA and getting more like soldiers all the time. Meaner, bossier. Try to enforce all the regs."

"Skunks are better company."

"Slootly."

"Coming to my birthday?"

"When?"

"Not sure. Maybe couple more sundowns. Whenever Gran's ready."

"I'll be around." Rafu took off, waving, bounding up the road like the whitetail deer.

Hom plopped his backpack on Elve's counter.

"Got a couple rabbits for my birthday," he said. "Got the guts for the cats too."

"We shall have a feast," said Gran. "Rabbit stew and flatbread. Dandelion greens."

"Raisin cake?"

"Absolutely! It's a tradition." Elve in the old recliner pulled down the boy's head to rub his cheek against hers and sneak a hint of a kiss.

Hom went to stash his offerings into the fridge. "Hey, this fridge is cold!"

"Yup. We've got better power than I ever remember. Kal installed a bank of solar chips on the roof. The RAA has made them available in quantity so that nobody misses H of P. They brag about it every night."

"H of P. Heaps of Poop. Don't believe any of it." Hom already had the peanut butter jar and bread out of the cupboard.

"Still, it's important to watch. Need to know what they're on about. The new regs, so you know how to be careful."

"Yeah, I guess. So Kal is doing lots of stuff around the building?"

"Kal is a genius. Has the water working too. No more piddling stream from the taps. Slootly glor!"

"He needs to be careful," said Hom, thinking of Nik.

Day 9 was chosen for Hom's birthday celebration. The usual guests were invited. Added to the list were Lam, and Kal. The guys too, of course. It was perhaps dangerous to invite Grandma Jema, a dedicated pucer.

"Did you get the Birthday Licence Number, Gran?"

"Hara got it, no prob. The RAA believes in birthdays. Your right as a Loyel Sitizen. You know, now that you're twelve, you're sposta make a speech about accepting your sacred responsibility as a citizen of the Magnificent New World Republic."

"I'll make a speech all right. I got lots to say."

"Remember. . .Grandma Jema. . ."

Hom bit his lip. He knew he should be careful. He didn't want to be careful.

With a Birthday Licence Number, there was no worry about the gathering of too many unrelated people. At sundown, they began to arrive, bearing food. Jema brought two kinds of excellent cheese and sweet stewed rhubarb. The dishes multiplied. Fresh bannock, Hara's berry preserve, yogurt, soya cakes, dandelion greens and other kinds too, rice, plain and herbed. The *pièce de resistance,* rabbit stew. The raisin cake, of course. Some had brought plates and spoons too, knowing they would be in short supply.

Uncle Odro had exercised his privilege of seeking new and better sexual satisfaction, leaving Doro with the twins. Bez and Boz were now proper schoolboys with regulation blue tunics and earlobe haircut.

Boat was out on the balcony grilling four fine fish. Elve and Jema were setting out food on the counter. Jog struck up a beat on the old plastic pail. Bim and Rafu soon picked it up, weaving their claps and foot stamps into Jog's rhythm. Hara soon offered a three-note call—"Happy Birthday"—echoed by the others and repeated with variations.

Bez and Boz huddled in a corner, heads down, looking out from under furrowed brows at the older children and their strange noise.

The noise continued until Elve sang out, "Come. All is ready."

Hom took the place of honour at the head of the table. The adults, including Lam, took the other chairs. The barstools at the counter accommodated the four guys. Kal took the recliner. Bez and Boz sat in the corner where they felt safe from the unaccustomed proceedings.

Elve asked Jema to pronounce grace. She did so fervently with uplifted eyes and hands. Hom felt a welling of gratitude, not to the RAA and Owr Preshus Leeder, but to Boat and Gran and his friends.

Bez and Boz raised their hands and murmured the grace with their grandmother. They were well schooled in its phrases.

In the midst of the feasting, a knock at the door silenced everyone. To be safe, they should be watching H of P. Jema moved quickly to turn on the set. Boat went to the door.

A shout of relief and welcome went up. It was Nura, all the way from Camp 46. In six years, she had achieved a rank that was allowed certain privileges, such as a few hours leave from the camp. She enveloped Hom in a joyous hug.

Jema sat stone-faced. Her disapproval didn't make much difference to anyone except Bez and Boz, who mirrored her expression.

Nura took her plate to the corner and made her peace with her young nephews. They relaxed into the ease they'd always known with her. Apparently, they forgave her lapse from RAA-approved behaviour.

After Hom blew out twelve birthday candles with one magnificent exhalation, a cry went up for the speech.

Hom stood up. He reached into his back pocket and pulled out a package—a roll of pages wrapped in soft rabbit skin. A scroll of sorts. He untied its red string and straightened the rolled pages. The paper was a little yellowed, with pencilled diagrams on the back.

"This is a story," he said. "It's really old. From a time way before the old time that Gran and Boat lived in. Hundreds and thousands of suns ago."

He began to read.

> The hand of the Lord was upon me, and carried me out in the spirit of the Lord, and set me down in the midst of the valley which was full of bones.
> And caused me to pass by them round about: and behold there were very many in the open valley; and, lo, they were very dry.

The pages rolled themselves back up in his hand, but Hom continued, "This guy was Ezekiel and this was maybe a dream. The Lord God was speaking to him and he heard God ask, 'Son of man, do you think these bones can live?' And Zeke said, 'Lord God, you know. Not me.'

"And God told Zeke, 'Tell these dry bones, O you dry bones. Hear the word of the Lord. I will make you breathe and you will live. And I will put sinews and flesh and skin on you and you will live and you will know that I am the Lord.'

"And Zeke did it. He prophesied to the dry bones. And there was this humongous rattling. And the bones joined together in all the right ways and made skeletons. And they grew sinews and fat and then the skin. But there was no breath in them.

"And God said, 'Zeke, call the four winds to put breath in these dead people.' And Zeke did, and the people began to breathe and they were alive."

Hom wiped the glisten of sweat from his forehead. He laid down the scroll.

"And God said, 'These are all the people of Israel. They say their bones are dried up and their hope is lost. Tell them I will put my spirit in them and they will live and I will give them back their country.'

"And Zeke prophesied. He said, 'You will get your country back.'

The Lord God has spoken it.'"

In the hushed space, a soft click. The door. Grandma Jema had left.

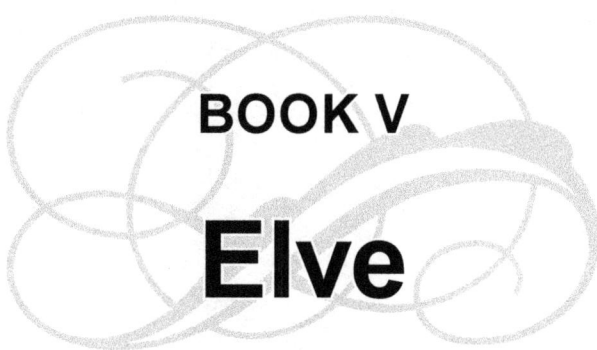

BOOK V
Elve

56

An early morning sky, purest blue, a woolly flock grazing high above. Elve leaned on her balcony rail, inhaling great breaths of coolness. It was her birthday. Or close to it. She had tried to keep track throughout the RAA's changes to the calendar, but might have lost a day or so. At any rate, it was midsummer and four full moons since the spring equinox.

Eighty-two. She'd escaped punishment for her resistance to the RAA's plan to exterminate her on her eightieth. She wondered if anyone noticed that she hadn't shown up for the party.

It was Day 5, she was sure of that. Hara always wrote the next day's number on the chalkboard before she went to bed. Hara was already up and off to check on O in the ravine. Elve had an hour of peace before Rafu would arrive for lessons. She would read the Ninetieth Psalm. It seemed suitable somehow.

She paused to inspect the houseplants inside the balcony glass. The aloe vera still flourished after all these years. An African violet seemed to be distressed: Elve moved it into better light. The pothos couldn't be contained. Leafy tendrils descended over the edge of the pot. When they reached the floor, Elve would cut them back ruthlessly, which would discourage the plant not at all.

Plants are so rewarding, she thought. Just soil, light, water, and they thrive. Deny them and they survive anyway, ready to recover if conditions improve. Like us. Elve smiled wryly.

The big room was rather dark now, as every available bit of wall had been painted black. There was just enough chalkboard to give each student a space. Lali's map took pride of place beside the TV screen. Large as a newsprint sheet of old, clear, and, by contrast with Elve's poor effort, detailed and in proper proportion. All the students studied it avidly.

Real chalk had become available in the Emp. Why, no one knew. It made as much sense as the writing machines without paper. Elve supposed that someone with influence in the Reespected Ministree of Proekyuerment and Distribueshun had chalk to sell.

Elve was finishing her bowl of porridge when Rafu knocked. He was still a daily attendee because of his interest in combing Elve's books for every bit of information about the natural world that they afforded. As Hom returned portions of Holy Bible that he'd studied to his satisfaction, Rafu claimed them for his own study. His summers with the RAAGERS seemed to have affected him very little. He had turned the hikes and canoe voyages designed to toughen him for service to the RAA into opportunities to study the natural world.

His absence from school removed him from the camp selection process. Like Bim and Jog, he wasn't missed. The older boys were more occasional students. They were spending most of their time in the Roons, enlarging the hideout and furnishing it with the comforts of home. They improved their access to the velo garage and the Statesfield entrance to the Octotrans by the addition of sturdy rope ladders.

After Hara complained that their makeshift latrine behind the wall stank to high heaven, they undertook to fashion something better in the area watered by the fountain. Jog took credit for an arrangement of piped water, elevated tank, a pit, a seat, and a pipe leading to a deeper pit. Forsythia gone wild afforded shelter and privacy.

The boys found the elements for these home improvements in the vintage velos. By the light of solar lanterns, they took them apart, sorted the pieces, found uses for many, and kept all in reserve for unforeseen needs.

"What're you reading today?" Elve asked, rinsing out her porridge bowl. Rafu had settled at the table with most of Holy Bible along with the blue schoolbook, which Lali had recently returned.

"I'm doing the HB parts that they used in the Blue Book. A bunch of sections about living things. All in The Book of Matthew. Like this one: The foxes have holes and the birds of the air have nests... What do you know about foxes? Did they used to live in Tranna?"

"I think foxes lived in the ravines and maybe in the wild park. I never saw one myself. But I've seen pictures. Rusty red, like Anne of Green Gables, with big bushy tails."

"Like squirrels?"

"Bigger than squirrels. So many animals died out in the decades of drought, and I don't know which ones have recovered."

"The skunks are OK," Rafu said with a grin.

"O will know. We'll ask her."

Rafu continued his reading while Elve blanched tomatoes and peeled them for sauce. She noticed with satisfaction how easily he dealt with Trad. Bim and Jog were still labouring with it, and she'd been tempted to rewrite difficult passages in Inglish for them.

The tomatoes were beginning to boil when Rafu leapt to his feet and dived into the tin box, no longer hidden, but left in a corner where all the students could get into it. He came up with the Anne book, mended now, but still showing the red-haired girl with her carpetbag.

"I found it! The part Anne was talking about. The picture of Christ blessing little children. It's in The Book of Luke." He leafed through the paperback, looking for the passage. He found it in Chapter VIII, 'Anne's Bringingup Is Begun.'

Elve pulled up a chair beside the boy. Together they compared Anne's imagined encounter with Christ and Luke's account of Jesus inviting children to come for his blessing. Elve was able to reconcile the names 'Christ' and 'Jesus'.

"It's all the same guy," she said. "After he was killed, the writers called him 'Christ'. And sometimes 'Jesus Christ'."

"Why?"

"Why was he killed?"

"Why did they change his name?"

"Not sure. I hafta read the books again to figure it out."

Rafu turned to the Anne book again, scanning the pages for references to Holy Bible. There were a few embedded in the stories of Sunday school and church and ministers. Rafu asked innumerable questions about these unfamiliar aspects of early 20th century society. Elve, while forcing the sauce through a dilapidated sieve, answered as best she could. She dredged up long-forgotten details from her years of wandering in the digital universe. We could find out anything, she thought ruefully, but we remembered nothing.

"I found another one!" Rafu yelled. "Marilla calls it 'The Lord's Prayer'. It's in Matthew's book, where Jesus tells all his followers the right way to pray. Marilla had it on a card and Anne had to learn it. What's praying?"

Elve cast about for a good answer. The RAA's required grace at meals was a prayer of sorts, but not one she wanted to set up as an example. Praying, if it was discussed at all in her younger days, was regarded as something that superstitious or ignorant people used to do in superstitious and ignorant times, rather long ago. Yet she supposed that her most intense wishes, as those for Mungo and Max—pleas for their safety, their happiness, their return—qualified as prayers, though she didn't consciously address them to any name.

Rafu was still looking at her. Elve felt a keen obligation. This boy should have her best truth. He deserved that from her.

"I—I don't know what to tell you. But I'll think about it."

"OK. I'll read the Anne book again. Anne prays quite a bit." Rafu packed up the books in the tin box. He took a piece of new chalk and went next door for Lam's math instruction.

As soon as Hara was home, she went down with Elve to begin clearing out Pen's apartment. There appeared to be no one else to take on the task, and Pen had clearly designated a few items as her legacy to the resistance: her radio, a box of old papers, vintage kitchen and workshop tools that Ovid had garnered in his adventures in the midden.

The latter they took up to Elve's, planning as they worked how these items should be distributed. Kal and Boat should have their pick of the heavy tools. Elve claimed the sieve.

"I really need that," she said.

Hara had her eye on the large shears. "I could use those," she said. "In my gardens." Hara had garden spots at O's place and in the Roons.

Elve confessed, "I feel odd. Not quite right. To be picking over all Pen's stuff so soon after she died."

"It all happened so fast. She seemed OK when I taked down the veggies in the morning. Not well, of course, but no worse than usual."

"And gone already when Kal checked in the evening. Died in that chair. I don't think she ever went to bed any more. Too much trouble."

"Her breathing was so bad. Can you die of that?"

"Oh, I think so. The heart gives out when it has no oxygen." Elve chastised herself yet again for failing to remember the multitude of facts she had once looked up but never committed to memory.

"Did you see her after. . .?" Hara had spent that night at Fel's doing kidwatch.

"Kal called me down. She looked peaceful enough. No sign of struggle or pain."

"What do you do after…?"

They both knew that O might leave them at any time. Hara would find her in the hideout, or under a chokecherry bush, or collapsed by the creek with a fishing line.

"Kal went out and found the patrol. Not Dum and Dee. The late patrol. The officer used her Apsam to call the Death Brigade. They come in a velovan and take the body away for cremation. It's done within hours."

"So they know. The Office of Citizenship and Documentation."

"I expect so."

"Will they claim the apartment?"

"They allow two days for family to clean it out. We're sposta have it washed and ready for new tenants." Elve sniffed. "So I guess we'd better work faster."

Kal brought Ovid's old cart to the door. Elve and Hara chucked buckets of trash into it. Sprem cans, dirty rags, broken dishes, holed pots, dead light bulbs, worn-out kitchen appliances, piles of Porgel packaging.

A couple of long outdated electronics lurked under the bed under discarded garments. They had escaped the RAA's sweep of electronics after Franklin's Folly.

"Let's keep these," said Hara. "Bim and Jog will take them apart to see how they worked."

"Kal, too. He's no slouch in figuring how to make things work."

Except for a few rags deemed beyond redemption, the two saved fabric of all kinds. Hara made three piles: dirty but useable; clean but worn out; clean and whole garments.

They worked in near silence, occasionally consulting each other about dubious items. Elve was inclined to save everything, an inclination shaped by twenty years of empty shelves at the Emp. Hara, accustomed to comparative plenty, was ruthless in discarding junk.

Elve's mind was only half occupied. It was Day 5, Jema's usual day to visit. But Jema hadn't shown up since the night of Hom's birthday celebration. Fear mixed with regret and longing lodged somewhere in her belly, or maybe in her brain. It seemed to wander, this amalgam of misery.

The afternoon was far spent. "I'm exhausted," Elve announced, collapsing into Pen's huge chair. "I can't do any more." She plucked a clean towel from the 'worn-out' pile to wipe away the sweat dripping from her temples.

Hara, experienced now in gauging the strength of her elderly friends, agreed to call it a day. They collected as much as they could carry and headed for the elevator.

Kal had worked one of his miracles on the aged machine. Though it rattled and groaned, it functioned reliably. Kal operated it with a key. He confined its use severely.

Hara went to ask for Kal's help. Elve leaned on the wall. The young people returned, Kal ready with the key. From the pimply gangler of a year ago, Kal had become a tall, sinewy frame. The work and responsibility sat well on his shoulders. He was a man.

"Need help with that?" For Elve had dropped her load on the floor. At her feeble nod, he gathered up the stuff and ascended with the women to Elve's place on the third floor.

"Want to stay for a bite? We have rabbit stew." Hara's invitation was warmed by her one-eyed smile. For Kal, the smile had its own peculiar charm.

"I gotta go home. My mom works late and I make supper for her."

Hara promptly dished up rabbit stew for two and pressed it into his hands. She was rewarded with a radiant grin and the ever so slight pressure of Kal's hands on hers as he accepted the gift.

Elve noted the exchange. "Hara is just fourteen."

Kal nodded. He understood.

Hara, tired too from a long day, went to bed with the sun. Elve took a folding chair to sit on the balcony. Behind the line of blasted spruce, the sunset dispersed its streamers of rose and gold, gilding all the sky as far as she could see. The hot day had subsided into a balmy, sweet-scented evening. She sighed.

She counted her losses. The foolish dream of writing her precious books in Inglish and spreading them everywhere. Just to broadcast the knowledge that the world is eons older than the RAA. That life can be different from the one prescribed by the regime. If only.

Jema. Caught in the RAA's web of lies. How could it happen? She'd found out how to work the system, to reap its rewards, to garner its honours. To sense how authorities would look the other way when it suited them. After all, with her lame leg, she should have been eliminated long ago.

Mungo. O my son, my son. So clear of mind, so full of truth. Where are you?

Of Max she dared not think. She knew so little, and feared so much.

She missed Hom too. He spent so much of his time with Boat and in the woods at the lakeshore house. The Troves had revived their night forays into the Octotrans. Another thing to keep him away from her. But he might turn up at any time, still her beloved Hom.

Elve's thought diverted from its yearning path into the stream of blessing. There was still Boat, after all. Loyal old Boat who came regularly with fish and rabbit and the odd squirrel. They repaired to the bedroom still. Elve thought with a smile how their utilitarian congress had become tender, a precious comfort.

And her web of friends: O and Lali, Fel and Lam, Sor, Kal and old Lem. Pen, who'd left her treasures, everything she had. And the kids. She mustn't forget Bim and Jog and Rafu—so clear-eyed and energetic. The RAA could never squelch them. And Hara—already a young woman of wonderful vigour and capability—and so kind. Kind in her very nature.

Not like me, thought Elve. I had to learn kindness. To apply kind principles in an intellectual way. And sometimes I still forget.

A rueful smile curled Elve's lips. A new problem. Kal's evident warmth toward Hara and the girl's innocent receptiveness. Life always threw a curve just when you thought you'd achieved some sort of equilibrium.

'Threw a curve.' An odd phrase, Elve thought. Its literal meaning lost in time.

57

Hara lugged a yellowed Styrofoam box from Pen's unit. It was the last thing. "I don't know what to do with it," she said, setting it on the table.

"I've been wondering about that," said Elve, giving the dishcloth a vicious wring. "Pen told me she had a box of old newspapers—really old, she said. Where was it?"

"It was tucked under her big chair. The fringe covered it."

"That chair kept a lot of secrets. Let's look."

Though chipped at all its corners, the box was in pretty good shape. Elve knew that such boxes had once been used for picnics. She'd seen a few others in her lifetime. "This stuff never breaks down," she said, "At least, as long as you use it gently."

Hara fingered the torn label on its side. " 'ERCULES' What's that?"

"Guess it was a HERCULES. The brand name. I'll explain brands another time." Elve was eager to get into the cooler. She couldn't dislodge the lid with her fingers, so resorted to using a kitchen knife. The lid yielded with squealing protest.

"Funny stuff." Surprised by its lightness, Hara almost dropped the lid.

"This is it! The papers. Pen said they were collected by her great-granddaddy. But I think she was kidding."

The topmost paper was discoloured to a brownish black, and the print was indecipherable. It fell into fragments under Hara's fingers. Several layers disintegrated in the same way. Elve and Hara removed handfuls of fragments before reaching a layer that could be lifted out, deeply yellowed, but intact except for its fragile edges. Elve laid the paper reverently on the table. It appeared to actually be a bundle of papers folded together.

"It's a newspaper, I think." Elve knew more about the Dead Sea scrolls and Babylonian tablets than she knew about newspapers. As far as she was concerned, all were equally obsolete types of communication. *Toronto Star* in large letters across the top of the page meant little. She didn't even relate "Toronto" to the "Tranna" she knew.

But the significance of the date didn't escape –Thursday, October 23, 2014. Over 1000 years ago. Not Fel's great granddaddy, but his great granddaddy's great granddaddy must have collected these papers. Elve couldn't calculate the generations that must have passed in the millennium. This paper was very nearly as old as her books.

The headline read "UNDER SIEGE" and more large print announced "PARLIAMENT HILL UNDER ATTACK." A photo showed uniformed men bent over a stretcher. One man wore a pale green jacket marked "PARAMEDIC".

"Assault shocks Ottawa and the nation as gunman kills soldier," Hara read aloud. Elve had never heard of this long-ago event.

Carefully, they turned the bundle to read below the fold. Hara read, not Elve, who had accepted that she could no longer see fine print.

A young man was pictured holding a dog. "The soldier was Nathan Cirillo," said Hara. "Why is he holding that animal?"

"We used to have dogs. They lived with us in our homes, and we fed them and petted them. People loved their dogs. Cats too. And other pets. Birds, iguanas, mice—but dogs were special. They were like family." Looking at the photo, Elve sensed the soldier's love for his dog.

"We had a dog when the kids were little. A silly mutt we called Spook." Elve felt her throat constrict.

"What happened him?"

"The RAA outlawed pets. Said that their presence was 'deleterious to kids' health. The care and maintenance of pets detracted from the proper care and maintenance of the RAA's youngest 'Loyel Sitizenz'. The trucks came, and the officers took them all away. They took Spook away."

"That was so cruel. If they were family."

"For a while there was new meat at the Emp. 'Savorpoo' and 'Savorpug.' Others too."

Hara shuddered. "It must have been awful."

"It was." Elve suddenly sat down. She shook her head and drew breath. "What else is in there?"

Hara laid aside the folded newspaper to bring out the next layer. It was similarly fragile at the edges, but otherwise well preserved. "**The Royal Wedding**" read the banner over a beautiful young couple, their smiles competing with the brilliance of their costumes. The date: Saturday, April 30, 2011.

Hara was transfixed. She had never seen such opulence. The grandiosity of the RAA ran to the elevation of military hats and a profusion of insignia. Flowers and drapery decked the officials' lecterns, but cathedrals and red carpets were not in evidence in the TV productions of the RAA. Day 10 gatherings were decorated only by super-size posters of OPPL.

It crossed Elve's mind to wonder why. Why wouldn't the RAA adopt the trappings of the republics and royalty of the past? Maybe none of the people in charge happened to study the relevant history. Between the silos of knowledge built by any person's Galaxy exploration lay chasms of ignorance. Information seldom or never accessed by anyone in Galaxy's uncharted wealth.

They pressed on to lift the remaining papers out of the box. Beneath **"Final Farewell"**, an issue devoted to the death of a pope (Saturday April 9, 2005), they came upon a different sort of publication: three booklets with the name, *Maclean's*. "Mack-leen's" said Hara.

These were printed on a different, glossier paper and were better preserved than the newspapers. Their smaller format had protected their edges within the bed of newspapers. The pages were only slightly yellowed.

A 2005 issue titled "**LEADERS AND DREAMERS;** CANADA'S GREATEST INNOVATORS AND HOW THEY CHANGED THE WORLD." featured photos of supposedly important Canadians. Not one face was familiar to Elve. But the picture of a zipper rang a bell.

Zippers! What had become of zippers? She recalled them from her childhood on her grandmothers' cotton knit sweaters. Sweaters they wore until the cuffs were in tatters and the hoods frayed at the edges. Grandma Atlanta salvaged zippers from worn-out garments and installed them in Elve's new ones, replacing the ubiquitous Velcro closings. Frog and toggle closings came later.

Hara was turning pages. "Why are all the men wearing their funeral clothes?" she said, pointing to the dark suits, collars, and colourful neckties. The regs for Ritual Funerals were clear: suit and tie for the male to be deceased and his male attendants; floor-length gowns for females and their attendants.

Elve recalled a photo she had once run across in Galaxy. A group of twenty-odd sepia-toned gentlemen, seated or standing near a table on which lay a large document and quill pen. Solemn dignity invested every pose and physiognomy. Every one was garbed in a dark suit, high white collar, and narrow bow tie. No date or title embellished Elve's recollection.

"Long ago, I think, important men wore funeral clothes—not just for funerals. For solemn occasions. And when they needed to demonstrate power." She recognized for the first time how the photo was a representation of power.

"But now the clothes are just for guys who're gonna die." Hara shook her head in wonderment and lifted out another *Maclean's*.

"Who's this?" The November, 2013 issue bore a picture of a white-haired brownish man with grizzled beard.

"That's Suzuki. The Prophet of the Great Disaster. He predicted the age of natural disasters that came along soon after he was dead. A long time ago now. But that's when the earth lost many of the animals, and the people came streaming from the hot countries into

North America and Northern Europe. Caravans of thousands. Most died in their tracks, we're told."

"ENVIRONMENTALISM HAS FAILED: David Suzuki loses faith in the cause of his lifetime." Hara read from the cover. "What was his 'cause'?"

"Saving trees was big. Stop using gas and oil. Stop polluting the air and the oceans."

Hara looked mystified. Elve had some knowledge in this field, and wanted to expand on David Suzuki's environmentalism. But another time.

"I wish I had those," she said, pointing to the lenses in front of Suzuki's eyes. Neither she nor Hara had ever seen eyeglasses, laser techniques having replaced them long since. But Elve thought they had once been common, even for relatively poor people.

"Would they fix my white eye?"

"Oh, my dear. I'm afraid not. I think the lenses improved people's vision but didn't cure anything."

Hara sighed and moved on.

The cover of the third magazine was utterly familiar. Two broken towers, grids of empty windows, against a smouldering sky. A streetlamp. And everywhere on the ground, a snowstorm of paper, small, white sheets.

"I've seen that lots of times," said Hara. "On H of P. The RAA uses it to show their military victories. When they've squelched 'a small but virulent rebel group. Disloyel peepel who fail to show their devotion to the RAA'."

"Oh, yeah. They always say that Sekuerity Consideraeshuns prevent the disclosure of the exact location of the battle." Elve examined the date on the magazine. "September 24, 2001. **SPECIAL REPORT AFTER THE TERROR.**" Something stirred in her memory. "That must be the actual 9/11. We used to mark 9/11/2001. It happened in a great city of the past. In the old country of the United States of America. I remember a solemn service streamed to huge public TVs. We went outside to watch. I was quite small at the time. I held Grandma Atlanta's hand very tight. The sounds were terrible."

"So it really happened? A thousand years ago?'

"About that."

"So war hasn't changed very much. If the pictures are still good."

Suddenly weary, Elve said, "I guess."

Hara began to pull out the remaining newspapers. A Sunday *Star* headlined "THE VICTIMS" lined up twenty photos of innocent, bright-eyed, six-year-olds with baby-toothed smiles. Dateline December 16, 2012. "A gunman shot them all," she said. "That's worse than the RAA."

Elve could only nod. She thought about how close Hom had come to being deemed ined, and therefore. . . shot? injected with poison? given as a plaything to officers? There were ugly rumours.

Hara dreaded the worst when she lifted out a heavily browned sheet showing nine young boys, most with broad smiles. But the news was good on Wednesday, July 11, 2018. ***"MISSION IMPOSSIBLE' ENDS WITH RESCUE OF 12 BOYS AND COACH FROM THAI CAVE."*** "Waw-waw, I'm glad something good happened back then,"

At the bottom of the box, the last blackened newspaper disintegrated under Hara's touch. In her hand a fragment. A photo. A red necktie. A grotesquely stretched mouth. A squinted eye and upraised fist suggesting rage. That was all.

58

Elve left Kal and Hara to finish the work on Pen's apartment. They'd decided to sweep, but not wash. The new occupants could wash it if they wanted.

Jema had moved four moons earlier. The address wasn't familiar, but the area was, and Elve thought she could find it. She had once known the streets of Rosethorn very well. Eons ago, she had canvassed them in support of a friend running for municipal office. Before municipalities lost all agency to central governance by the RAA.

A street called Loyalty Drive, though no one drove there, seemed likely. It had recently been built up with modest detached dwellings similar to Fel's house. Government houses for government officials. Number 56. Elve would start there.

Judging by the sun's progress, it was between five and six o'clock, old time. Jema should be home by now. She wouldn't want to miss H of P.

The youngster who opened the door at No. 56 pointed across the road. "Sitizen Jema lives there," she said.

Elve knocked, surprised at the apprehension gripping her belly.

Jema opened. A brief shadow crossed her face. Then, impassive, "Come in, Sitizen Elve," she said.

Two puce stripes on Jema's sleeve, a new, high (though only modestly high) hat on the shelf, the government house. Clearly, Jema had risen in the ranks. She was no mere pucer. Something with more authority. Elve's apprehension tightened.

Jema ushered her mother to a hard chair, one of three in a row along the puce-painted wall. She herself continued to stand with her back to the window so that her face was a white blob above a darkly outlined body. A heavy form with slightly uneven shoulders, Jema presented a solid, boding presence.

"So?"

"I was just wondering how you are," said Elve softly. "We haven't seen you for a couple of moons. Is everything OK?"

"More than OK. The RAA increases in efficiency and right action with every hour. We should all be filled with gratitude."

"And the little boys? Bez and Boz? Doro was worried that her new partner wouldn't take them on."

"They reside under the umbrella of the RAA's unfailing diligence in the welfare of all kids."

'Which means?"

"They are officially in my care."

"So where are they?" It was late afternoon, Elve thought. They should have been home, playing about in the house.

"It is not your concern, Sitizen Elve. They are suitably ensconced."

"For grood's sake, Jema. Cut out the official lingo. This is your mother talking. What has become of Andro's kids? Your own grandkids. And sit down where I can see you."

Jema didn't move. "All is well. The true magnificence of the RAA is its concern for the wellbeing of all Sitizenz. There are no exceptions."

Elve had been prepared for a scolding. For an enumeration of her sins— not saying grace properly, for growing flowers—whatever. There were lots of other infractions. But not for the denial of their family relationship. Or for this robotic rehearsal of RAA propaganda. "You've gone mad, Jema. They've done something to your mind."

Jema moved now. Moved so that her face was illuminated by the western sun. "Oh yes, oh yes. I have seed the glory. We move towards the excellent fulfillment of our Deer Leeder's Promises. I am a privileged sitizen of this new age."

"Hmph. Privileged, yes." Elve suspected then that Jema's "black market" offerings were foods that she now, as an officer of the RAA, accessed legally. She stood up.

"Before you depart," said her daughter, "there's something you should be looking after. Without delay."

Elve registered the embedded threat.

"Good-bye, Jema." Without thinking, she reached for Jema's hands in their old gesture of affection.

Jema drew back primly. She smiled as at an unseemly child. "Only the RAA. Love only the RAA."

Elve turned home, the sun burning in her eyes, its heat still heavy on her limbs. She took a path into welcome shade where three skull cairns stood sentry on the dead. The first had lost a number of its components, whether by accident or design, so that a seat was formed in its side. All was covered in moss and vines; no bones were visible under the veil, and none lay errant in the path.

She dropped gratefully onto the mossy seat.

She recalled her sweet brown lass, stubborn, quick to anger, yet just as quick to make amends, to forgive, to dissolve dissension with merriment. Yes, Jema was the funny one. She made her brothers laugh.

It was after Max and Mungo were taken away that merriment faded, Elve thought. Always a conscientious child, Jema became preternaturally diligent in learning the precepts of the RAA. She became solemn, hard-working, and humourless. Was it that thing—what was it called—Sweden something? Something Syndrome. As usual, Elve's memory of her long ago Galaxy searches yielded fragments of dubious information. Sweden or maybe Oslo. Where hostages developed a bond with their captors and took on the kidnappers' cause. A necessary tactic for survival while under threat of death, she thought.

That was it for Jema. Love the RAA. Keep its commandments. Gain favour. Protect herself from liquidation. How much did she know at that time, Elve wondered, about the RAA's summary disposal of defective children?

"I tried to keep her from being afraid," Elve said to the trees. "I tried, but I had to make sure she was careful too. Never let the pain show. Stand up straight. Walk like a soldier." So I lost her either way.

She licked salt from dry lips and realized that she had been weeping.

59

The three flights of stairs were undoubtedly getting steeper. Elve grasped the wobbly handrails to drag her way up. A heartening aroma wafted under her door.

"Hom!"

Hom stood at the cooker, spatula in hand, turning a mix of fish, rice, and carrots in the wok. "I was hungry, so I got supper started. Knew you'd be home. Wouldn't miss H of P for anything."

"OK, Saucebox. You know we need to keep abreast of the regs, even if we don't plan to observe them." Elve washed her hands in a tiny stream. Saving water was still ingrained. She filled the boiler for tea.

"Dear Gran. You are a first-class heretic. Where's your true belief in the beneficence of the RAA?" Hom grinned and raised his hands in mock worship.

"I never had any true belief. I haven't diverged one bit from my hope in truth and decency. When the RAA lied—watch what you're doing with that spatula."

Hom scooped the fallen rice back into the wok. Judging that the food was ready, he began to serve up two platesful.

"Save some for Hara. She should be in soon."

"Where is she?"

So Elve explained about Pen's death and the necessary work in her unit. "We have her radio. Probably better than ours. I'll give it to Bim to study and maybe break up for parts."

"Or use as is and improve the others. Radios are popping up all over Tranna. The Troves have a great network now. We have the Octopus clear all the way to Steeltown."

"Who organizes it now?"

"Another guy from the docks. We got lots of fishermen in the gang."

"Boat too?"

"Sure thing."

"Silly old geezer. He should take better care of himself."

H of P droned in the background as they ate and talked. A reiteration of hair length regs and condemnation of female head coverings.

Elve touched her rose-and-blue polybag head-wrap. She didn't take it off.

Early apples from the ravine served as dessert. Elve and Hom took them to the balcony. They bit into the crisp fruit and leaned elbows on the rail.

Sunlight sifted through piled cloud, gold-lighting the broken edges to send a spray of lights into the sky's blue bowl. "The heavens declare the glory. . ." Elve murmured.

The Roons stood silent and brooding, its crumbling tower a presence, a token of old power.

The dusk was alive with sound. Crickets and tree toads. A liquid birdsong. A gusting wind that trembled the leaves of an aspen (a self-seeded upstart in the condo grounds), and swished the decorative grasses planted there long ago.

Rasping shrieks rent the evening's serenity. Two winged shapes rose from the tower, circling. The peregrines! A smaller raptor showed against the sky above the dead spruces and disappeared.

"They have young ones," said Hom. "Fledged, but not flying yet. They still need the old ones."

"Surprised they didn't take out that intruder."

"Yeah, I've seen them catch a pigeon in mid-flight and carry it off to the tower."

Hom paused. A sparrow twittered. "I'll be leaving with them in the fall."

Elve's heart dropped. "Leaving! What do you mean, leaving?"

"I gotta start sometime. There's something I hafta do. Don't know what it is yet. When I walk in the trees by the lakeshore, and when I feel the wind, I know I have work to do."

"But Hom—you're only twelve. What can a little boy like you do in this awful world?"

Hom chuckled. "Gran, you've *never* called me a little boy. I always worked and had to read hard stuff and set the sail, and haul the cart up the bank." He showed her his hands, brown, sinewy, callused.

"But"—Elve dropped her hands in a gesture of resignation, "where will you go?"

"I'll follow the peregrines south."

"To live there?" Bewildered.

"I hafta see the world. I know it isn't like the RAA says it is, but I need to see it for myself. Like, are the regs we hear on H of P really sent out over the whole world? Or is it just for us? Tranna? Are there places where the RAA isn't even doing anything? And what happens all the soldiers—the guys like Mungo that march off when they're eighteen and you never see them again?"

Elve grasped at a straw. "But you don't have good boots."

"Look at my feet, Gran." He held up a toughened sole. "I can go anywhere."

Another straw. "But the cold—"

"The winter nights were long. I saved all the rabbit and squirrel skins. Boat helped me and we made boots and a fur vest. A helmet too."

"So Boat knows you're going?"

"Yeah. Wants to come too, but he's too old, he says. But he'll take me a ways by boat. Don't care if the RAA doesn't like it. Camp 46 can do without their fish, he says."

Elve sniffed, feeling slightly peeved that these plans had developed without her knowledge. "You might have told me."

The face Hom turned to her was alight with anticipation of adventure. Whatever lay ahead, the joy of discovery would be his.

She shook her head. "I never could do a thing with you. Not since you were seven." She reached and pulled his head down to nestle under her chin. But it felt awkward, and Hom reversed the roles, cradling his little old granny's head against his chest.

"Wherever I go," he said, "I take you with me."

60

They came for her on Day 9 at dusk.

Hara, working in the garden, saw the dilapidated velovan pull up and the uniformed group proceed into the building. She saw them leave with Elve and bowed her head against her hoe as they passed.

It was a police operation, of course. A shamefaced Dum, who had accepted countless snacks from Elve's hand, was one of the arresting party. There were two others and a driver.

A bracing gust from across the Roons bathed Elve's face before they hustled her into the velovan.

Hands bound behind her back, Elve balanced on the edge of the seat, bracing her head against the driver's seat in front of her. She listened for clues. Why had they picked her up? What were the charges? Would there be charges? Would there be any semblance of justice?

The velovan's occupants talked in grunts and numbers. "She's 29.06.-35.43.79? "Umph-umph. "She's the 006 for Day 10?" "Umph." "Gotcha."

Tomorrow. H of P had been very clear yesterday. All and sundry were ordered to attend Day 10 Celebrations. There were to be no exceptions. Even ambulatory hospital patients should be there. "All should present themselves before the spectacle of RAA justice which will unfold before you in all its majesty, decorum, glory, and power," the puce-robed reader proclaimed with a rising voice.

Elve and Hara had giggled over "majesty." "Thought the RAA was supposed to be a republic." "Shouldn't have no truck with kingishness."

The reader concluded, "It is your duty and pleasure as a Loyel Sitizen of the Magnifisent and Glorius Noo Wrld Reepublik uv Azhu and de Amerikas."

The screen displayed a waving flag, puce with a multitude of white stars, accompanied by military music distinctly reminiscent of "Stars and Stripes Forever". Elve recognized that. The flag waved a full five minutes before fading to black.

In the velovan, Elve reviewed the H of P message. 006 for Day 10. This surely had to refer to the Day 10 Celebration. And her. Or maybe not. She was being paranoid. She hadn't come to police notice. Oh, yes, she had, recalling her adventure with Officer High-hat at the Awesome Force for the Administration of Law and Order.

But that was long ago—well, not so long—Elve struggled with the fuzziness of time under the RAA. So maybe...

006. Which meant? She was the sixth? Sixth what? Day 10 Celebrations were usually innocuous enough. School choir performances, dedication of new posters, awards to Loyel Ofisers, an inspirational talk by a high-hat brought in for the purpose. But every so often, a bloody execution. Death by stoning. Meemee. Have there been five? Am I No. 6?

If she was to be a scapegoat for the RAA's amusement tomorrow, there would be no justice tonight.

How should I prepare for my death? Elve, who had steadfastly refused to prepare as the RAA decreed, began to consider how to use her last hours.

The velovan jolted on. No one spoke. The only sounds were the vehicle's squawks as it plunged along the cratered road. It was hot. The driver rolled down the windows.

Elve sat back, though it hurt her hands. She let the cleansing wind bathe her face. A deep calm overtook her. Words entered and vanished: true, honest, just, pure, lovely, and of good report. She didn't question their origin or reason their aptness. She let them flow. She breathed deeply; the wind and the word.

She recognized the warehouse shape of the Awesome Force for Law and Order. The velovan went round to a back door where a sentry allowed the group to enter: the two arresting officers first, then Elve followed by the reluctant Dum.

The cell: a cot; a sink/toilet combination; walls painted a bilious green; a high, grated window; the door a barred gate. Elve sat on the cot. The superior officers exchanged a few words and left. Dum found a chair and sat down outside the gate. Sat staring straight ahead, hands on his meaty thighs.

Elve spoke first. "What happened to your partner?" She had never learned his real name and didn't want to call him "Dee". "He hasn't been with you for a while."

"Busted. Doin' hard time in AF 5."

"AF5?"

"Awesome Facility 5. The worst."

"What for?"

"Accepting a bribe." Dum wiped his brow. "A goddammed piece of apple pie."

"Just a piece of pie?"

Dum nodded.

"Could have happened to you too."

"Yeah. All those tomatoes. Man, they were good." Dum turned to look at his prisoner. "Look, I. . . sorry…like. . .you know I can't do anything. Anything to help. They'll do what they're gonna do. . ."

"And just bust you into the bargain. Stay safe, my friend. Stay safe."

After a time, Elve said, "You could turn out the light. That would be a help."

Dum considered. "I'm sposta be relieved at 10 m. When the guy comes, I'll offer to take his shift. If he goes, I'll turn it out then. Don't wanna get caught with it turned off now."

The relieving officer was happy to trade shifts. Dum snuffed the high-lumen light.

Elve lay down. Her restless mind ranged in waking dream from Grandma Kumi's daisied field to Hara's garden. Through distant lovers to steady old Boat. All her laughing brown boys, Hom and Rafu, Bim and Jog, Max. Mungo. Mungo. Mungo. She may have slept.

Dum certainly did. Slumped on the hard metal chair, hands dangling, head back and mouth agape, he maintained a chorus of snores, peculiar in their volume and variety.

The meagre window permitted dawning light to alter the shadows in Elve's cell. To her compromised eyes, the grill of her door seemed illuminated—edged in gold, and diaphanous, as if she might pass through it. A shimmering gate.

Elve sat up to watch the gate. Perhaps someone would come. Or was it her exit? A way out? She shook her head. Not a way out of whatever fate the RAA had in store for her. Not for what they would do to her body—whether prison or execution as No. 6 candidate for stoning. A way out for something else—something she'd never claimed to be or have—a spirit.

I've escaped them already, she thought. In a thousand ways. And when they kill my body, I will fly free. Like the dove—the wing Hom carries.

Dum's watch ended. He was replaced by a dour woman who brought water and a little food which Elve refused. It must have been close to mid-morning when she brought a voluminous red garment—a sort of caftan. "Put this on", she said. "The blood won't show so much."

At Elve's questioning look, she explained. "Some of them gets queasy when they see the blood. Then they don't throw the stones so good. So we use a red one."

So it was to be a stoning. "Thanks for letting me know."

The woman gaped. Then her face crumpled in a grimace of terror. "I didn't say nothing. Please say I didn't say nothing."

"Your secret is safe with me." Forever and ever, within the hour, Elve thought. Likely this poor woman will have to clean up the mess too.

The moments or hours passed as in a dream. Elve was aware of the van ride, the walk through the Emp's shadows and out the grand doors to the stage prepared with the x-shaped frame. She winced, but didn't cry out as her wrists and ankles were wired to its extremities.

Piles of rock were still being augmented by the barrowful when a high-hat officer took the stage. Rocks tumbled. Silence fell.

"Behold!" the officer shouted. "This woman, one Elve 35.43.79, a viltrid worm who fails every test of Loyel Sitizenry. Who flouts our sacred regs. Who breaks the supreme laws designed by Owr Preshus and Perfect Leeder for the well-being and happiness of all the people. It is through the regs and the laws that we as Loyel Sitizenz maintain our historic greatness and our dominance in the world of all men."

The crowd roared, "Long liv Owr Preshus Leeder. Long liv Owr graet Reepublik. RAA. RAA. RAA," a chant rehearsed daily in the classrooms of the world—well at least in Tranna.

With a flourish, the high-hat unfurled a lengthy scroll and began to read. "First charge: the shame of violating the sacred reg of our esteemed republic. Head coverings for women are strictly forbidden."

At this, a lesser officer stepped forward to rip away Elve's bright headdress, revealing the strange, white "train-track" through her hair. For people unused to disability or disfigurement, this was a disturbing sight. A mark. An evil mark? A mark of the devil? The crowd murmured uneasily.

"Second charge: the shame of failing to observe the sacred reg of our esteemed republic. All Sitizenz return thanks to our Preshus Leeder before partaking of their food."

The crowd responded feebly, perhaps realizing how carelessly they themselves observed this rite. The reader signaled to the pucers and petty officers stationed at intervals in front of the crowd, Jema among them. They approached, and she gave low-voiced instruction. They returned to their posts and turned to face the crowd.

"Third charge:" Here the reader hesitated. She felt that the third item, the shameful practice of keeping flowering plants in her domicile, would fail as the first two had.

"The charges are many and serious. Let me say only that they show this female scum to be of such character as to perform shameful and criminal acts deleterious to the well-being and happiness of all her fellow citizens. You—dear Loyel Sitizenz are the victims of her criminal acts. Such acts require retribution."

Led by chanting, stamping pucers, "Re-tri-bue-SHUN-KILL," reached a satisfactory pitch.

The cheerleaders were able to elicit enthusiastic opprobrium for the several more infractions, described always as shameful sins against all Loyel Sitizens and deleterious to their well-being and happiness.

The reader moved to the last and worst crime. "This vermin, this perpetrator of evil, has violated the sacred law, established since the beginning of Time itself that each Loyel Sitizen prepare at the age of 75, and carry out upon reaching their 80th birthday, their Ritual Death as decreed by Owr Preshus and Perfect Leeder."

"Ooooh" in a tone of disgusted reproof.

"This Holy Law, imparted to the wisest and most excellent of all law-makers, Owr Preshus and All-knowing Leeder, provides for the elimination of senescence. The elimination of dementia. The elimination of imperfection among us."

"Pre-shus LEE-der! Pre-shus LEE-der!"

"The Law of Ritual Death ensures the achievement of Perfect Well-being and Happiness. You, dear Loyel Sitizenz, are the losers when any one of these hunks of rotting flesh, these doting, deteriorating intellects (here the reader gestured toward Elve) selfishly prolongs its unlawful life."

The pucers called and leapt and gestured, punching the sky. The crowd replied in terrible unison, "BLOOD!" "BLOOD!" "BLOOD!"

The high-hat rolled up her scroll to the continued chant. She waved it imperiously. "Who," she called, "will cast the first stone?"

A young boy stepped forward. His black hair was drawn into a thick braid down his back; a strange amulet swung against his bare brown chest; his countenance was a study of concentrated will. He took a central, commanding position. Something about him silenced the shouting.

The boy carried a slingshot. With maimed left hand, he pulled a single, round stone from his pocket.

The crowd watched, breath suspended.

Hom's aim was true. The stone flew straight to its mark. Elve collapsed against her bonds. Blood tracked gently from the wound on her forehead.

The people gaped, terrified.

No one moved as the boy and two others mounted the stage. Hara, at Elve's side, faced the crowd, fixing her terrible white gaze upon them all. They beheld a devil, surely. A presence from the pit.

Boat cut the wires holding Elve's hands and feet. Her body fell into Hom's arms. A man appeared from the back of the crowd. A lean, brown stranger in alien clothes with grey-streaked locks and a white scar on his cheek.

Jema gasped one word, "Mungo," before collapsing against the stage.

The man reached up and gathered the body from the boy's arms to his own breast.

The crowd parted to allow the little retinue to pass—Elve's body transported on the shoulder of her son, then Boat, Hom, and beside him, Hara,

High-hat and pucers hurried back through the grand doors. The crowd with frightened whispers began to disperse.

They laid the body, wrapped in Mungo's cloak, on a bed of tender branches in the Roons. Lali was there, and O. The children too. They covered it with rocks and earth, so that soon green things would grow and cover it. They placed a larger stone at the head. Hom would, before he left, carve it with a dove's wing.

And when, on another, later day, the south tower too collapsed, all was covered.

But in Tranna and in the net of explorers and bards that went out from its core, the story never died. The story of an old woman who dared defy the RAA, of a boy with a slingshot, and a girl with the terrible eye.

Acknowledgements

"The End of Summer" by Edna St. Vincent Millay is now in the public domain, as are the lines quoted from "The Walrus and the Carpenter" and "Jabberwocky" by Lewis Carroll. Rose Wilder Lane's *The Peaks of Shala*, excerpted in *Life and Literature* with the title "A Mountain School in Albania" figures importantly in the story. Canadian author Lucy Maude Montgomery is to be thanked not only for *Anne of Green Gables* but also for all her other brave and resilient heroines. Holy Bible (King James Version of 1611) and Mother Goose are of course the bountiful heritage of generations of listeners and readers in the English-speaking world.

Thanks

First of all, to Elizabeth Marshall and Claire Moran, who read the chapters in their roughest form, offered their critiques and encouragement, but who did not live to see the manuscript completed.

I also owe much to the diligence and talents of my editor, Ann Birch, and to those of my beta readers, Barbara Nobel, and Marianne Hamilton. Their discerning eyes and literary sensibilities were invaluable.

All of these readers helped me to offer a presentable manuscript to the great people at Tellwell Publishing: Jennifer Chapin, who first got in touch; my Project Manager, Jonveth Tabar; my cover designer, Benjam Mosquera, and the interior designer Joemar Becbec. I am grateful to all for their quality work.

CPSIA information can be obtained
at www.ICGtesting.com
Printed in the USA
LVHW030727260919
632300LV00002B/2/P